Maitlyn Flutters

Timothy Braatz

French Point Press

French Point Press

Maitlyn Flutters

Timothy Braatz

1

Don't act impressed, Maitlyn had told herself when she hopped from the van and checked her hair in the side-view mirror. *Be confident, just another day on the job*, she had added as she strode past the palm trees and the splashing fountain, up the carved stone steps, and through the ivied arch. But here he was, opening the front door himself—*Nathan!*—even more handsome in person, football star turned corporate spokesman turned rising politician, taking her hand in both of his.

"Maitlyn, gosh, a real pleasure. Come in, please. I'm so glad you agreed to this."

Was he serious? A leading candidate for U.S. Senate and a national celebrity—Nathan, last name unnecessary—invites a local reporter for an on-camera sit-down in his living room—did he think she'd say no?

"Good to meet you, Congressman."

"Please, call me Nate. You look terrific."

Nate! She tried to ignore the compliment, but could feel a blush heating her face. "What a beautiful house."

He grinned, and the crinkles around his blue eyes deepened. *What is it about older men*, she wondered, *that makes you want to curl up in their arms?*

"I'll show you around while your crew sets up."

Maitlyn had two guys with her. Scott was her news photographer and frequent companion as she tracked down house fires, traffic backups, and celebrity sightings. She would stake out her spot in front of the drama, Scott would shoulder his big Sony and hit record, and breaking news would beam into forty thousand households. When she complained about the tedium of local interest stories, Scott would reassure her, "One day we'll catch a scoop, I can feel it. Your talent, my karma."

She was skeptical about his karma, mostly because Scott was a committed smoker, didn't exercise, and seemed to subsist entirely on food truck burritos, but *something* had gotten them invited inside the fabulous mansion of Congressman Nathaniel Saltenstall (R-CA)—which is why Charles was also along, sporting his signature baseball cap bearing the slogan You Can't Fix Stupid. Charles was a studio tech, a whiz with lights and sound—the hat was misleading—and he had a nickname: The Mouth from the South. "Gonna make y'all look professional," he had said that morning as he loaded his equipment into the van, and Maitlyn had remembered why she disliked working with him.

Congressman Saltenstall directed them to the living room. The news team trio couldn't help staring out the sliding glass doors to the back patio, where more arches and palm trees graced a glassy waterfall and a meandering swimming pool.

"Aloha!" Charles enthused, emphasizing the last syllable.

"Good thing we're not in a drought," Scott said under his breath.

Maitlyn had been thinking the same thing ever since they'd driven into Rancho Santa Fe, passing sprawling lawns and verdant golf courses interrupted by picturesque water hazards. With the state's reservoirs half empty, California had been under water restrictions for months, yet this ritzy little community looked like a tropical oasis.

"I thought maybe we'd sit by the fireplace," the congressman said, interrupting their gawking. "Make it look cozy."

"Works for me," Scott agreed, turning away from the windows to survey the room. "Mind if we move a few chairs?"

"Anything you want. Make yourself at home. I'm going to give Maitlyn the grand tour." He put his large hand lightly on her shoulder blade and ushered her out of the room.

The congressman didn't seem to notice, but Maitlyn distinctly heard Charles say, "Gotta be the tits."

Back in college, Maitlyn and her roommates had sworn they would never go in for "voluntary mutilation." Positive body image, they agreed, only came from within. In fact, it was Maitlyn who had said, "Girls who do that stuff have self-hatred from looking at fashion magazines."

Then she graduated with a degree in communications, took a summer internship at the news station, and found a mentor in an on-air meteorologist named—no lie—Sunny Snowden. One Saturday night, over drinks, Maitlyn had shared that she was interested in investigative reporting—"I mean, like, totally dig up the facts"—but really aspired to be a news anchor "like for CBS Evening News—wouldn't that be amazing?" As politely as possible, Sunny hinted that a few "enhancements" might help her chances because "at that level, the competition is bitch-eat-bitch, seriously, you've got to stand out, it's not enough to be cute, you've got to be, like, dazzling, that's just how it is."

After her third glass of wine, Sunny confessed that she didn't really understand the science behind global warming, or even El Niño. "Something about hot water," she laughed, "but who cares?" She'd made Sunny her legal name, "had a little work done," and could read off the daily temperatures as well as anyone. "Seriously, the only ones watching the news are old farts, right? And Grandpa controls the remote. So who's he going to chose, gay Kevin on Seven or Sunny Snowden and her marvelous rack on Four?"

Mentored and inspired, Maitlyn began her professional development. Teeth-whitening was her gateway drug. *It's not self-hatred, it's hygiene*, she convinced herself, and she liked her shiny new smile, liked the confidence it gave her. She took spinning classes and Pilates. She tapped out her savings—most of it a graduation present from her grandmother—to pay for breast augmentation. *It's not self-hatred, it's self-improvement.*

But how do you explain to your mother, who has told you over and over again that you were made in the image of God, that sometimes genetics aren't enough? "Everyone does it," Maitlyn pleaded, "it's really no different than bleaching your mustache or plucking your eyebrows"—neither of which her mother bothered with anymore.

"It just doesn't seem right," her mother maintained.

"It's harmless," Maitlyn assured her.

Better than harmless. Mr. Cooper, Channel Four News editor-in-chief, unexpectedly created a full-time position for Maitlyn, mostly running errands for him, and the ripe new boobs paid for themselves in six months. Sunny may not have understood hemispheric oscillations, but she knew which way the wind blew.

With steady income, Maitlyn was able to invest in a thinner nose and smaller chin. When the bandages came off, she had buyer's remorse and severe guilt. *Why did I do this?* It was like renouncing her inheritance. She still had her father's green eyes, but the obvious resemblance to Mom was gone. She got over it. Within days of the bruises disappearing, a handsome lawyer asked her out while she was leaving the gym, and they started dating. He introduced her to local big shots—"heavy hitters," he called them—including the mayor, who flirted with her unabashedly.

Then she discovered that her dreamy lawyer was married. Sunny was proved right again: "Guys are pigs, Maitlyn, but they run the world, so you better know how to play them." Mr. Cooper wasn't an outright swine—the women at the station found him generally supportive—but he had the porcine instincts. His glances suggested that he approved of the enhanced and augmented Maitlyn. She rewarded him with gleaming smiles, and soon she was holding a microphone in front of Scott's lens with the red light glowing.

And now Congressman Saltenstall had summoned her to his trophy home in Rancho.

"Let's start in the kitchen."

"Oh. My. God."

It was straight out of a glossy magazine—the marble-topped island, the hanging jungle of ladles and copper pots, two brushed-steel refrigerators, four sinks, built-in wine rack.

"Do you cook, Maitlyn?"

"Sure, but, I mean, if I had a kitchen like this, I would quit my job and get serious." She ran her fingers along the smooth countertop and covetously eyed the industrial-size cappuccino maker.

"Then we should have dinner sometime. Whip something up together."

At that point, she later admitted to herself, she should have said she needed to get back to her crew, see if they were ready to roll. She was being charmed, she knew she was being charmed, and she should have nipped this seduction business in the bud. But she knew how to play this guy, she thought.

"What about your wife?" There was a wife, but they were rarely seen together—that was one of the issues Maitlyn planned to raise during the interview.

"Valerie is her own woman. Let me show you my gallery. Do you like modern art?"

Again, the gentle hand guided her forward, through a formal dining room, the table set for six, and into what could have been a wing of the art museum in La Jolla, only the pieces were better. Maitlyn had long since given up her self-imposed marching orders—how could she *not* be impressed? The kitchen was irresistible. The oil paintings were stunning—abstract female figures, geometric designs, a forest of pointillistic sunflowers.

"I didn't know football players were into art."

"It's my guilty pleasure. Well, one of them."

He put an arm around her shoulders, and she forgot to pull away. She was imagining a selfie in the kitchen with Nathan—*the* Nathan—and how nice that photo would look when she sent it to the phone of Whatshisface, the married lawyer whose calls she had finally stopped taking.

"Which painting do you like best, Maitlyn?"

"They're all so amazing. I mean, really, I wouldn't have guessed you for this."

He took his arm off her shoulders. "Dumb jock, huh?"

"No. I'm sorry, Congressman." *Is he offended?*

"Nate."

"I didn't mean it like that."

"Want to see what's behind door number three?" He pointed to the next room.

"At this point, I'm kind of expecting the Mona Lisa."

"I wish." He opened the door. "It's just my little studio."

First she saw several easels. "You paint?"

"I try. Campaigning kind of gets in the way these days."

Then she noticed the sliding door, which opened onto a small patio of miniature trees and raked pebbles. "Is that like a Zen garden?"

"Exactly. Those bonsais are my babies. They calm me down. Well, what do you think?" He gestured toward his canvases. They were all female nudes.

Maitlyn was starting to feel awkward. *You're an investigative journalist*, she told herself, *stay steady, there's a story here*. "I notice a theme," she said, trying to sound unfazed. "Do you use, you know, models?"

He chuckled. "Off the record?"

"Sure. Off the record."

"The answer, Maitlyn, is no. I work from memory." The paintings weren't quite pornographic, but clearly the former jock standing behind her was a breast man. Now he was massaging her shoulders. "I could paint you, if you like."

She froze. A boundary had been crossed. "They're probably ready for us out there."

"A body like yours should have a portrait done."

He kissed her neck, and this time she remembered to stop him. "No," she said, stumbling out of his grip and almost knocking over an easel. "No means no." It sounded almost childish. She didn't care. She was scared but kept her eyes locked on his.

He held out his hands, fingers splayed, as if surrendering. "I'm sorry, I'm sorry. I misunderstood."

"I'm a professional, Congressman. I'm here for the interview, that's all."

"I'm very sorry. I didn't—." He looked remorseful. Puppy dog eyes.

"It's okay," she said stupidly, instinctively wanting to ease his guilt.

He reached for her cautiously, as if to straighten her rumpled blouse, then suddenly his hands were around her waist and pulling her close.

"Congressman, no."

"It's okay," he said, repeating her words. "No one can see us." He had her trapped in the corner of the studio. His strong hands were sliding up her rib cage.

"No! Get off me!"

"You're so beautiful."

"Let me go!"

"I'd make you my queen." His hands were cupping her breasts and pushing her against the wall.

Gouge his eyes out! She remembered that from self defense class. But he was too tall and her shoulder blades were pinned. *Knee him in the groin!* She swung a knee upward and banged it against his knee cap. He didn't seem to notice. He bent down and was forcing his mouth against hers. Her right hand rummaged across a nearby tabletop for something heavy or sharp. She found a metal can instead. It felt half full. "Nate, wait." She wrenched her face away from his mouth to get a better look.

He paused. "You want to be queen of my castle?"

She faked a smile while her palm worked the can's safety lid: press down and turn. She felt the lid give. Using her finger tips, she twisted it off. "Nate." She reached her left hand up to his chin. He took her fingers lightly in his mouth and was reaching down for her thigh when she splashed the paint thinner in his face.

"Shit," he sputtered. "Goddammit!"

Two splashes, then she jammed the can into his chest, ducked under his arms, and headed for the gallery. He beat her to it, still spry despite his famously rebuilt knees. But rather than grab her, he scooted past the paintings and disappeared into the dining room.

She heard a faucet come on in the kitchen. *Hide!* The door to the Zen garden slid open. She lost her footing on the pebbles and landed on a treetop, crushing tiny branches with her hands. She scrambled back up, slid open another glass door, and found herself in a bedroom.

"Maitlyn?" The congressman's voice came from the studio.

She fled the bedroom and headed down a hallway. She couldn't find the living room. "Scott!" No answer. "Hey, Scott!" Was she going the wrong direction?

"Maitlyn, wait. I want to apologize." The congressman was following her.

She kept going, looking for a bathroom, for safety. Instead, she was in some sort of entertainment room with a big screen television and a pool table. She dashed for a door in the corner and closed it behind her. The room was pitch black. She fiddled with the doorknob but there was no locking mechanism. She listened for approaching footsteps but only heard her heart thumping in her chest. She slid to the ground and sat with her weight against the door. For a few minutes, she hardly moved. She focused on her breathing, trying to slow it down. "You're okay, you're okay." She was whispering to herself when a vibration jolted her leg. She almost screamed, then stifled it. The buzzing sensation was her cell phone. "Scott!" she answered.

"Where are you? We're all waiting."

"Is he with you—the congressman?"

"Yeah." The cameraman seemed oblivious to the panic in her voice. "You're interviewing him, remember?"

"Scott, he—."

"Where are you? He said you went to freshen up."

"He tried to—."

"Are you okay? You sound winded?"

"I—I need to talk to you."

"Hold on one second, Maitlyn." When Scott came back on the phone, he was whispering. "Maitlyn, listen, he's getting impatient. If you've got stage fright or something—."

"He grabbed me."

"What? Hold on. The reception is bad in here." He said that louder, maybe for the congressman's benefit.

"Scott? Hello?"

"Okay, I'm outside now."

"He—."

"What happened?"

"He tried to—." She didn't want to say it.

"Did he molest you or something?"

She answered by not answering.

"Are you hurt? Maitlyn? Where are you?"

"I don't know. In some closet. Hiding."

"You're not hurt?"

"I can't stop shaking."

"Listen, I don't want to sound callous, but I think he's about to cancel on us. If you're not hurt, then you've got to pull yourself together and get back to the living room. Can you do that? This is our scoop, Maitlyn. If we blow this—."

"I—I just need a minute."

9

"Okay, I'll stall. But hurry, okay? Maitlyn?"

She didn't want to end the call. Scott's voice was a lifeline. "Okay. Okay. I'm coming."

The congressman was seated by the fireplace, looking placid, unruffled. He stood and smiled when Maitlyn re-entered the room. "Ready when you are, Maitlyn."

Maitlyn had retraced her steps, through the bedroom, the Zen patio, the studio, then back to the kitchen, stopping only to inflict further damage on the bonsai with her heel—"Fuck you, tree"—and to daub her face dry and fix her hair in a bathroom off the dining room. "Just let me—I need to get organized here," she told her crew.

The congressman chuckled. "It's easy to get lost in this house. It's my fault. I should have waited for you. I'm sorry. Really, Maitlyn, I'm very sorry."

Maitlyn turned away. Scott was whispering instructions and looking worried. "Remember, one camera on you, one on him. When he's talking, you can check your notes. You've got your notes, right?"

"Yeah." She had a little stack of cue cards. She was squeezing them with both hands.

"Okay, then. Big smile."

She nodded. She knew how to do this—block everything else out, get in "the zone." Her high school tennis coach used to say, "Just you and the ball."

"Let's mic you up," Charles said, handing her a tiny microphone to attach to her blouse.

When their eyes met, he was leering from under his crass ball cap—You Can't Fix Stupid—with something between disgust and a knowing grin. At least, that's how Maitlyn read it. *Fuck you too*, she thought, and went to work.

"Congressman, let's start with your family life, if we may."

"Certainly."

His eyes were a little bloodshot—from the paint thinner, she assumed. *When did he have time to change his shirt?* She pushed that thought away. *Just you and the ball.* "You claim to stand for family values."

"I do. The family is the heart and soul of America."

"But sources claim that you and your wife, Valerie, are separated. That your relationship is, shall we say, troubled."

She couldn't bear to look him in the eye and was afraid to look down and see his meaty hands. Instead, she focused on the wall behind him. Just over his shoulder was a small pastel portrait of an old fisherman with a rumpled cap. *Just you and the painting.*

"Sources say a lot of things, Maitlyn. But I'm glad you brought this up so I can clear the air. Valerie and I are happily married, have been for almost twenty years. I think people kind of jump to conclusions because they don't see her campaigning with me. But she's a businesswoman, as you know. She's a remarkable woman. Has her own career, right here in San Diego. I'm not saying all woman need to be working outside the home, but if that's their dream, they should pursue it, absolutely."

"So your marriage is solid?" she asked the pastel fisherman, who had a jolly gleam in his eye, like he knew his nets were filling up or maybe just life on the coast was good.

"We have our differences sometimes, but yes. Solid. I wouldn't be who I am without her."

"And who you are right now is a United States congressman."

"A *hardworking* United States congressman. My constituents know that. I rarely miss a vote in the House."

"So can you tell us why you are running for the U.S. Senate?"

"That's an easy one, Maitlyn. My opponents are going to accuse you of serving up softballs." He smiled broadly. She looked down at her cue cards. "I'm running for Senate because it's time to take back America. In my playing days, I crisscrossed this country many, many times. I know the American people as well as anyone. I know California as well as anyone. Being a professional athlete gave me a privileged life, and I want to give back. I'm not interested in partisan bickering and Beltway deal-making. I think America means values that we can agree that—."

"Just what are those values, Congressman?"

"Freedom. Honesty. Hard work. Rule of law. Family, as we've already mentioned. Family is so important. My father taught me to play football. His father taught him. There's nothing more American than that."

And so it went—well-oiled, vacuous answers offered with heartfelt conviction and a winning smile. She had gone over her list of questions with her assignment editor. "Nothing that makes him uncomfortable," the editor had said. "No gotcha's, otherwise you'll never get invited back." Now, though, a second invitation seemed unlikely. *Might as well throw him a curve.*

"Congressman, there's been a lot of talk lately about bombing Iran and potentially starting yet another war in the Middle East. Where do you stand on this?"

"First, no one wants another war. But Iran is a threat to its neighbors. A threat to regional stability. A threat to world peace."

"So you would support the bombing of Iran?"

"Well, it's like, you know, we can't stand by and let World War III happen."

"So you don't want a wider war?

"Of course not."

Maitlyn's mind flashed back to the studio. She stared hard at the fisherman on the wall, at the spidery cracks in the tarnished frame that bounded him, but all she saw were flesh-filled canvases and groping hands. "So what you're saying is, sort of" — she was trying not to panic, trying to think of what to say next— "you're against the bombing?"

"Well, I...now, don't put words in my mouth. Let me put it this way: as a senator, I would support my commander-in-chief."

For the benefit of the cameras, Maitlyn smiled at the fisherman and thanked him for the interview.

"Thank *you*, Maitlyn." When the camera was turned off, the congressman stood, adding, "I think that went well. Again, Maitlyn, I'm truly sorry for any misunderstanding."

Once out of the living room, Maitlyn made a beeline for the van, climbed into the passenger seat, and locked the door. Waiting for the guys to load out their equipment, she replayed in her mind the incident in the studio. She could feel his rough hands on her torso, pressing her back into the wall. Just the thought of it made her want to get home and take a shower, wash off his scum.

"Hey, are you okay?" It was Scott, opening the driver's door.

"I don't know." She was shaking again.

"You were great in there. Really pulled it together. The network will pick it up for sure."

"I feel nauseous."

"Uh, oh. Let's get you some fresh air. No barfing in the Four-mobile." He helped her onto the lawn, then lit up a cigarette.

Charles walked past them, carrying lights out of the house. "Y'all ready to roll?" he drawled, then noticed Maitlyn's distress. "What's going on?"

"She's not feeling well."

"That was fast." He winked at Scott and arced a hand over his belly — the universal symbol for pregnancy.

Scott followed him toward the back door of the van, and Maitlyn could hear them talking in hushed voices. *Great*, she thought, *now everyone will know*. At least she wasn't throwing up on Nathan's designer driveway. He was probably watching from a window somewhere.

"Is it true, Maitlyn? Did he try to mess with you?" Charles was coming toward her in a huff.

"It was nothing."

"It wasn't nothing," Scott corrected her. "Not if he tried to molest you."

"He rape you?" Charles asked.

"Charles, come on," Scott interrupted, trying to keep things decent.

"Seriously, Maitlyn," Charles growled, "what did —?"

"He didn't rape me. Jesus."

"He try to have his way? Not taking no for an answer?"

Maitlyn hesitated. She wanted to forget the whole thing.

"He did *something*," Scott said. "I've never seen you like this."

"Can we just go?" She climbed back into the van.

"Give me a minute," Charles said. "I think I left a cable in the house." He pulled his cap down lower on his brow and headed back up the walkway toward the front door. Halfway there, he called back to Scott, "Get that camera ready. Lock and load."

Maitlyn watched as Charles continued up the steps and disappeared into the arched entryway. Suddenly angry, she rolled down the window and scowled at Scott. "Did you have to tell him?"

"He thought you and Nathan were getting it on in the kitchen. You want The Mouth telling people *that*?"

"He's a jerk." She thought back to the kitchen. *Yes, I was friendly in the kitchen, but in a professional manner. I wasn't flirting. No way was that flirting. If anything, I was hitting on the cappuccino maker, not the congressman.*

"Here he comes," Scott murmured.

Charles had reappeared from the archway and was walking toward them, rubbing his hands together, but not carrying the missing cable. Then the congressman appeared, descended the steps, and broke into a jog, like he was trying to catch up with Charles.

"Now what?" Scott asked, tossing aside his cigarette and shouldering a camera.

Charles glanced back at the large man pursuing him, then pointed at Scott. "Get that fucker rolling!"

2

Maitlyn kept her composure, sort of, until she was back in the news station, until she had hurried into Sunny's office and pulled the door shut.

"What's up, girl?" Sunny asked, and Maitlyn burst out crying. Sunny stood up from her desk. "What happened? Did you screw up the interview?" When Maitlyn couldn't speak, Sunny wrapped her in a hug. "That's okay. You just cry it out. We all have bad days."

They sat on the couch, Maitlyn bawling, Sunny handing over tissues, until the tears stopped and Maitlyn could stammer through her story, starting with Prince Charming in the kitchen and ending with King Kong in the studio.

"That asshole," Sunny said. "That fucking asshole."

"I shouldn't have gone back there with him." Maitlyn started crying again.

"You did nothing wrong, you understand?"

"I'm so stupid. I thought I—."

"Maitlyn, it's not your fault. Do you hear me, Maitlyn? If you said no, if you said stop, that's sexual assault. He's a fucking criminal."

"Should I, do you think, call the cops?"

A knock on the door, and some staffer poked her head in. "Sunny, you've got to come see this footage."

"Not now. I'm busy."

The staffer noticed Maitlyn. "Oh, sorry," she said. "But this is huge. Tell her, Maitlyn." Then she disappeared again.

Maitlyn stared at the closed door. The way the staffer had looked at her—she already knew, the entire station knew—slutty little Maitlyn got felt up.

"Tell me what?" Sunny asked. "What footage? Maitlyn?"

"Nathan pushed Charles. Knocked him to the ground. In his front yard."

Charles had talked and laughed the entire drive back from Rancho Santa Fe. "You caught that, right, Scott? Tell me you caught it." Scott kept assuring him it was in the can, and Charles kept laughing. "We got him. We got him dead to rights. Don't you worry about that, Maitlyn. Ol' brother Nathan gonna get his. You sure you got it?"

Charles was driving the van. Maitlyn was in the passenger seat, knees curled up to her chest, face hidden in her hands. Scott was in the back seat with his camera. "I got it, Charles," he muttered. "Relax already. I'm watching it right now."

"This will play in Peoria, I guarantee you. Gonna sizzle like sunup in summer."

"You're lucky you hit the lawn and not the driveway."

"No luck involved, Scottie. After what I said to him, I knew he was on my tail. I *went* for that grass."

"What did you say to him?" Maitlyn asked.

"I told him what I thought about him messing with you."

"How did you put it?" Scott asked.

"Oh, I put it good. I told him, all that money and he still can't get a girl to say yes."

Maitlyn cringed and shrunk deeper into her seat. Had she gone into that studio because of the money, because of the fame? Was she that pathetic?

"I told him," Charles continued crowing, "he'd never have a chance with a lady as fine as Maitlyn."

"He chased you down just for that?" Scott asked.

"Well, I might have mentioned about his wife screwing that talk show host."

"You did not."

"Yes, sir." The Mouth from the South drummed the steering wheel and bounced his shoulders in a celebratory dance. "I waved the red cape and that bull come a-running. You got it all on tape, right?"

"Ask me again, Charles, and I'm erasing it."

"When this hits the internet, his campaign is over. Crash and burn. Not taking anything away from you, Maitlyn. That Iran question was off the hook. But Nate the Great jumping a skinny black man from behind? Family values, my ass. Black folk in Cali gonna come out and *vote*.

"He did that to you *and* he pushed Charles?" Sunny asked incredulously. "Was he drunk?"

"No. I don't know. The interview went fine."

"Wait. You did the interview? Nathan assaulted you, and you still did the interview?"

Maitlyn nodded, but she was confused by the tone of Sunny's disbelief. It wasn't admiration for professional courage, for bravery under fire. It was almost scolding.

Sunny stood up from the couch. "Oh, girl."

"No, it was good. I held it together." A tough assignment, and she had aced it. She could be proud of that. "I just had to avoid his eyes."

"I think you can forget about calling the cops." A beeping computer drew Sunny back to her desk. She tapped her keyboard and stared at the screen. "Oh, goody. It's actually going to rain for once." She picked up her office phone and started rattling off instructions about storm graphics. "Probably just a sprinkle, but let's work it. See if they'll give us a bullet for the end of the A-block. Precipitation in the forecast, stay tuned." Then she hung up and looked at Maitlyn. "Do you have any scratches? Or bruises?"

18

"He didn't hit me."

"Right. I'm mean, that's good. But the cops are gonna see that interview and say, 'She doesn't look distraught.'"

"I told Scott. Right away. He can confirm that I was upset."

"Yeah? I mean—look, Nathan's gonna get a slick lawyer, and he'll say the same thing—'Does that interviewer look traumatized?'"

"I was doing my job."

"He'll say, 'Yes, Nathan tried to kiss her, but that's a misunderstanding, not a crime.'"

"He didn't just try to kiss me." No more tears. Now she was angry.

"I know, honey, I know. But it's your word against his. Famous Nathan versus little Maitlyn Flutters. You're a reporter—you see this stuff all the time."

"What I see all the time is the guy gets away with it because the woman is afraid to come forward, and then he does it to someone else. I have to at least file a police report, so there's a record."

Sunny tapped the keyboard a few more times, then came out from behind her desk, but this time she didn't join Maitlyn on the couch. She leaned against the front of her desk, arms folded across her chest, in mentor mode now, no longer the gentle comforter. "Okay, I'll just say it. Do you want to be damaged goods?"

It took a moment to sink in. *Damaged goods?* "Is that what you think, Sunny? Blame the victim?" Maitlyn stood up. She was back in the painting studio. She needed to escape.

Sunny put a hand on her shoulder. "Maitlyn, wait."

Maitlyn spun away. She'd had enough hands on her shoulders.

"Maitlyn, please, just listen. There's going to be one dominant narrative out there—there always is. Either it's Maitlyn the rising star who scooped the interview with Nathan, or Maitlyn the naughty girl who was in a backroom alone with Nathan. Just think about it. Maybe we should keep this quiet."

"It's too late. Charles knows."

But to Maitlyn's great relief, The Mouth from the South had taken a vow of silence. "It was his idea," Scott explained, as he walked with Maitlyn to the conference room. "He told me, 'Gotta protect the talent.'" They were hurrying to meet with Mr. Cooper. They'd been told it was urgent. "Going to be show and yell," Scott warned.

Charles was already seated at the conference table. He greeted them with a wink. His baseball cap was on backwards and a toothpick poked from the side of his mouth, like he had gone out of his way to look unimpressed by the suits and ties and serious white faces across the table. Two men flanked the editor-in-chief. Maitlyn knew one of them—Jerry, the communications director. After asking Scott to close the door, Mr. Cooper introduced the other as a lawyer. Scott gave Maitlyn a wide-eyed look—when a lawyer shows up, you know it's serious—but she kept her face blank. She was steeling herself for the impending unpleasantries.

"First of all," Mr. Cooper began, "fine job on the interview, Maitlyn. You looked great, you held your own. This could open some doors. We'll get a little guff from Nathan's camp for the Iran question, but I don't think you made any enemies. Always a good thing."

She nodded, and he blessed her with his rabid grin. His pointy ears were too big for his narrow face. He always reminded her of a coyote.

"Item two," he continued, loosening his tie. "Charles, what the hell was that all about? You piss on the man's toilet seat or something?"

"Just a little disagreement between two hall-of-famers."

Coyote Cooper laughed. He fancied himself one of the guys even though everyone addressed him as Mr. Cooper. "Remind me, which hall of fame are you in?"

"Barbecue. You never had my ribs?"

The communications director managed a smile at Charles's routine, but the lawyer was all business. "Forgive me interrupting, Mr. Cooper. Mr. Lockett, we need to know precisely what happened between you and Congressman Saltenstall. What motivated him to run after you and knock you down?"

"That's the million-dollar question, ain't it?" Charles leaned back in his chair and fiddled with his toothpick, like a man holding all the cards. "Hard to say what goes through a man's mind."

The lawyer persisted. "Just tell us what happened in the house, if you would."

Maitlyn braced herself. So far as she knew, only three people—Scott, Charles, and Sunny—could say what had happened between her and the congressman in the painting studio. That number was about to double. She was about to be humiliated in this room full of men, including a lawyer. She hated lawyers. This one was nerdy and balding, not broad-shouldered and tan like Whatshisface, who, after Maitlyn had discovered the wife, still wanted to maintain their adulterous relationship. Was she drawn to treasonous husbands, or they to her?

Charles caught her eye. She stared back. *Just get it over with*, she wanted to tell him. Her walls were up. She wasn't going to cry in here.

"Mr. Lockett?"

Without warning, Charles pushed back from the table and jumped to his feet. "When I walked past Nathan on my way out, I did this." He held his right arm at his side, elbow at an acute angle, and brought his left arm across his belly so his hands overlapped.

"What's that?" the lawyer asked.

"This, Your Honor, is how you cradle a football when you're running through traffic." Charles shuffled his feet in a two-step dance. "Two hands on the ball, Saltenstall, Saltenstall," he chanted. "Two hands, please, on the ball."

Mr. Cooper laughed again. "That song was all over the radio," he explained to the lawyer, "after Nathan fumbled in the Super Bowl. It's still kind of famous around here."

"I saw the game," the lawyer said, defending his manhood.

"*Kinda* famous?" Charles hooted. "That fumble cost us the championship."

"Did you say that to him?" the lawyer asked, scribbling notes on a yellow pad.

"Course I did. Two hands on the ball, motherfucker. I had us and the spread. I had the under. I'll never forget that. Cost me five grand. Not to mention the enduring heartache. We had that game. Two minutes to go, and he doesn't wrap up the rock. We *had* that game." Charles slapped the table with both hands and sat back down. "We had it." The heartache was still there.

"What did the congressman say in response, Mr. Lockett?"

"In response to what?"

"In response to" — the lawyer checked his notes — "two hands on the ball, motherfucker."

"Nothing. He just kind of looked over his shoulder, like see this house I got, what do I care about some game fifteen years ago? Hell, his front door alone probably cost five grand. Looks like it come off some old barn outside of Nacogdoches. A sweet pad like that, you don't have to say nothing to nobody."

"So I'm guessing there was more repartee on your part?"

Charles raised his eyebrows at *repartee* — was the lawyer being cute? — then pursed his lips and glanced down at his feet. "Okay, so now I'm fixin' to exit the premises, and he says...he says something about my hat."

Scott looked at Maitlyn and appeared to be suppressing a grin because this wasn't the story Charles had told them in the van.

"What did he say about your hat?" the lawyer asked.

"Nice hat." Charles took off his backwards cap and turned it so the lawyer could read the slogan on the front.

Maitlyn couldn't remember ever seeing Charles bareheaded. His short, kinky hair was flecked with gray. He was older than she had guessed.

The lawyer looked up from his scribbling. "Nice hat?"

"Yeah. But in a sarcastic way. *Nice* hat. Where I come from, you don't go denigrating a man's lid. So I say something about him never winning a championship for us."

"What exactly did you say?"

Charles replaced his cap, brim forward. "Never did win that championship for us."

It was too much—Charles lying through his teeth while his forehead announced You Can't Fix Stupid, and the lawyer assiduously taking it all down. Scott laughed out loud. Maitlyn, despite her misery, almost smiled.

"Anything else, Mr. Lockett?"

"Non. Fin de la répartie."

"Sorry?"

"Nothing," Charles said, his voice suggesting disappointment at the lawyer's lack of French.

"Then he followed you out?"

"I thought we were just talking a little trash, but I guess I hit a sore spot. Halfway to the van, I hear him coming after me. Scott got it all on tape."

"Digital, to be precise," Scott inserted, for the lawyer's benefit.

"Next thing I know I'm kissing the lawn. I tried to break my fall, but—."

"We've seen it," Mr. Cooper said.

"Okay, then," Charles added, bumping fists with Scott, "gonna win my boy here the Pulitzer."

The Mouth from the South wasn't simply telling lies, Maitlyn realized, *he's lying to protect me.* If what he had said in the van was true, Charles had upbraided Nathan for two hands on something else, and this football story was so Maitlyn didn't have to explain to the rabid coyote and the communications director and the bookish lawyer what had happened in the studio. She had started the morning resenting Charles's presence on the interview assignment, and now she could have hugged him, except that she never wanted to touch a man ever again.

"Okay, Jerry," Mr. Cooper said to the communications director, "lay out the game plan."

Jerry stopped fiddling with his cell phone and set it carefully on the table. "Maitlyn, so you know, we're going to sit on your interview for a few days. First we get Charles's bellyflop out there." With thumbs and forefingers, he drew lines in the air, indicating a headline. "*Nathan attacks news crew.* If it goes viral, then your sit-down with the congressman is golden." He mimed another headline: "*Nathan gives interview moments before attacking news crew.*"

"Crash and burn," Charles said with a smile.

"We've already talked to New York," Jerry continued. "They want to run hits on evening news. Then we'll air the entirety local and post it to the web. Excuse me." He picked up his phone to check a new message.

Mr. Cooper jumped in. "Going forward, we're going to blanket the Saltenstall campaign, stay out ahead on this. Nathan may be forced out of the race. Others might jump in. Main thing, we are now the go-to affiliate for this story. Charles, you work closely with Jerry. Don't just go blabbing your mouth."

"Moi?" Charles asked.

"We need to be strategic, right, Jerry?"

The communications director looked up. "That's right. Charles, we'll have you release statements, but on our schedule.

We control the cycle. If the buzz slows, we'll stir it up again. Maybe some Twitter stuff. Keep building, keep building."

"Bring the cyberworld to orgasm," Mr. Cooper clucked. "No offense, Maitlyn."

3

Maitlyn woke up the next morning with a dry mouth. It had taken her several glasses of wine and half an Ambien to get to sleep. She rolled over and reached for her cell phone, then remembered she had turned it off for a reason. She had told Mr. Cooper she was taking a day off, then imposed a 24-hour media blackout on herself: no internet, no messaging, no television. She fixed coffee and tried to squelch the memory of Nathan's kitchen. Then she caught herself. *Push away nothing.* She needed to process yesterday's trauma, not bury it. *I was flirting with the cappuccino maker, not with him. Even if I was flirting with him, that gave him no right. I said no. I said stop.*

She opened the curtains and looked out the window, but it was the nudes in the studio that flashed through her mind's eye. All those large breasts. Had she brought this on herself? Her hands were shaking. Maybe coffee wasn't such a good idea. She poured it down the sink and returned to the window. This was going to be a long day.

Her third-floor condo on Banker's Hill faced west toward the ocean. From her balcony, she could watch the planes land at the San Diego airport and the cruise ships fill the harbor. She could see the red roof of the hotel out on Coronado Island. Though she no longer noticed, an endless roar rose up from Interstate 5. The rent was ridiculously high, but an up-and-coming television reporter should be well located. Live as if your dream will come true.

It wasn't just her opinion. *San Diego Reader* had named her 28th out of 50 Young Professionals to Watch. Well, if San Diego was watching, catching her live reporting weeknights at 6 p.m.

and re-aired at 10, spotting her out shopping on weekends, she'd better be living in a neighborhood with cachet. "In our business, it's not who you are," Sunny had told her early on, "it's who they *think* you are."

Maitlyn's career plan was to rise from local-interest reporter to investigative journalist to anchorwoman. She wanted to become "the face of San Diego news" and "a name you can trust" — Channel Four's current franchise pieces — not just, as Scott had so charmingly put it, "the hot news chick." From there, she hoped that a national network would think she was celebrity material, ready for prime time, and pluck her up. Yesterday's interview was supposed to be a big step in her ascendance. Now Sunny's stinging words replayed in her head: *Do you want to be damaged goods?*

She hadn't yet called the cops. She was giving herself time to think it over, like Sunny had suggested. She wasn't hurt, not physically. She had been felt up uninvited before — back in high school. You feel violated, but it passes. *So why this anxious feeling?*

Maybe some exercise would calm her nerves. She tucked her hair up in a baseball cap, hid her face behind sunglasses, and went for a jog in Balboa Park. The morning was warm enough for shorts, but she opted for loose sweat pants and pulled a saggy sweatshirt over her most repressive sports bra. She would have worn a fake mustache if she had one.

She stayed on the sidewalk along 6th Avenue, and no one bothered her, no one recognized her, the guys who passed her didn't look back over their shoulders, and she didn't check out their calves. *Men are gross.* Maybe she could call Nathan's wife, tell her what happened. Or get a lawyer and file an affidavit, whatever that means. *No, no lawyers.* There must be some way of putting Nathan on notice without getting the law involved, without becoming breaking news yourself, some way of teaching him a harsh lesson so that he never did that to a woman again. *I should have smashed* all *those stupid bonsai trees.*

After her run, Maitlyn took a shower and dried her hair. She ate some toast and drank green tea instead of coffee. And still she felt jittery. She stood by the window again, looking out at the expanse of ocean. *Okay, he scared me. I was cornered. He had his hands up my shirt. Of course, I was scared. He would have raped me. Who wouldn't be scared?* She had read enough books on clearing out emotions and staying in "the now." She knew how to do this. *Fear is nothing to be ashamed of. Fear is what told me to fight back. Fear is what told me to run.* Acknowledge and affirm. *Thank you, fear. Thank you for saving me.* Then release. *But I don't need you right now, fear. The danger is gone. I'm safe.* That was a good mantra. She wrote it on a notepad and stuck the page on the refrigerator door: "The danger is gone, I'm safe."

Out of habit, she went looking for her phone but left it turned off. *He would have raped me.* If she had screamed, would he have stopped? Would Scott and Charles have heard her cries for help and come running? Would they have saved her? *Not Scott.* He would have told her to calm down, don't upset the congressman, don't lose the scoop. *Charles, though.* Charles would have torn that house apart to get between her and Nathan. Charles was tough.

At the end of yesterday's meeting with Mr. Cooper, the lawyer had suggested that Charles might have grounds for a lawsuit against Congressman Saltenstall. "I could give you the names of some attorneys who handle that sort of thing."

Charles had responded with a snort. "I'll give *you* a few names. Dwayne, Marvin, Alden. My brothers would die laughing if I sued someone for a few grass stains. In our house, you got hit harder than that before breakfast. No, I think we'll just call it even."

He had seemed in a hurry to leave the station building. Maitlyn had to run to catch up with him. "Charles, wait, I owe you a thank you." She wasn't quite sure what to thank him for, or how to phrase it, so she just said it again. "Thank you. That was good of you."

He nodded. "Just looking out for the talent. You'd do the same for me." Then he lowered his voice so he wouldn't be overheard. "You got someone to talk to? About what happened."

She answered quickly, "Yeah, sure. I'll be fine."

But she wasn't fine. *He would have raped me.* She looked over at the frig. *The danger is gone, I'm safe.* She was crying again, and who could she talk to, really? Her friends couldn't be trusted with such a scandalous secret. Sunny was busy at work. She could call her mother in Arizona, but Mom would only freak out about what happened, and that wouldn't help anyone.

I could drive over to Whatshisface's office, tell him about my famous new boyfriend who doesn't take pains to hide his marriage and really knows how to make a girl feel special. Asshole Number One, meet Asshole Number Two. She caught herself. *Hello, bitterness. Of course, I'm bitter. That's perfectly understandable. It's okay to feel bitter. But don't act bitter. Just feel it.*

So, feeling bitter and feeling mostly okay about it, Maitlyn drove to her grandmother's house.

Before an early and unexpected death, Maitlyn's father had carted her to and from elementary school in a 1967 Volkswagen Beetle. She had loved the gentle rattle and whine of the engine and the old-car smell of peeling upholstery and rubber floor mats.

When she got promoted to reporter and went shopping for her first brand new automobile, nostalgia got the best of her. The New Beetle didn't sound or smell like Dad's old Bug, and the low gas mileage was probably irresponsible, but the turbocharged engine accelerated effortlessly up freeway ramps. Maitlyn would have chosen a white exterior, in tribute to Dad's old ride, except pale blue was her favorite color—VW marketing called it "denim".

So, a splashy new Bug, with flower decals on the windows. Scott called it a "chick mobile," which was alright by Maitlyn. She called it Ciela. Whatshisface hated riding in it, and always insisted they take his Nissan Xterra, like they needed four-wheel drive and eight-inch ground clearance to drive downtown. *Prick mobile.* He especially didn't want to ride in Ciela with the top down. Maitlyn, though, loved zooming over Coronado Bridge with the wind in her hair, like she was soaring through the sky, pale blue on pale blue.

But not today, no windswept tresses, she wasn't in the mood. Cruising the bridge, two hundred feet above San Diego Bay, her mind was on what Scott had said about Charles. "He goaded him, that's what I think. Maybe he said something about you or about the fumble, maybe it was something else, but I'm pretty sure he wanted Nathan to come after him. That's why he told me to get the camera ready."

Maitlyn's grandmother lived on 1st Street, not far from where the bridge descended onto Coronado Island, population 24,000, the flattest city in California. Grandma only went out on Mondays and Fridays—for shopping and duplicate bridge games—so Maitlyn knew she'd be home. The house was nothing fancy—a one-story box with wood siding and composition shingles, a typical southern California residence from the 1950s, back when new arrivals were trying to replicate the Midwest. A white picket fence surrounded a neat square of lawn. A row of rose bushes, heavy with white blossoms, lined the walkway. Near the front door, a small U.S. flag fluttered in the midday sun. Indeed, every front yard on 1st Street was tidy, the sidewalks were clean, flags were plentiful—a picture of domestic tranquility, the all-white, all-American neighborhood where Maitlyn's father had grown up, a place where Maitlyn had always felt secure.

"Grandma, it's me." Maitlyn knocked on the screen door and let herself in. A well-groomed Sheltie came on the run. "Hi, Sugarpie, hi there." The dog yipped with joy and jumped against Maitlyn's knees.

Grandma appeared from the kitchen and greeted her with a hug. "Mattie, what a nice surprise. You're not sick, are you?"

"They gave me the day off."

"Well, they should. They work you too hard."

Maitlyn's eyes were drawn to the dining room wall. "You got a new painting?" The sun-drenched beachscape was instantly recognizable as La Jolla.

"It's cliché, I know—palm trees above The Cove—but I couldn't resist. See, look, it has the little clubhouse where we play bridge. You'll stay for lunch, won't you?"

Maitlyn couldn't say no, not to the woman who had practically raised her after Maitlyn's widowed mother had found full-time work, and a clandestine affair, in a chiropractor's office. But if Maitlyn hadn't wanted tuna salad on toasted English muffins and strawberries with milk and sugar—comfort food from her childhood—she wouldn't have come at noon.

She followed Grandma into the kitchen and helped her set the table. She had something she wanted to ask. "Do you know an old painting of a boy with a hat? Like a floppy hat. With a feather."

Grandma thought for a moment while placing napkins under forks. "Sounds like *Blue Boy*. We saw it at the Huntington, remember? He's holding a hat at his side." She had taught art history once upon a time and had introduced young Maitlyn to the finer museums of Los Angeles.

"No, this one's *wearing* the hat. And his blouse is black and white stripes. Could be a Rembrandt. You know, dark and shadowy. It's real small."

"Maybe Frans Hals. Are you in the market for seventeenth-century Dutch?"

"What would they go for?"

"The *Laughing Cavalier*—you can't put a price tag on a true masterwork. But a minor Frans Hals might be worth a million dollars. Same as this house."

Her residence might have been unremarkable, but the island was prime real estate. "I'm told I'm rich," Grandma had said one time, "but I can barely afford the gardener." She was sitting on a gold mine, "but if I sold it, where would I go?" In truth, property taxes were low, the house was paid for, and Grandpa had invested well. Grandma could live out her days in island repose.

After lunch, Grandma brought out a coffee table book of important Dutch paintings. Maitlyn flipped through the pages until the Sheltie jumped onto the living room couch and started barking at the front window. "What is it, Sugar?" Grandma asked. "Is it a ship? Do you want to see the ship?"

The word *ship* sent the dog racing to the front door, then to Grandma, and back to the door. You couldn't see the harbor from the house, and you couldn't hear a ship chugging by, but somehow Sugar always knew. And a ship meant a walk.

"It must be the navy. She doesn't get this excited about the cruise liners. Are you coming with us, Mattie?"

They walked down the street to Bayview Park, which reached to the water's edge. A gray warship, bristling with communications structures, was headed out to sea, led by a patrol boat and flanked by security men on jet skis.

"She's a destroyer. Looks like 106. USS *Stockdale*. Keeping us safe and sound." Grandma knew her Pacific Fleet. "Say hi, Sugar. Say hi to the ship." Grandma waved and Sugar barked excitedly. "Wave, Mattie. You might meet a nice sailor."

"That's the last thing I need." Maitlyn looked past *Stockdale* and across the harbor to the city, trying to pick out her building on the hillside. It was two miles away, but she guessed that the turret-mounted cannon in the bow of the ship could easily reach her apartment and ruin it with a quick barrage. *Maybe I should start carrying a gun.*

"Mattie, what's bothering you?"

Maitlyn didn't answer right away, and Grandma didn't push it. She knew Maitlyn's moods—you had to give her time. Rather than open fire on Banker's Hill, the ship disappeared around the naval air station at the north end of the island.

Maitlyn remembered the mantra on the refrigerator: *The danger is gone, I'm safe.* She took a deep breath and started to explain. "I interviewed Nathan yesterday."

"Nathan? You mean *Nathan* Nathan? Why didn't you tell me? Why didn't you take me along?" Nathan's success on the field had inspired the entire city, even Grandma, who had taken to football like she took to the art world—more enthusiastic observer than expert connoisseur.

"You can watch it on Four in a few days."

"I'm still a card-carrying member of Nathan's Nation. The fumble wasn't his fault. His blockers let him get blindsided. He'll always get my vote. What's he like in person?"

"Not what I expected." *He would have raped me.*

They stood for awhile without speaking. A little blue-and-white ferry boat burbled past on its way to the mainland. A screeching passenger jet took off from the airport. Maitlyn usually found the busyness of the harbor reassuring—a city at work. Today, the noise irritated her.

"Is that why you took the day off?"

Surprised by the question, Maitlyn glanced at her grandmother, then looked away, wondering how much more to say. The afternoon sun gleamed off the office towers downtown. The harbor stunk of fuel and stagnant water and pelican shit. "Grandma, he made a pass at me. A not very nice one."

Grandma studied Maitlyn's face. "It made you uncomfortable." She always had been able to read her granddaughter.

"Very." Maitlyn closed her eyes. She had revealed enough. When she felt her grandmother's hand on her arm, the tears started.

"I'm sorry, Mattie. Maybe he meant well. He seems like such a good man."

Back at her condo in the evening, Maitlyn finally turned on her phone. She had a long list of texts, mostly from Scott and Mr. Cooper. Something was up. Rather than wade through the messages, she dialed Scott's number.

He picked up on the first ring. "Where have you been all day? You know what's going on, right?" He sounded worked up.

"Tell me."

"Charles punched Nathan."

"What?"

"Haven't you been online? Charles slugged him in the jaw. They caught it on a security camera."

"When?"

"Yesterday. That's why Nathan chased him. The internet is blowing up. You really haven't seen it? First it was my footage of Nathan pushing him—which was everywhere, by the way, I mean big time—and people were calling Nathan a bully and saying he should resign from Congress. So then Nathan's office released their video from the doorway. First you see Charles ring the doorbell, and Nathan opens the door, and it looks like they exchange words, and then Charles just goes and pops him."

"While we were waiting in the van?"

"Uh-hunh. So now Charles is a thug and Nathan is the victim. It's getting real ugly out there. Fox News is having a field day."

Maitlyn turned on her laptop, but it was taking forever. "Have you talked to Charles?"

"Can't. He's been huddled up with management. Cooper's been trying to get a hold of you. Did your phone die or something?"

"Does Cooper know about—? Did Charles tell him?"

"You mean about what happened to you? I don't know. Maybe not, because Cooper wants us camped outside Nathan's house first thing in the morning."

"I can't go back there." Her home page finally came up, and the news headline was enormous: *SUCKER PUNCH!*

"You don't have a choice. They're working on getting a second interview. It's going to be all Nathan, all the time, and you're the one with access. I told you this would be our big break."

Maitlyn hung up. The implications spun through her brain, accompanied by a wave of panic. Her heart pounded, her hands shook. No way could she interview that creep again. She couldn't go back to Rancho Santa Fe — just thinking about it made her want to scream — which meant she would have to tell Mr. Cooper why she couldn't do it, and he wouldn't keep it a secret. No, he would put it out there, everywhere, big time, and *she* would become the story, reporters would be camped out on *her* street, because that's what they all wanted — scandal. *Nathan pushed the news guy because he punched Nathan because Nathan was in a back room groping the reporter.* There's your dominant narrative. *Did the hot news chick try to seduce the congressman? Is that why she asked about his wife in the interview?* Maitlyn could feel sweat dripping from her armpits. *Damaged goods.* She would never become a news anchor. "Anchorette," Scott had called it.

She paced around the apartment. She was going to be sick. *Mr. Cooper, I need to stay in bed. I can't hold anything down. Maybe it's the flu.*

Her phone rang. She assumed it was Scott again and answered without checking caller I.D. It was Grandma. "Mattie, I just saw the news. Why didn't you tell me?"

"Tell you what?"

"That black guy attacked Nathan. It's just terrible. Why would he do that? Did it have something to do with you?"

"No. I don't know. I just found out. What do you mean — to do with me?"

"Is the black guy — ?"

"His name is Charles."

"Is he your boyfriend?"

"No!" She immediately regretted denying it so forcefully. Did she sound defensive? Racist?

Grandma must have sensed she had gone too far because she abruptly changed the subject. "Oh, I found another book of Dutch paintings. Lots of portraits with feathered hats. You can take a look next time you visit."

Earlier, after the walk to see the ship, Maitlyn had finished skimming through the first book. The portrait of the boy in the striped blouse — the one she had seen in Nathan's house — wasn't there.

4

Maitlyn tossed and turned all night, but in the morning somehow found the zone—*just you and the ball*—and drove to work. She walked through the building with her game face on, ignoring the stares, and headed straight for Mr. Cooper's office. He hung up his phone and gestured toward a TV screen, where the video of Charles punching Nathan was playing in slow motion, frame by frame, the sound muted. The grainy picture and shadowy faces suggested a crime scene.

"How could you have your cell off when all this is happening?" Mr. Cooper asked.

"I was—."

"I know. Scott said you weren't feeling well."

"Yeah, I—."

He waved her off. "He and Sheila have been outside Nathan's gate since six this morning." Sheila was Mr. Cooper's latest find. "I'm sorry, Maitlyn, but you didn't call in and we couldn't wait." Scott called her the "new hot news chick."

"Does she have an interview?"

"As soon as Nathan's PR people call back, we're sending her in. Unless he insists on you. Are you okay? You look pale."

A surge of panic had sent her heart racing. She couldn't go out there. She couldn't go near him. She reached for the chair behind her. "Yeah. Fine. Just a little—."

A secretary's voice announced, "Jerry on three."

Mr. Cooper picked up the desk phone. "Is it a go?" He listened, occasionally murmuring "good" or "okay," then "I'll take care of it" and "keep me posted."

Meanwhile, on the screen, Nathan staggered back into the house, disappearing from view. Maitlyn had already seen it several times—it was hard not to watch. Charles turned and walked away, but, in one still frame, you could see his face and almost read his hat: You Can't Fix Stupid. A few empty frames clicked by, then Nathan reappeared, following him. The video ended, and immediately the broadcast cut to Scott's footage of Nathan pushing Charles on the lawn.

Mr. Cooper hung up the phone. "Sheila's doing the interview."

"Right now?"

"I'd rather it was you, believe me, Maitlyn, but it would take you an hour to get up the freeway, and we want live feed as soon as possible. You understand."

"Yeah. Okay. I just...I need to—."

"Maitlyn, if you're sick, go home, for Christ's sake. We've got this covered."

She rushed down the hall to her office and called Scott. He picked up after three rings. "Maitlyn, I can't talk, I'm at—."

"I know. Did you warn her?"

"What?"

"Sheila. You have to warn her. Don't take the house tour."

"Okay," he laughed.

"Scott, I'm serious."

"Okay. I gotta go."

"Listen to me. Don't let him get her alone."

"Roger that."

Maitlyn closed her eyes. She needed to slow down, get grounded. *I'm right here, right now. I'm okay.* She wouldn't have to face Nathan again. *The danger is gone, I'm safe.* She took deep breaths, focusing on the flow of air. *But I can forget about prime time.* No one was going to care about her asking Congressman Saltenstall why he was running for Senate, not when they could watch raven-haired Sheila with her pointy little nose asking him what was said in the doorway that led to fisticuffs with Charles. *Thank God for Charles.* Charles had become the story, not her. She could go home if she wanted. *I should go home, turn everything off again. Let Sheila have her big moment.*

A knock on the door, and Sunny stuck her head in. "Hey, you busy? Howya doing? Crazy stuff, hunh?"

"Crazy."

Sunny pulled the door closed and sat down. "Are you okay? I mean, with — ."

"Yeah."

"I mean, Charles punched him because of you, right? I mean, because of what Nathan did."

"Who knows?" Maitlyn had heard two different versions from Charles, and the security video suggested neither one was complete. "Is he around today?"

"Who, Charles? You haven't heard? They let him go."

Maitlyn burst back into Mr. Cooper's office without knocking. "You fired Charles?" The lawyer was there, staring at her. Maitlyn tried to catch her anger. "I'm sorry, but — ."

"Maitlyn," Mr. Cooper interrupted, "close the door and have a seat."

She didn't sit. "He's our best tech guy. You've said so yourself." She didn't know how else to defend Charles, not without telling the whole story of their visit to Nathan's house.

"I'm not happy about it either," Mr. Cooper said wryly, "but Channel Four policy is you don't slug congressmen. Especially not Republicans."

The lawyer laughed.

"Right there." Maitlyn pointed at the TV screen, where Charles and Nathan were talking in the doorway again. "Nathan said something to Charles right there — insulted him or called him a name. Nathan instigated it."

"It was the other way around," the lawyer injected. "Mr. Lockett was mad about the fumble. You heard him."

"Yeah, but that...." *That was a lie*, she wanted to explain. *Charles didn't punch a guy because of some football game fifteen years ago.* But she couldn't say it.

"Maitlyn." Mr. Cooper was getting impatient. "Charles sat in that chair right there for two hours yesterday. He told us it was his fault. He took full responsibility."

"So give him a second chance. He made a mistake."

Mr. Cooper sighed and picked up the remote control. "Maitlyn, Maitlyn."

"What?" She hated when his tone became condescending, like he really wished she could understand the obvious. He probably thought he was being kind.

"This isn't a little mistake. This is assaulting *Nathan*. On camera. This is the lead story on the networks." He flipped channels to show her. Every news station had the video going.

"Mr. Lockett will probably end up in court," the lawyer added.

Maitlyn turned to face the lawyer. "Nathan won't press charges, if that's what you mean."

"Oh, we're pretty sure he will."

"He won't," she retorted. *Why are lawyers always so smug?* "I mean, Nathan... he's going to want this to go away. It's a distraction. Politicians don't like to testify in court. They get nervous when they have to tell the truth." *Especially about sexual assault.*

"That's true," Mr. Cooper agreed.

"You could just let Charles...I don't know...give him unpaid leave or something, until this blows over and something bigger comes along. Charles is...he's a good guy."

Mr. Cooper leaned back in his chair, propped his feet on his desk, and flipped another channel. "You're being noble, Maitlyn, sticking up for your crew member, but you're not seeing the whole picture. Nathan's gonna milk this. Look at Fox. They're framing this as a white homeowner defending his property against a black invader. Then it becomes a discussion of illegals crossing the border. Suddenly, Nathan's a hero among a certain segment of voters. He's strong, he's tough, he fights back. When was the last time California sent a Republican senator to Washington? And if polls are correct, he's going to make it a real race. He's like the new Schwarzenegger — without the misogyny."

Maitlyn's legs felt wobbly and she had to sit down. The studio full of breasts flashed through her mind. The hands on her shoulders. The hands under her shirt. "Nathan is...." Her voice was shaking. She didn't know what to say. *A creep? Molester?* She probably wasn't his first victim. Or his last.

"Maitlyn?"

"All I'm saying — asking — is don't cut off Charles completely. A month from now, no one will remember his name, and no one will care that he comes back to work. I mean, we're still getting the interview, right?"

Mr. Cooper rubbed his temples with a thumb and middle finger, as if to say all this nagging was giving him a headache. "We're getting the interview — Sheila's out at Rancho Santa Fe — because we escorted Charles out of the building yesterday."

"Immediate dismissal," the lawyer explained. "Nathan's people insisted on it."

Rather than go home, Maitlyn drove straight to Coronado. She was tired and wanted to lie down in her old bedroom, with a gentle sea breeze floating through the window screen, and fall asleep to the sound of her grandmother busy in the kitchen. It was the safest place she knew.

She burrowed her head into the familiar pillows, but sleep didn't come. Charles had lost his job, and Sheila was stealing the scoop, all because Maitlyn had allowed Nathan to lure her into his studio. *No, it's not my fault, I did nothing wrong.* But Charles taking the fall—that *was* her fault. If she came forward, told her story, then Charles is the hero who stood up for her and gave Nathan what he deserved. *And I'm damaged goods.*

She started crying but felt better when she decided that coming forward wouldn't do any good. Nathan would just deny it, and everyone would see that she had smiled and gone ahead with the interview—*that was so stupid*—and no one would believe her. *A misunderstanding. Nathan's Nation versus little Maitlyn Flutters. Probably he meant well.* Even her grandmother gave Nathan the benefit of the doubt.

On the dresser by the bed stood an old photo of Commander Calvin Flutters. Grandpa spent twenty years in the navy, then worked as a liaison for a ship-building company. A heart attack took him on the job at fifty-eight. "Menfolk die young in our family," Grandma had told her, "the women flutter on."

Growing up, Maitlyn had spent so little time around adult males—maybe that's why she didn't understand them. "You're looking for a father figure," her college roommate had told her, when she was fooling around with her English professor. Then came a guy closer in age, only six years older but so much younger. She wanted to be "the name you can trust." He liked bartending because "Dude, I'm a night person." Then it was Whatshisface, already in his forties with two kids. She liked older men—no shame in that. *But that's why I get into these messes. You can't fix stupid.*

Giving up on the nap, Maitlyn went out to the kitchen, where Grandma was taking peanut butter cookies out of the oven. "I know you don't eat sweets, Mattie, but these were always your favorite."

A hot news chick has to watch her figure, but a little cheat wouldn't hurt, just this once, after all she'd been through. When Maitlyn dipped the warm cookie in milk, she was a kid again, spending afternoons after school with Grandma. Back then, her mother would either pick her up after work or call to say she was "staying late again," and then Maitlyn would sleep over on the island. No doubt the chiropractor, Mom's employer, had called his wife with the same "staying late" message. Young Maitlyn hadn't understood about extramarital affairs and the way a lonely widow might be drawn to her good-humored boss, but somehow she had known.

"Grandma, how come you never remarried?"

Grandma arched a quizzical eyebrow before answering. "It never seemed right. Your grandfather—we'd known each other forever. There *were* offers. But I had you for company, and then I got Sugar. A man would only hash things up."

"Weren't you friends with the popcorn guy?"

"Orville and his wife had a condo on the island. His second wife—Nina. She died, and I talked with Orville on the phone once in a while. That was all. He wasn't exactly a looker. Now if Paul Newman had been available, and if he played duplicate bridge...."

When Grandma and Sugar left for a walk, Maitlyn flipped on Channel Four to find Sheila's interview—she was going to have to watch it eventually. Again, it was staged by the fireplace, with the old fisherman looking on. People always said Sheila was naturally beautiful, but that nose and those carved cheekbones, caked with makeup for the camera, were acquired—Maitlyn was sure of it. Nathan, too, was fake, trying hard to look sincere as he told Scott's camera, "I apologize to Mr. Lockett if I offended him in some way. If I overreacted when he hit me, I apologize for that too. I harbor no hard feelings against him."

"What an asshole," Maitlyn said aloud, gripping a throw pillow for security. "You had him fired."

Sheila nodded, trying to appear thoughtful. Maitlyn had never before seen her wearing eyeglasses and guessed they were clear lenses. Not a bad idea, actually, the schoolmarm look.

But the glasses didn't make Sheila's questions any smarter. "Did it hurt?" she asked Nathan.

He laughed and rubbed his handsome chin. "I've got a pretty tough jaw. Of course, had I known what was coming, I would have put on my old helmet."

Maitlyn studied Sheila, searching for evidence of Nathan's grubby hands at work, but the blouse looked untroubled and not a hair out of place.

"So, Congressman," Sheila smiled, "you still don't know why Mr. Lockett took a swing at you?"

Because he would have raped me.

"Well, Sheila, you never know when the media is going to hit you, or from which angle." He put up his fists, pretending to guard his face.

Sheila laughed. "Don't worry, this is a friendly interview. Do you really still have your old helmet?"

"Jesus, Sheila," Maitlyn said to the television, "ask something serious."

After a few more empty questions, the interview ended. Maitlyn called Scott, who was in a good mood. "She did good, don't you think?"

"A total fluff job," Maitlyn snorted back.

"What did you expect? They told her keep it light."

"Did he offer her the house tour?"

"She never left the living room, and he disappeared as soon as we wrapped. Some of his campaign people were there."

The relief Maitlyn felt should have been for Sheila's safety, but, in fact, Maitlyn wanted to believe she was special, that Nathan didn't hit on every hot news chick that came his way. *Am I really jealous of that creep's attention?*

"Are you there?" Scott asked when she went quiet.

"Yeah. Uh, have you heard anything from Charles?"

"Not a peep. Supposedly, he's been strongly advised not to speak with the media, including us. My guess is he's already back in Texas, lying low."

When Sugar burst into the room, panting from the walk, Maitlyn was peering at more photographs of old Dutch paintings. "I found it, Grandma. It's by Frans van Mieris. A self-portrait. It's called *A Cavalier*." In the painting, a man was holding a sword and wearing a striped blouse and a big black hat with a red feather.

Grandma came over for a look. "I thought you said it was a boy."

"I only caught a quick glimpse of it." *I was running from a rapist.*

"You saw this painting?" Grandma sounded skeptical.

"Yeah. It's real small."

"Are you sure? This exact one?"

"See, it says sixteen by twenty centimeters."

"Mattie, that piece was stolen ten years ago."

5

To Maitlyn's relief, Mr. Cooper kept Sheila and Scott assigned to Nathan. To Maitlyn's dismay, Sheila was getting raves for her live reporting from the campaign trail. A flock of reporters shadowed the celebrity candidate, elbowing for position at his rallies, but Sheila always managed to catch his eye and get in a quick question or two before he ducked away. Maybe it was because he could trust her to ask feely questions like "Congressman Saltenstall, how do you feel your campaign is going?" or "Congressman, the polls suggest you're now the front runner, are you feeling good about that?"

Only once, so far as Maitlyn could tell, did Sheila pose something of substance. "Congressman," she asked, "how do you respond to accusations that you're too close with the military industry, that you would be the senator from Lockheed-Martin?" Nathan gave her forearm a convivial pat to show he wasn't threatened by this line of inquiry and responded with a smile, "Sheila, I hope to be the senator from California. And Lockheed-Martin and Raytheon, General Dynamics, Northup Grumman— these companies employ thousands of Californians, not to mention they help keep our armed forces the finest in the world. I'll keep these jobs in our state and work for more."

While Sheila was starring in Nathan Watch, Maitlyn was back to local interest stories. With a young cameraman named Hassan, she rushed off to Carlsbad, where a great white shark had taken a bite out of a surfboard. Maitlyn lollipopped her microphone in the surfer's face, and he lit up. "I shoved my board in its mouth and rolled off. My buddy got it on his GoPro, so everybody should check it out on YouTube. It's gnarly."

As they left the scene, Hassan wondered aloud, "This is news?"

"They'll use it for the kicker at 10," Maitlyn told him. The producers always ended the late broadcast with a soft piece.

Maitlyn also covered the departure of an aircraft carrier. She'd been watching these big ships come and go most of her life, yet, up close, their immensity always astounded her. "A floating airport," she told the camera, as she stood at the naval base on the north end of Coronado, not far at all from her grandmother's house. "Now, this ship is longer than three football fields, carries ninety aircraft and a crew of six thousand. It has a TV station and its own zip code. You really can't appreciate the size unless you come down to the dock and take a look. I'll leave you with one more detail as we watch *USS George Washington* head out to sea. The two anchors each weigh thirty tons. That's the equivalent, I'm told, of five adult male elephants." She had looked it up on her smartphone. For the benefit of the camera—and for her grandmother, who would catch this at 6 p.m.—she turned and waved to the ship lined with sailors in their dress whites. "Godspeed."

"Funny thing," Hassan said as they drove back over the bridge, leaving the island, "that ship does nothing to keep us safe. Can't prevent wildfires. Can't end the drought. Can't protect the border. Can't stop the next 9/11. You should do a story like that."

"Why?"

"Twenty billion dollars down the drain. That would be killer reporting."

"It'd never make the air. In case you haven't noticed, San Diego is a navy town." She pointed out the window to the flotilla of gray ships lined up at the piers.

"Which actually makes us less safe. When China decides to bomb America, where to do you think they're gonna start? Probably the nuclear reactors up in San Onofre and then this harbor. This bridge we're on is doomed."

"Hassan."

"What?"

"Just...." She wanted to tell him to shut up, but she had to work with him again the next day.

"What?"

"Take a chill pill." *Sheila gets Scott*, Maitlyn thought to herself, *and I have to drive around with this bozo.*

"San Diego may not want to hear it, but it's the truth. All them rich folks back on Coronado are gonna be at the center of the bull's eye. If global warming doesn't drown them first."

Apparently what San Diego *did* want to hear was Nathan. In the two weeks since the incident with Charles, his poll numbers had soared. A local rally at a football stadium drew five thousand Nathanites holding signs with slogans like "Nathan fights back" and "Nathan stands his ground." An equally large and boisterous turnout greeted him in Los Angeles, normally a Democratic stronghold. The latest poll had him as a lock to win the Republican primary and gave him a better than even chance at defeating the Democratic incumbent in November. National pundits were calling him "presidential material."

Maitlyn just wished he would disappear. She wanted to forget about him and get on with her life. But the man who would have raped her was constantly in the news, shaking hands at car shows in the Inland Empire, kissing babies at farmers' markets in the Bay Area, making the rounds on late night talk shows. His wife was completely absent from his campaign, yet he was still polling well among women. White women, anyway. Maitlyn wanted to tell them what Nathan was like at home, in his studio—the *real* Nathan—but how could she? He was suddenly so popular that if she accused him of sexual assault, filed a complaint with the police, it would be dismissed as a political move, sour grapes. *I could produce a corpse with his fingerprints all over the murder weapon and no one would blink an eye.* Nathan was untouchable.

And that wasn't all. "You know about Sheila and Nathan, right?" Sunny asked casually one day. "Hot and heavy."

"Yeah, right." Maitlyn scoffed at the gossip, but the future flashed before her eyes: Nathan taking up residence in the Senate, and Sheila, with little experience and less talent, promptly promoted to Capitol Hill reporter. The latest power couple, dining at the White House, sitting for the cover of *Time* magazine, leaving little Maitlyn Flutters behind in San Diego, nothing but collateral damage, road kill, just her and her big, searing secret.

That evening, Maitlyn paced around her apartment, took an Ativan, which her doctor had prescribed for her lingering anxiety, and finally decided to make the call. "Someone has to do it," she said aloud, and started dialing the police department. She quit after three numbers and tossed her phone onto the couch.

Instead of reporting the assault, she went online and again searched Google for "theft of *A Cavalier*." She wanted her facts straight. The tiny painting was stolen from an art gallery in Australia while the gallery was open to the public. Someone with a Phillips head screwdriver had simply removed two fasteners, grabbed the frame off the wall, stuck it in a jacket pocket or under a sweater, and walked out. The gallery room had no surveillance cameras and guards rarely came by. The piece was probably for sale on the black market in Amsterdam before anyone noticed it was missing. The perfect crime.

Maitlyn poured a glass of Pinot Grigio, sunk into her couch, and, for the first time in two weeks, relaxed. The Ativan was kicking in. A second glass of wine, and she was floating. The phone rang. She rarely answered calls when she didn't recognize the incoming number, but *what the fuck.* "Hello?"

"Maitlyn?" She knew that deep voice. "Charles Lockett here." And that hint of Texas twang. "How y'all doin'?"

"I'm okay." Why would he be calling? Was he pissed at her for not coming to his defense? "How are *you*?"

"Hanging in there. They gave me three month's severance, so I'm just kicking it. I saw you on that shark attack. Ooh-wee, that surfer boy was checking you out."

"Great." Being ogled by a teenage dumbshit did nothing for her.

"I see they got Sheila on Nathan."

"Better her than me."

"I hear you. But you're doing okay? That was a rough time of day out in Rancho. Anything I can do for you?"

Maitlyn's eyes teared up. Sunny, Scott, Grandma—none of them had asked her that. "Charles, do I owe you an apology? I mean, if people knew why you hit him...."

"*He* knows why. That's all that matters."

"But you got fired."

"Blessing in disguise. I'ma find me something better. This cat lands on his feet."

"In that case," she giggled, "could you hit him again?"

"Hell, yeah. And this time I ain't going easy. Gonna give him the business. Course, then they'd go and make him commander-in-chief."

"No kidding. Have you seen his polls? Scott's calling it the Lockett Bump."

Charles laughed. "Sounds about right. Nothing says 'vote for me' like getting punched by a black man."

"Hey, do you know anything about art?"

"Art who?"

"No, like paintings and stuff."

"Oh. Like my man Basquiat? That dude tripped me out. Wish I could afford one of his. All I got on my wall is an old Leroy Neiman print of Olajuwon. Hakeem the Dream, baby."

The names meant nothing to Maitlyn. Her grandmother had only taught her the European greats. "I think Nathan has a stolen painting in his house."

"Say what?"

50

"I went into this closet—I thought it was a closet—but there was this famous portrait that's been missing for a decade."

"Seriously? What's it worth?"

"One-point-four mil."

Charles let out a low whistle. "Ol' Nate the Great gets everything. Could be a fake though."

"That's what my grandmother says. But why hide a fake in a back room? I took a picture of it. I can show you."

The next day at work, Maitlyn went to see Mr. Cooper, who was in his usual chipper mood. "Maitlyn, super work on that aircraft carrier. You looked good."

"Thanks." It was always about her looks.

"I got a real nice phone call from the navy thanking us for the coverage, and another from the Marines. They want a story on their helicopters fighting that wildfire up at Pendleton."

"Yuck." Camp Pendleton meant a long drive up the freeway, followed by a public relations officer extolling "the Corps" while trying to hit on her. Naval officers could be attractive, if she was in the right mood, but marines gave her the creeps. There was something sinister under all that aggressive politeness.

"You got something better?"

"Actually, yes. I want to pitch a story."

Mr. Cooper looked a little surprised. "Shoot."

"Global warming is causing the oceans to rise."

"Maitlyn." He shook his head, like he felt sorry for her naiveté.

"Just hear me out. One day, all those houses in Pacific Beach and Ocean Beach will be flooded. Coronado might be gone. Same with the airport."

"So they say."

"How can that not be of local interest?"

"Because it hasn't happened yet. This is something for Nightline or National Geographic, not a three-minute cutaway on the local news. It's too big for us." He sorted some papers on his desk, signaling that the conversation was over.

Maitlyn was prepared for his objections. "So we make it a series. I'll go see the scientists up in La Jolla. I'll talk to insurance companies. I'll talk to the Coast Guard. There's a scare story here—the kind that gets ratings. How will sea-level rise affect San Diego?"

"Maitlyn, Maitlyn."

"What?" How she hated his condescension. "We did killer bees coming from Mexico."

"I'm sorry about Nathan. That was your story, and I let Sheila run with it. I'm sorry your interview got pulled." They hadn't bothered to air her full conversation with Nathan. They said it was already old news.

"You aren't even listening, are you?" She was ready to walk out in a huff.

"I'm listening, Maitlyn. You want to break a ratings buster—I get it—a real scoop. San Diego under water. It's a great story. In fifty years."

"It's already happening. In fifty years, it will be too late."

"That's just speculation—this whole global warming business." He waved a hand toward the muted television, which was airing CNN. "No one knows for sure."

"Then how about a story on a stolen painting? A Dutch masterpiece. Right here in San Diego County."

"That's crime. That's Jeffrey's beat. Okay, listen, bring me an outline on what this sea-level series looks like. You need an angle. Are homeowners in trouble? Is the city ignoring the issue? But first go do that Pendleton thing. Those military guys love you."

So forty-five miserable minutes on Interstate 5 northbound, the usual slowdowns at Del Mar and Carlsbad, and Hassan, like everyone else in California, wanting to talk about the congressman who was taking the Senate race by storm. "I'm not into his politics, but he was my hero growing up."

"Yeah?" Maitlyn wasn't in the mood for friendly chatter. Working with Hassan felt like a demotion, like she was back on the B team. Maybe Mr. Cooper was right—she *was* looking for a big story to reclaim her position as the top hot news chick. *No, I'm worried about Grandma's house becoming fish habitat.*

"If you ever get another interview with him, I hope you take me along."

"Talk to Sheila."

"I should. Sheila's cool."

So I guess I'm not, Maitlyn thought, as she flipped through the photos on her phone. The last two were from when she was hiding from Nathan. Those moments in the closet were still vivid. After she had hung up with Scott—"This is our scoop, Maitlyn"—she had felt around in the dark for a light switch. It was blinding at first, but her eyes adjusted, and the closet, glowing with shiny metal, turned out to be a large shrine to Nathan's football career. Glass display cases held trophies and signed footballs. Plaques and game photos covered the walls. A life-sized cardboard Nathan gave her a start. When she kicked it in the groin, it collapsed forward at the waist, revealing *A Cavalier*. The tiny portrait hung in a back corner, hidden from casual view. Despite panic rising again—she had to go interview her attacker—she somehow thought to snap a few pictures before turning off the light and quietly closing the door behind her.

"I met him once," Hassan said proudly. "At a wedding. I wanted to ask for an autograph, but I was taking photos and didn't want to look unprofessional. So I walked by him and said, 'Hey, Nathan,' and he said 'What's up?' And I said, 'Yo, MVP." Hassan looked over at Maitlyn for approval. "Righteous, huh?"

Maitlyn wasn't sure what to say. She didn't want to talk about the creep. *He would have raped me.* "You took photos at weddings?"

"Still do. Can't pay the rent just doing this. Hey, do you want to have kids?"

"What?"

"I don't mean with me. That was random, hunh? I just think, I mean, kids would be great and all, but I'm not sure I could afford it. Unless I marry a Kardashian."

Ignoring Hassan's prattle, Maitlyn studied her close-up photo of the red-haired Dutchman with the striped blouse and floppy hat. Was it authentic? Her grandmother had said there was no way to know just by looking at the painting, never mind a hurried photograph. You had to study the brushstrokes, the chemical makeup of the pigment, even the thread pattern in the canvas. "Sometimes, Mattie, even the experts get fooled." When Maitlyn told her the painting was in Nathan's trophy room, Grandma concluded, "Oh, then it's a fake for sure."

Lieutenant Gomez greeted them at Camp Pendleton with pleasant words and a hard smile. The dullness in his eyes suggested a lack of imagination—or maybe Maitlyn just assumed that of all marines. He directed them to a Humvee, where a driver was waiting to take them on a tour of the Pendleton backcountry. Dirt roads crisscrossed the dry, brown hills. Heavy vehicles had pulverized the tracks into soft sand.

They stopped on a knoll to watch helicopters emptying their water buckets on the burning mountains. Hassan set up his tripod, and, with the fire in the background, Maitlyn let the lieutenant deliver his spiel. "Those are Bambi Buckets," he explained, "but they aren't just saving deer. If that fire spreads, Fallbrook is in danger. We want to be proactive to mitigate property damage and prevent human suffering."

"You go off the base, too, right?" Maitlyn prompted him.

"Absolutely. We have a memorandum of agreement with CAL FIRE to address combustion events throughout San Diego County. As you can see, this is risky work, but our pilots are topnotch. Most have been in combat overseas. They can control a wildfire."

"Thank you, Lieutenant Gomez."

"Yes, ma'am."

"Now, as you can see right now," Maitlyn pointed back to the mountains, "these pilots are hot on the job." Hassan zoomed in on a helicopter circling the blaze. Then they recorded the toss-back: "This is Maitlyn Flutters reporting live from the Big Cave Fire on Camp Pendleton. Back to you in the studio."

As they climbed back into the Humvee, Gomez encouraged Hassan to sit up front with the driver. "You'll get a better view of the ocean. If you see a photo op, just tell him to stop." Then the earnest lieutenant climbed in back for a better view of the hot news chick. "When we get back to my office, I can give you a tour, show you around Mainside."

Sunny had said that the right enhancements "get you in the door." What she hadn't explained was that every guy you met would be holding a door for you. You had to be constantly on guard, and it was easy to become cynical about every smile, every act of politeness. In college, Maitlyn was cute. Now she was a head-turner—guys just couldn't ignore firm, full breasts—and sometimes it felt like a burden.

"I'll have to check with my station," Maitlyn replied to the lieutenant, already planning to get off the base as quickly as possible. "I think we have to rush to another assignment."

But marines don't give up easily. "Nathan Saltenstall is giving a speech on base next Saturday," Gomez informed Maitlyn hopefully. "You should come back. I'll get you right up front."

6

The Botanical Building in Balboa Park is advertised as "one of the largest lath structures in the world," meaning it consists of wood strips spaced to allow in air and light. The effect is the sun-dappled understory of a tropical jungle, filled with ferns, cycads, and orchids. Light and shadow—Maitlyn wasn't sure which was for her. She removed her sunglasses, looked about the foliage, and spotted the hat—You Can't Fix Stupid.

He was sitting alone on a bench next to a mossy pool. He put a finger to his lips, signaling her to stay quiet. "You bring the photos?" he whispered.

Maitlyn thought that a bit dramatic. "Are we spies or something?"

"Can't be too careful."

He had called the night before and asked her to meet him. "I've got a plan," he had promised, but declined to elaborate. She had offered to send him the pictures from her phone, but he replied, "No, no, don't do that."

Now, sitting next to him in the exotic garden, she retrieved the first photo—the trophies with the little painting in the background. "This is the room," she explained. "The closet where I—."

"Okay, that's the MVP trophy right there. He stole that too. Should have gone to Dunbar that year. Even I know that, and I never liked Dunbar."

"And this next one…there it is." She flipped to the close-up of *A Cavalier*.

"That's it? A million four for this?"

"On the black market you supposedly pay a lot less. Like only ten percent."

Charles studied the photo until a woman pushing a baby stroller passed out of earshot. "The first thing you got to do is call the FBI. Then you've got to confront him. Force him to deny it in public. Even if he says it's a fake, he looks bad. What's he doing with a fake?"

"I can't."

"You said you wanted to hit him again. This is how you do it. Nothing else, you just go knock on his door."

Knock on his door? "No way." A wave of anxiety was gathering. She stood up. Should she leave? She sat down.

"Are you okay?"

"I never want to see his face again. Ever." She stared at Charles with watery eyes, and he didn't flinch. She expected him to argue, but The Mouth was silent. The calmness in his face was priestly, inviting her to confess. "If I didn't escape, I mean, if I didn't get out of that corner, out of his studio, he wouldn't have stopped. He would have…he would have…." She couldn't say it out loud, and a few people were walking by, looking at her, drawn to her agitation, or maybe fascinated by the mixed-race couple having a public moment.

"I'm sorry, Maitlyn. That ain't right what he did."

She nodded. She tried to say something. Only tears came out.

"Come here, darling." He put an arm around her. She didn't resist. Charles was the only guy at work who'd never hit on her. Even Scott had given it a shot. "He ain't gonna hurt you no more," Charles said softly. "I'd kill the motherfucker before I let that happen. You know I would, right?"

She nodded. She actually believed him.

"Alright, then," he said. "You're gonna be alright. And Nathan gonna get his."

She took a tissue from her pocket and dabbed at her eyes. Hopefully, none of the gawkers recognized her—the weepy news chick. She put on her sunglasses. She laughed quietly at her embarrassment.

"Thatagirl. Can you give me a smile?"

"You know what, Charles? You need a new hat."

Call the FBI? Back at her condo, Maitlyn opened up her laptop. A Google search took her to the FBI Art Crime Team website, which listed *A Cavalier* in their top ten unsolved cases. She could submit a tip online. But it wasn't anonymous. They wanted name, street address, and phone number. She imagined the conversation that would follow when they contacted her:

Let me get this straight, Ms. Flutters. Instead of calling the police, you went out and interviewed him?

I'm a reporter. That's my job.

And while you were running from this would-be rapist, you happened to notice a stolen piece of art?

My grandmother says I have a good eye.

Okay, thanks for the tip. Now call your local police department and tell them exactly what he did to you.

Maitlyn popped an Ativan and tried to relax. *I need to get back to meditating.* There was a time when she had known discipline, sitting in the lotus position thirty minutes a day. But then she got out of the habit. Work, the gym, Whatshisface—she didn't have time. *You have to make time.* She closed her computer, switched off all the lights in her condo, and sat on the living room floor, facing the balcony and the setting sun. She shut her eyes. She followed the rise and fall of her breath.

"Lordy, lordy, look out, shorty"—that's what Charles had said after she told him about throwing paint thinner in Nathan's face—"talk about giving him the business." Maitlyn caught herself thinking and tried to refocus on her breathing. *Breathing in, breathing out.* But she kept hearing Charles's deep twang. "You fought back," he had told her. "He's a big dude, a professional ath-a-lete, and you got away. Far as I'm concerned, you're the hero." *Just breathe.* She used to be good at clearing her mind. *Breathing in, breathing out. Was that woman with the stroller in the garden a single mom? Breathing in, breathing out. She looked happy. Breathing in, breathing out. Breathing in. I should call Mom. Breathing in, breathing out. Breathing in, breathing out. Breathing in, breathing out.*

When she opened her eyes, the condo was dark. The sunset was long gone. She had lost track of time. Her breathing was slow. She felt a gentle vibration in her chest. Her phone rang. She ignored it. She unfolded her legs and wiggled her toes. She stretched her arms straight up toward the ceiling. *Far as I'm concerned, you're the hero.*

"Maitlyn, come in. Nice package from Pendleton the other day." Mr. Cooper was behind his big desk, as usual, telephone in one hand, remote control in the other. The television was running Fox.

"I've got an outline for the sea-level story, like you asked." She had spoken on the phone with a humorless but helpful researcher at the Scripps Institute of Oceanography. He had explained that the debate was over, the only question was how quickly the land ice would melt and when, not if, the rising water would inundate low-lying communities. She had spent several evenings reading through documents online. She handed her carefully typed pages to Mr. Cooper.

He set them aside and muted the TV. "Give me the short version."

"Sure. Okay. San Diego and the surrounding cities have something called an Adaptation Strategy. It's based on sea-level projections by the state—10 to 17 inches by 2050, 31 to 69 inches by 2100. That would be my first report—the science." She had memorized the numbers. She wanted to sound well-versed.

"So the city is already working on it?"

"They're talking about it. But so far no action. That's my second report. Will anything actually be done—for example, to save Mission Beach, to stop coastal flooding? *Can* anything be done?"

"Hmm." He put on his reading glasses and glanced at her report.

"And there's more. Rising sea levels up in San Francisco Bay could turn delta freshwater into saltwater, and that's the source of twenty-five percent of San Diego's drinking water."

"Sounds bad."

"I know, right?"

"But most of our viewers will be long gone by 2050."

"That's the hook. That's where this leads. Do we have an obligation to future generations?"

He took off the glasses. "Do we?"

"*I* think so." But, really, what did she care? Maybe she would inherit the house—she was clearly her grandmother's favorite—but then what? Would she have children to pass it on to? Would she be an old maid, sitting on Coronado, watching high tide roll up 1st Street? Her high school friends were all married and raising kids. Her college roommates were all married and talking about raising kids. And she spent her evenings alone in her fancy condo with the spectacular view—far above the water's rising edge—trying not to get agitated about her latest humiliating encounters with men.

"You know what Nathan says?" Mr. Cooper asked. "He's not going to let the climate-change scaremongers—his words—get in the way of economic recovery."

"So?" *Fuck Nathan,* she wanted to say.

"So, our advertisers want economic growth, not doom and gloom."

"Well, what happens when our reservoirs are empty and we lose one third of our beaches and Sea World is under the sea and tourism disappears? Ask the advertisers *that*. The city planners, the Coastal Commission, even the navy — they're all taking this very seriously. This is *the* issue for the next hundred years. More important than the Marines dumping water on a little wildfire."

"You looked great, by the way, with the breeze whipping your hair and the smoke in the background."

"Fuck Nathan." She said it out loud when she was back in her office with the door closed. Then quickly, before second thoughts arose, while she was still pissed, she called the FBI's San Diego office. They put her on hold, and she was about to hang up — *This is crazy!* — when someone picked up.

"Agent Hansen."

"Hi. My name is Maitlyn Flutters. I'm a reporter with Channel Four News." *No turning back now.*

"Oh, sure, what can I do for you?"

Maitlyn felt reassured by Agent Hansen's pleasant voice, but still was nervous. "I'm doing a story on stolen art. Could you answer a few questions?"

"I can try, but maybe you want to talk to an art investigator."

"Well, it's kind of a local story. See, a few weeks ago, I interviewed Congressman Nathan Saltenstall. At his house."

"Yes."

"And when I was there…when he showed me around his house, I saw a painting. It's like famous…a famous painting. I mean, I don't know if it's a fake or whatever, what I saw, but the painting…it's actually on the FBI website because it's stolen. The original."

"Could you repeat that?"

Maitlyn tried it again, this time describing the painting and explaining the theft in Australia. Agent Hansen asked a few questions and sounded skeptical until Maitlyn mentioned the photos. "They're not great, but the painting looks like the real thing." As if she would know.

"Ms. Flutters, could you come out to our office and discuss this with us?"

Maitlyn hadn't expected that. "Uh, sure." She didn't have time to think it through. "That would be great."

After hanging up, she felt like she might vomit. She hurried down the hall to the bathroom, locked the door, and looked at her pale face in the mirror. *Am I really doing this? Did I just kiss my career goodbye?* Agent Hansen had seemed straightforward, hadn't shown any excitement at the mention of Nathan. And a female FBI agent—Maitlyn hadn't expected that either—but it somehow made things safer.

In fact, it turned out to be no big deal. The FBI building was just off the 805 Freeway. Maitlyn went through the security screening, produced her press credentials, then met with Agent Hansen, who immediately took charge of the proceedings, asking her to describe Nathan's house and where exactly she saw the painting and how she had identified it. No big deal—until the agent, whose brown hair was drawn back in a tight bun, wanted to know about the circumstances of her house tour. "You were in this trophy room alone, right? I thought he was showing you around."

But Maitlyn was prepared. *Just you and the ball.* She had rehearsed her answer. "He showed me the kitchen and his painting studio. But then he had to get ready for the interview. Change his shirt, I think. So he told me I could look around."

"So you opened this door that looked like a closet?"

"He was like 'feel free to snoop.'"

"Feel free to snoop?"

"Something along those lines, yes." *Why did I say that?—feel free to snoop.* That's what Whatshisface had said the first time she visited his live-aboard sailboat on Shelter Island. Of course, there wasn't much snooping to be done inside a 50-foot yacht, and he didn't mention that the floating bachelor pad was actually his second residence, unknown to his wife and kids, with whom he lived in a big rancher way out in La Mesa.

"Did you ask the congressman about the painting?"

"No, I...no."

"Does he know you went in his trophy room?"

"I don't know. Probably not. I didn't touch anything." *Except the life-size cardboard Nathan.*

"Okay, thank you for bringing this to our attention, Maitlyn." Agent Hansen relaxed a little. "What kind of story are you writing?"

"It's kind of—I'm not sure yet. I guess it depends on that painting." Maitlyn opened her notepad, trying to recall the questions she had planned—*Is there a lot of stolen art in San Diego?*—trying to maintain the pretense of a disinterested reporter.

Before Maitlyn could organize her thoughts, though, Agent Hansen again took charge, her voice still pleasant, conversational. Her eyes, though, betrayed her—a hint of narrowing, the slightest tightening of facial muscles—the kind of physical cue that Whatshisface, who frequented card rooms to play poker, called a "tell." Sharper eyes, and then a glance at the computer screen on her desk. "Say, Maitlyn, while I've got you here, what can you tell me about Charles Lockett?"

"You got a new hat." It carried a warning in red letters— Don't Mess With Texas.

"Just doing what I'm told."

They were meeting again in the Botanical Building. Charles seemed to think a bench in a public garden was a safe place to talk—safer than telephone conversations, which he insisted were all being recorded by the government. Considering that Agent Hansen had spent more time asking about the infamous sucker punch than about the stolen painting, maybe he was right to be paranoid.

"She wanted to know why you hit him. I said I didn't know."

"San Diego P.D. asked me the same thing. I told them it was between me and my man Nathan and not their concern."

"I said I didn't really know you. Only that you are really good at your job."

"*Was* really good. Currently unemployed."

"I also...I told her what you said about the Super Bowl."

"The fumble?"

"I had to say something."

He pressed an open palm against his forehead. "We had that game in the bag, you know that?"

"So I've heard."

"Jesus. All he had to do was take a knee, and we're going to Disneyland." He shook his head in dismay. "Two hands on the ball." He stood up, walked over to look at a cluster of tiny orchid blossoms, then returned and sat down again. "So, this agent—did she say she would investigate the painting?"

"She said she'd pass it along to their art crime people."

"Okay, that gives us a few days. We've got to ask Nathan about it before they do, put him on the spot, on camera, before he knows what's up. Then *he's* the one in the corner."

"I can't—."

"I know. You don't want to get near him. I don't blame you. Maybe we can get Sheila."

"She won't do it."

"Tell her it's a scoop. If he denies having the painting, he's gonna look silly when your photos come out. If he admits it, it's either stolen or a fake, and, either way, the Democrats will jump all over his ass, raise questions about his character, about his lifestyle, the whole shootin' match, anything to burst his bubble."

"Sheila's sleeping with him."

Charles stared at her. "You're shittin' me."

"That's according to Sunny."

"Unbelievable. That sonofabitch gets everything."

"It's probably just a rumor." She hoped.

"They got Sunny in the wrong job. Don't know a Santa Ana wind from a hurricane, but she's got the dirt on everybody. One day she goes to me, 'Charles, my friend has a vacant apartment, if you're interested.' She knew I was getting divorced before I did."

"You were married?" Maitlyn had always thought of Charles as the tech with the attitude—the only black man above janitor working at Channel Four—The Mouth from the South and nothing more. That he might have a biography had never occurred to her.

"My daddy tried to warn me. He said Monique had more than a few holes in her screen door. But I had my love blinders on. She was the reason I moved to California in the first place. You ever been in love?" When Maitlyn looked away, when she had to think about it rather than just reply, he answered for her. "You're still young."

"Yeah." *But not as young as Sheila, and getting older every day.* "I always go for the wrong one." Had she just said that? What was it about Charles Lockett that caused her to reveal herself?

"Par for the course. They're all the wrong one until the right one comes along."

7

When Hassan met Maitlyn at the Channel Four building early on Saturday morning, he was wearing a tuxedo. "I'm working a wedding this afternoon," he explained.

"You couldn't change later?" Maitlyn asked, not trying to disguise her irritation. She didn't want her cameraman embarrassing her in public.

"This way Nathan will remember me from last time—the photog dude in the penguin suit. I'm gonna be all, What up, Nathaaan? What, what!"

Traffic on the freeway was thin, and Hassan kept the van zipping along in the fast lane. When they arrived at Camp Pendleton, cars were backed up at the gate and news vehicles were everywhere—including the truck from Channel Four with the satellite uplink. "Is that Sheila and Scott?" Hassan asked. "Are we on the same story?"

It had been no trouble recruiting Hassan on his day off, but Maitlyn hadn't mentioned that they weren't officially covering Nathan's rally. "Okay, Hassan, listen. We're here to follow up on the fire."

"You're joshing, right?"

"Cooper's orders."

"We're not interviewing Nathan? I thought—."

"Just listen. We came up here to do the fire, that's our assignment. We didn't even know Nathan was going to be here."

"I got all dressed up for nothing?"

"But since we're here....see what I'm saying? Since we're here and he's here...."

Hassan glanced over to see if she was serious, then finished her sentence. "Then we might as well check out the rally."

"I'm mean, if that's alright with you."

"Awesome sauce." He pumped his fist. "Saltenstall in the *house*."

The sun was beginning to burn off the morning fog. Hundreds of people, giddy with anticipation, were crowded together before a large stage in the middle of a yellowed crabgrass field. Large speakers blasted nationalist tunes—"And I'm proud to be an American, where at least I know I'm free"—and red, white, and blue bunting and balloons added to the festive air. Campaign volunteers were handing out signs that read "Saltenstall for Senate" or "Nathan's Nation."

Maitlyn picked up a hand-lettered one that read, "Nathan Don't Run." "This one needs a comma," she said to Hassan.

"Or two," he replied. Camera on his shoulder, he'd been trailing her as she worked her way through the crowd.

Maitlyn flinched when she heard someone say her name. She had hoped to avoid this encounter but knew it was inevitable. She managed a smile as she turned to greet her colleague. "Sheila, hi."

Sheila eyed Hassan's tuxedo, then turned to Maitlyn with a puzzled frown. "What are you doing here?"

"Cooper's idea. For the fire."

"The fire's out." That sounded accusatory.

"Yeah, I know. He wants us to call it, like, a big win for the Marines. I wasn't expecting a circus." Maitlyn looked about, indicating the rally. "What's he going to say?"

"Nathan?" Sheila squinted in the sun. "How would I know?" That sounded defensive.

"I mean, don't they give you press releases?"

Sheila's phone buzzed. She glanced at it before responding to Maitlyn's question. "Nathan does three of these a week. They just tell us where and when. I've got to go check in with Scott. Are you sticking around?" That sounded suspicious.

"Might as well. For a little bit, anyway."

"They always start real late," Sheila warned, then hurried off toward the encampment of satellite trucks with their white dishes pointed skyward.

"Aaw-kward," Hassan commented.

Maitlyn ignored him and watched Sheila go, thinking, hoping, that the new hot news chick had put on a little weight.

What *was* she doing here? Mr. Cooper wanted a follow-up from Pendleton—that was true—but it didn't have to be today. She had an angle—the smoke has cleared just in time for the congressman's visit—Cooper would like that. But she'd only just invented it on the drive up. *I'm here*, Maitlyn told herself, *to exorcise my fears*. She couldn't let what happened in Rancho keep her from doing her job, from pursuing her dream. *I'm here to fight back*. She had fought back in the studio. She was a hero, not a victim—it had taken Charles to point that out. *I fought back then, and I'm fighting back now.* "Let's do my stand-up," she said to Hassan. "Get the mountains in the background."

"Ready when you are." He focused his camera and gave her a nod.

Maitlyn picked up a "Saltenstall" sign and took a deep breath. "I'm here at Camp Pendleton where, as you can see, the wildfire is finally out. Base officials are crediting the efforts of airborne firefighters, assisted by a shift in weather earlier this week, as onshore breezes brought cool, moist air to the region. And just in time, too, as today the base is hosting a political rally for Senate candidate Nathan Saltenstall. Now, organizers are handing out signs like this one." She raised the sign for the camera. "I'd say maybe five hundred supporters are here. There's a lot of excitement on the ground. A lot of excitement in the air. And, thankfully, no smoke. Reporting from Camp Pendleton, this is Maitlyn Flutters, Channel Four News."

Next, Maitlyn interviewed one of the women handing out signs. She wore a straw hat with a flag-colored band. She sported a large "Nathan" button. "It looks like you're a big Saltenstall supporter," Maitlyn began, and held out her microphone.

"I am." The woman could barely contain herself. "I'm a proud member of Nathan's Nation. I support everything he stands for. Go, Nathan." She waved to Hassan's camera and giggled self-consciously.

"What does he stand for?" Maitlyn asked encouragingly.

"He stands for...for taking back America. He stands for America. He stands for us. And family. He's always talking about family."

"That's important to you?"

"Yes, of course. I have three children."

"What do you think of Mrs. Saltenstall?"

"I don't really know her. I'm sure she's great. I mean, she's married to Nathan, right?"

Then Maitlyn recorded a conversation with a heavy-limbed, crewcut man who had stopped by to pick up a sign. "You're a football fan, I see."

"Oh, yeah." He was wearing a jersey with "Saltenstall" stitched across the back. "Absolutely."

"What brings you out here today?"

"We came to see Nathan. All the way from Huntington Beach. Nate's da man!"

"You live in Huntington Beach?"

"That's right."

"Are you worried about global warming?"

"No. Why?"

"Scientists say the rising ocean will flood low-lying coastal areas."

"Yeah, I've heard that. But we're already used to some flooding, so I'm not worried. We've got sandbags."

Sheila was right—they started late. Finally, a man in a blue suit and red tie appeared onstage to thank everyone for attending. Despite a voice going hoarse, he led a hearty Pledge of Allegiance, followed by a complicated joke about a Republican and a Democrat playing golf with the Cat in the Hat and Jesus, and it turned out that it wasn't Jesus, it was a gardener named "Hey, Seuss." The crowd was ready to laugh, but the punch line fell flat. A second joke, about the bankruptcy of Social Security, fared worse. Unfazed, the hapless comedian croaked out, "Now please join me in welcoming THE NEXT U-NITED STATES SENATOR FROM CALIFORNIA, NATHAN SALTENSTALL!"

The crowd hooted and screamed, the speakers switched to reggae music—"Get up, stand up, stand up for your rights"—and Nathan gallantly took the stage, hand held high in a confident wave. He stood for a moment in the late morning sun, absorbing the adulation, then positioned himself behind the lectern and adjusted the microphone. "Thank you, so much, ladies and gentlemen. One nation under God. Isn't it great to be here this morning at Camp Pendleton?"

More cheering and some "oorahs." Maitlyn had noticed there were very few uniforms in the crowd. It was mostly civilians— retired military men and their wives, from the looks of them. Pendleton buses, someone had told her, were shuttling people in from Oceanside.

"The U.S. Marines never run," Nathan proclaimed, almost shouting, "and neither do I."

Cheering.

"Except forward. I used to run for first downs. Now I'm running for the U.S. Senate. And I need your vote to make it happen."

More cheering.

"We're going to make this country great again. That's my game plan."

Standing at the back of the crowd, Maitlyn gauged her response to seeing him again, the jerk who felt her up—*Asshole!*—the man who would have raped her. *I fought him off—I'm the hero here.* She was surprised when anxiety didn't arise. Maybe it was the distance—fifty yards away—with hundreds of flag-waving, star-struck Nathanites in between. *At least what he felt up was fake.*

A cluster of reporters, Sheila among them, was standing off to one side, shielded from the sun by a military tarp. Scott was there too, sucking on a cigarette. Maitlyn picked out the familiar faces from the other network affiliates and the *Union-Tribune*. She felt the ache of resentment that she had been pretending wasn't there. She should be working with Scott—*he* would never think of wearing a tuxedo in the field. She should be in the press tent, chatting and laughing and showing a veteran journalist's disdain for Nathan's stump speech. No doubt they had heard it a dozen times before. There was nothing really to report on, except for his presence. *Breaking news: Nathan is here!* It was a silly assignment, she told herself in consolation, *Sheila can have it.*

"Here's what we're going to do," Nathan crowed, "we're going to fund the military. One hundred percent."

Cheering.

"We're going to take out the terrorists."

Cheering.

"We're going to take on Russia and China...and Iran and North Korea...and Venezuela and Cuba and...."

With each country mentioned, the crowd response grew until Nathan couldn't be heard. He grinned and waited until it subsided.

"I get the impression I'm among patriots."

Bedlam.

Nathan spoke for thirty minutes, then departed with a wave. The reggae resumed—"Don't give up the fight"—and the Nathanites waved their signs and bounced up and down, dancing despite themselves. Nodding his head to the music, Hassan said, "I didn't know so many white people liked Bob Marley. I mean, *really* white people."

"Let's go." Maitlyn led him around the perimeter of the field and past the press tents. She saw Sheila and Scott disappear through a gate into the backstage area. They would be getting a few exclusive clichés from the candidate before his handlers hustled him off.

"Are we leaving?" Hassan asked, his voice sounding winded, as they hurried toward a lineup of sand-colored Humvees.

"I think he's going to exit this way. Be ready to roll." Lieutenant Gomez had divulged the schedule—campaign rally, driving tour of the base, private lunch with the top brass—when Maitlyn had phoned him for a press pass.

"I'm on it," Hassan assured her.

"If he stops and takes my question, zoom on his face."

"Roger rabbit. Close-up on N-Salt."

Maitlyn asked one of the marines posted by the Humvees which vehicle was for the candidate, then staked out her position alongside the one he indicated. Could she do it? Could she watch Nathan approach without running away? Could she stand next to him without freaking out? *I'm safe here. I've got Hassan and his camera. I've got marines. He can't hurt me in public.* She popped an Ativan under her tongue just in case.

"Ma'am, you'll have to back up."

Obeying the marine's instructions, Maitlyn and Hassan moved away from the vehicles, and suddenly they weren't alone. "Let the pig-fuck begin," Hassan said under his breath. The press corps had spotted them, had seen Maitlyn standing with her microphone ready, and decided something was up. Civilians followed, breaking into a run and elbowing for position.

"Folks, please, move away from the vehicles, thank you." Several marines, their arms spread wide, herded the crowd backwards, clearing a path for the VIP.

A roar rose up when Nathan and his people emerged from the security fence behind the stage. The crowd surged forward, trapping Maitlyn and Hassan four or five bodies back. When the Nathanites waved their rally signs, the candidate disappeared from view.

"Shit," Maitlyn muttered in resignation. She had intended to confront him, catch him off guard. She had convinced herself she could do it. But part of her had been dreading it, and, stuck behind a large man holding up two signs, it was easy to give up the chase. *Oh, well,* she told herself, *I tried.*

"Coming through. Make way. Press coming through. Thank you, folks." It was Hassan. People in front turned to look at him, saw the tuxedo, and let him squeeze by. He grabbed Maitlyn's hand and pulled her forward.

"Channel Four News," she explained apologetically to a frowning woman who had inched aside for Hassan but clearly didn't want to enable the news chick. "Thank you, ma'am."

It took a few moments to reach the front of the throng, and they just missed Nathan. He was already past them, shaking the hands of supporters further down the path as he moved toward the waiting vehicles. The sight of his broad shoulders sent Maitlyn's stomach churning. She was glad she didn't have to face him. *Sorry, Charles, I tried.*

"Nathaaan! Nate the Great. From the N to the T to the G. What up, MVP, what up?" Hassan was loud. Everyone turned to look: security men, marines, campaign assistants. And Nathan. He released a handshake and came back toward them. "Remember me from the wedding?" Hassan asked. "In Torrey Pines. That was me. MVP, MVP."

The Nathanites around them took up Hassan's chant: "MVP, MVP." Hassan reached out for a fist bump.

Nathan obliged, but his eyes were on Maitlyn. "Ms. Flutters, good to see you." He extended his arms and leaned forward, looking for a hug.

She wanted to run but was trapped. Reflexively, she flipped on her microphone and held it between them. "Congressman, one quick question."

"Of course. How are you? I'm very sorry about our misunderstanding. I hope you believe me."

She looked to Hassan. The red light was on, his camera was rolling. "Congressman, you're a big supporter of the arts."

Nathan smiled. A non-question was his kind of question. "Yes. California has a great arts community. Our film industry is the finest in the world."

A booming voice behind Maitlyn called out, "We're number one!"

"That's right," Nathan laughed, and reached out to shake more hands.

Maitlyn flinched at his sudden movement but managed to keep her voice steady. "Congressman, in your art collection, do you have a painting by Frans van Mieris?"

He hesitated, but only for the briefest moment. "I'm not sure." His eyes locked on Maitlyn. "Maybe my wife...."

It was just the two of them. Like in the kitchen. Like in the studio. *Just you and the ball.* "It's called *A Cavalier*," Maitlyn continued. "It's stolen. Do you have a painting that's stolen? Congressman?"

He pulled back and turned away, pretending he hadn't heard. He whispered to an aide. Maitlyn could read his lips: "Get me out of here."

The aide put a hand in the small of Nathan's back and pushed him forward, toward the Humvees. The "MVP" chants rose again as the great man waved goodbye.

8

"Hassan, could you please slow down?"

Grudgingly, he brought the van back to a less frightening speed. "Sorry. I can't afford to be late."

And I can't afford to be dead. Maitlyn looked out the window at the rows of tile roofs on the hillsides overlooking the freeway. The next exit was the one to Rancho. She could hear Nathan's voice— "I'm very sorry about our misunderstanding." Was it really a misunderstanding? Was it because she had led him on? *No, it wasn't my fault. I said no. But maybe he didn't hear me. He's not the rapist type.* "Who's getting married, anyway?" Not that she cared. She was just tired of thinking about Nathan.

"Some random couple. I just take the shots and...ka-ching. Easy money. And free food. Why, you wanna go?"

"No. Are you kidding me?" She didn't care if her snicker sounded insulting. She didn't want Hassan getting any ideas.

"Hot date tonight?" He looked over with a smile.

She looked away. They were passing the Del Mar horse track. She'd gone to the races once with Whatshisface. They'd sat in somebody's private box. He had only taken her places where they weren't likely to be seen. *What does the rapist type look like?* she wondered.

"Hey," Hassan continued, "have you ever used one of those online dating sites? No, probably not, hunh? You don't have any trouble getting asked out."

"I'm seeing someone," she said brusquely, and immediately felt her stomach roil. Lying always did that to her.

After a moment of silence, Hassan asked, "Are you okay?"

"What's that supposed to mean?"

"Nothing. Just, I mean, like, you don't seem yourself today."

"Whatever." *Maybe it's because I have to work with a moron all day in a tuxedo who won't shut up, and this trip was a total waste.*

She had expected her question about the painting to catch Nathan unprepared, cause him to stutter and stumble and contradict himself. Charles had convinced her it would work. It hadn't occurred to her that Nathan could simply walk away. Hassan had recorded the close-up, but Mr. Cooper would never allow it to air. She knew what he would say—same thing he said after she asked a Sea World spokeswoman on camera if captive orcas ever cried—"Not answering is not an answer, Maitlyn. We don't do gotcha journalism."

"What's his name?" Hassan asked. "The guy you're seeing."

"I don't know." Now *she* was the one caught unprepared.

"You don't know?"

And she couldn't just walk away. "I mean, I don't know if I should…."

"You don't want to tell me. That's cool. I'm seeing this girl named Sana. But I'm not really into her. My friend is dating her friend, so we—it's, like, just for fun."

"Congratulations." Maitlyn was in a mood, no doubt about that.

For dinner, she reheated takeout Thai noodles from the day before. She wanted to open a bottle of wine, but all she had was an expensive Chardonnay—too good to drink alone.

The sun went down. City lights sparkled in her window. Nightlife in the Gaslamp Quarter would be picking up—college kids, navy guys, tourist couples—San Diego after dark. Maitlyn regretted being rude to Hassan. It wasn't like her. She'd been irritable. *And he can be so annoying.* She thought to call and apologize but remembered he was busy, somewhere, snapping pictures of a beaming couple. *A wedding would be fun. Some champagne*. Maitlyn had been a bridesmaid for three different friends. *Everyone is married except me.*

Later, looking back, she couldn't recall deciding to go out. She remembered feeling depressed, another Saturday night at home. She was going to wash her hair, watch a movie, go to sleep. Getting out the door was involuntary. Exiting the underground garage and steering Ciela down Laurel Street, she was on autopilot. At the stoplight before the freeway, in the glow of a streetlamp, a man with a cardboard sign was begging for change. Maitlyn avoided eye contact. "I could use change myself," she said aloud, then gunned Ciela up the onramp.

Had she stopped to consider what she was doing, had she engaged herself in serious conversation — had she been mindful! — probably she wouldn't have gone. Definitely. She would have reminded herself that the house of the man who would have raped her was the last place on earth she wanted to be. Yet that's where she ended up. Rancho.

Nathan's house looked dark. The big gate across the driveway was closed. Maybe he was already on a plane to the next campaign stop, or maybe tonight it was a dinner with fat-cat donors.

Maitlyn parked down the street and waited in the car. Had he really misunderstood her intentions? Had she given him mixed messages? She tried to replay the opening scenes, to identify her missteps. *Did he open the studio door or was I the one leading the way?* She couldn't remember. *I should never have gone beyond the kitchen.* She regretted being flirtatious. *I gave him the wrong idea. I told him it's okay.*

A security patrol vehicle pulled up beside her. She gave the rent-a-cop a friendly wave, and he drove off. A few minutes later, the gate rolled open, allowing a long limousine to enter. Maitlyn drove forward slowly, lights off, until she could see up the driveway. Nathan was climbing out of the back seat of the limo. She recognized his broad shoulders.

When the limo began pulling out, Maitlyn flipped her lights on and circled the neighborhood. It was a maze of curvy, unlit lanes, large properties shaded with eucalyptus trees, mansions set back from the road, so different from the rectangular block of apartment buildings where she lived.

She looped back around. The gate was still open. *I could drive right up to his front door.* Another car beat her to it, pulling in right in front of her without slowing down. *Who's that?*

Maitlyn parked up the street, out of view from Nathan's house. Safe in the darkness, she got out of her car and walked back to the gate in time to watch a woman exit her vehicle and disappear into the front entranceway. "Breaking news," Maitlyn whispered, holding an invisible microphone to her mouth, "Sheila Patterson is screwing Nathan Saltenstall. Stay tuned for live coverage."

She had a scoop. *The* scoop. Congressman Saltenstall, self-proclaimed pillar of American family values, was having an extramarital affair. Sheila, the new hot news chick, was compromising her journalistic integrity. Forget rising oceans — this was *serious*!

But all too soon, Maitlyn was in over her head.

"Charles, I need help."

"Maitlyn?" The Mouth from the South sounded like he'd been sleeping.

"I can't get out. I'm trapped. I'm —."

"Slow down, now. Trapped how?"

"I can't get back to my car."

"Where are you?"

"Rancho. Nathan's place." The phone went silent. "Hello? Charles?"

"Y'all fuckin' with me?"

"No. I know. It's a long story."

She had crept up the long driveway to confirm her discovery. With her phone, she had recorded a video of the car parked in front of the house and zoomed in on the license plate. She recognized the plastic crates with file folders in the backseat. Sheila was so organized.

More lights had come on in the house—anyone inside wouldn't be able to see out into the dark—so why not sidle up the carved stone stairs and slip through the ivied arch and peek in a window or two? No one was visible in the foyer, no one at work in the magnificent kitchen. Again, not making a conscious decision, not pausing to weigh the pros and cons of a television reporter trespassing on the property of a Senate candidate, not to mention peeping into the house of the man who would have raped her, Maitlyn had continued around to the backyard.

Nathan's back was turned toward her. He was standing by the swimming pool, talking on the phone. Maitlyn froze—a deer in headlights. Had he turned around, he would have seen her, illuminated from below by the glowing blue water. She backed up slowly, holding her breath.

Once safely out of view, she turned and ran across the lawn toward the driveway—Bambi in startled flight. The gate was now closed. "Are you kidding me?" She couldn't locate a button to reopen it. She couldn't squeeze between the wrought iron bars. "Shit." The fence was too high to climb. "Shit, shit, shit."

A cold sweat came over her. Pressing her head against the bars, she could see the shadowy outline of Ciela waiting up the road—so close and so far, with her anxiety pills in the cup holder between the seats. Thank goodness she had her phone.

"I'm on my way, Maitlyn," Charles said calmly, "I'm walking to my car right now. Just sit tight. Stay away from that house. Don't do anything stupid."

"Yeah, too late for that."

She stood at the gate, peering out helplessly, *like a prisoner of war*, she imagined, *like a starving refugee*. Whenever she saw footage of reporters at refugee camps, she wondered where they ate. Was there a dining tent for journalists? *I could do that. I could be an international correspondent*. Did they have a tent for showers?

She was tempted to sneak around to the back patio again. She craved a quick peek in the back windows. But she heeded Charles's warning and stayed near the front of the property. Hoping to find a way out, she walked back and forth along the hedges as they followed the fence line. *Like an elephant in a pen*. She lived a mile from the San Diego Zoo and hadn't been there in years. Whatshisface had refused to go with her. *Strange, cuz he was a cheetah*. She laughed at her own joke. *And a lion*. She said it aloud: "A lion cheetah. A cowardly lion cheetah." She looked through the fence. "And Dorothy wants to go home. Now."

She checked her phone for messages and found nothing of interest except a text from Scott: You smothering Nathan now? It was a reference to her appearance at Camp Pendleton, possibly snide — the tone in texts is easily ambiguous. She thumb-typed a reply — Yes camped outside his house — but heard Charles's admonition again — *Don't do anything stupid* — and quickly erased it. She typed a new reply — Cooper wants me on military — and sent it off, then powered down the phone to preserve the battery, in case she needed it later. She sat down on bare dirt and leaned against a tree. *This is ridiculous. I should have just gone to bed.* She closed her eyes and tried to focus on her breathing.

The sound of a car engine woke her up. *How long was I asleep?* She walked to the gate and peered through the bars, expecting to see Charles. Instead, she saw the security vehicle parked behind Ciela. And Ciela was up in the air. Maitlyn blinked her eyes and stared, trying to make sense of the scene. Her car was aglow and floating above the patrol car. Ciela was ascending to heaven. Then the patrol car drove off, and the illusion was revealed: her VW was seated atop a flatbed truck.

"Hey, that's my car!" Maitlyn yelled. "Hey, you! Hey! Hey!" But the truck driver only yanked his door shut and roared off. Maitlyn went for her phone. "Charles, they took my car!"

"Who did? Are you okay?"

"A tow truck. They just—."

"We'll find it, don't worry. I'm almost there."

I ran out of gas. The engine died. She was going to need an explanation for her car being illegally parked in a Rancho neighborhood. *I was walking around, trying to get a sense of the place—for a story. Not on Nathan, on Rancho Santa Fe. I got the idea when I interviewed him. All that water usage. I want to ask Rancho residents if they know about the drought and will they vote for a candidate who doesn't care about global warming and what they will do when their golf courses turn brown.* Would anyone actually believe her—doing background late on a Saturday night? *I know, crazy, right? I have no life.*

She was rehearsing her story when Charles drove up. He parked across the street. She met him at the gate. "I'm sorry, Charles." She started crying when their eyes met through the bars. "I ruined your night."

"Got me out of the house for once," he said with a reassuring smile. He was wearing his new cap—Don't Mess With Texas. "A brother can only watch so much *Law & Order.*" He looked around. "That's good—no security cameras." He inspected the gate and tried to slide it open. It wouldn't budge. "Okay, I'm coming over." He turned his cap backwards, grabbed the bars, pulled himself up, swung his legs over the top of the gate, and stuck the landing. "Buenas noches, señorita," he whispered, with a tip of his cap.

"I wish I could do that," she said, admiring his quick maneuver.

"Maybe if I give you a lift." He bent his knee so she could step up on his thigh. With his hands on her hips, he boosted her up.

"I can't." She wasn't strong enough to hoist herself any higher. "I'm sorry." As he helped her down, she reached for his shoulders. For a moment, they were holding each other in a tight embrace. She had the urge to stay right there. *What is it about older men?*

He let her go and looked up at the house. "He's here, right? Ol' Fumble Fingers."

"Yeah. And that's Sheila's car. Sunny was right."

"My, my." He shook his head. "Ain't that sweet as a beet to eat."

"You think we should just go knock?"

"Last time I knocked on that door, it didn't go so well." He was inspecting the gate again. "I think I can jumpstart this bad boy open. Be right back." He scaled the fence again. He made it look so easy.

Maitlyn saw a light blink on and then off at the nearest neighbor's house. She glanced back at Nathan's entryway to be sure that no one had come outside. Across the street, Charles opened the trunk of his car—an old Jetta—and dug through the contents. *My hot date*, Maitlyn thought to herself, shaking her head at the absurdity, *my knight in shining armor*. Then it seemed hilarious: *He drives a Volkswagen. We were made for each other!*

She heard something, getting louder. "Charles, there's a car coming." Square headlights flashed into view.

"Aw, shit." Charles waved at Maitlyn, motioning her back. "I'll handle this."

"PUT YOUR HANDS UP!" It was a police cruiser, not the security vehicle.

Maitlyn shrunk farther into the shadows of the hedge. She could see Charles standing by his open trunk, hands held high, bleached by the cruiser's spotlight.

The police officer opened his car door and crouched behind it. "Keep 'em up, asshole," he ordered in a tough-guy voice. "Who's with you? Where's your partner?"

"It's just me, officer," Charles shouted back. "There's no problem. I'm with Channel Four News."

"There were two of you climbing the gate."

"It was just me. You can call — ."

"Don't fuckin' move."

Maitlyn twisted her body, trying to get a better view through the hedge. She heard the cop say "requesting backup" and "black male adult," then saw him step away from his car. He had a pistol trained on Charles. "You got a weapon?" he barked.

"No, sir."

"What's in your pocket?" He was inching toward Charles, one cautious step at a time.

"Nothing."

"Don't lie to me, asshole, I can see it."

"I got a screwdriver."

"Don't fuckin' move. Is that a gun?"

They both sounded scared.

"It's a flathead screwdriver."

"You move, swear to God, I'll fuckin' shoot you. Turn around. Turn...around! Put your hands...on the back...of your head!"

Charles did as instructed, turning slowly so that he was facing the rear corner of his car on the driver's side. The officer approached, pistol still extended. He hesitated, then raised his right leg and delivered a heavy kick to Charles's lower back. Charles's hips slammed into the car. His hands smacked the trunk door, knocking it shut. "What the fuck?" he gasped.

The officer took a step back and swiveled his head around. "Where's your partner?"

Charles had one hand on his stomach, the other on his hip. He looked in pain. "You broke my fuckin' spine." He bent forward and placed both hands on the car to steady himself, like a man exhausted.

"Hands!" the cop ordered. "Hands up! Let me see 'em!"

Charles lifted his hands. Without warning, the trunk door sprung back open. Startled, Charles spun away to protect his head.

The cop jumped backwards. "Don't move!" he shouted. His gun went off with a metallic bang.

Charles lurched forward, then collapsed backward to the ground. His head thumped against the pavement.

The gun snapped again. "I said don't move, motherfucker!"

Maitlyn bit her lower lip and tightened the muscles in her face until her eyes squinted shut. She was trying not to scream. She could barely breathe. *I'm passing out.* She grabbed for the hedge. The cop was walking toward the gate, pistol in one hand, a flashlight in the other. *I'm dead.*

The uniformed man stopped and looked away. He was listening to sirens. He swept his torch beam across the bars of the gate, lighting up the driveway, but only for a second. The sirens were getting closer. He walked back across the street. He stopped to holster his weapon, then changed his mind and drew it back out. He went to the open trunk and looked inside. For a moment, he was in shadow, out of Maitlyn's view. Then he stepped back into the light and dropped something beside Charles's lifeless body. He reached down and moved Charles's arm. Unsatisfied, he nudged the lifeless arm with his foot.

Lights and blaring sirens cut through the night. A cruiser sped up, flashing blue and red. Then another. And another. Brakes squealed. Doors swung open. "It looked like a gun," the cop shouted, pointing down at Charles, "I thought he had a gun!"

9

After Charles fell, Maitlyn wanted to let herself faint, but the reporter in her said keep the camera running, keep the phone trained on the police officer. Watching the action on the little screen, she saw him drop something next to Charles, saw him kick at Charles's arm.

When more police cruisers roared onto the scene, when the cop yelled, "I thought he had a gun," she ran back up the lawn to the far side of the house. Her heart was pounding at her chest and throat. Over her shoulder, she saw two flashlight beams moving at the gate. The cops were looking for her. If they jumped the fence, she had no place to go. *My car ran out of gas. I was backgrounding a story. I have no life.*

More sirens. Another cop car arrived, followed by an ambulance. *They're taking him to the E.R.,* she thought—she hoped—but she knew he was dead. "I'm sorry, Charles," she whispered through her tears, "I'm so sorry."

Lights came on in the front yard. The gate across the driveway began sliding open. Peering around the corner of the house, Maitlyn saw someone—*Nathan!*—walking down the driveway. He had a phone to his ear. Two cops met him at the open gate. Sensing movement out of the corner of her eye, Maitlyn pulled her head back. After two deep breaths, she slowly leaned forward for another look. Sheila was standing by her car, talking on her phone and watching the activity in the street. One of the cops swept the yard with his flashlight. *Hide!*

Spurred by panic, Maitlyn pushed away from the wall and ran to the backyard. She stopped on the patio for a moment, not thinking, just looking, then pulled open a sliding glass door and closed it gently behind her. Once inside, she turned and looked straight into a familiar face. She squealed in fright. The pastel fisherman was watching from his perch on the wall. *Hide!* he urged.

Still in a panic, Maitlyn hurried out of the living room and down a hallway. This was all familiar — the pool table, the trophy room door. She pushed it open, slipped in behind it, and slumped to the ground, struggling for air.

Paralyzed, afraid to move, Maitlyn sat against the door in the darkness. She didn't think. She couldn't think. She lost track of time. She only breathed. She was safe in her breathing. Once or twice she thought she heard the murmur of voices. *Are they searching the house?*

When she finally checked her phone, it was almost midnight. *Call Charles — he'll know what to do.* She started to dial, then remembered. She lay over on her side and pulled her knees to her chest. She tucked the collar of her blouse up around her mouth and cried into her shoulder. The tears kept coming.

At some point, after her weeping had eased to sniffles, she heard a door slam shut. *That's Grandma, returning from bridge club.* She groped around in the dark but couldn't find her pillow. She sat up with a start. She had to go home. Her phone, thank God, still had juice.

"Maitlyn, you're up late." He sounded surprised.

"Scott." She didn't know what to say. She almost hung up.

"Hey, guess where I am," he said, but didn't give her a chance. "I'm in Rancho. The cops shot a black dude in front of Nathan's house. Seriously. We're totally scooping it. No one else is here. That's my karma again."

"You're at — ?" She could barely speak.

"Yeah, we're staked out in the street. The deputies won't tell us anything, but — okay, I gotta bounce. Sheila's about to go live with Nathan. I'll call you later. This is big."

Maitlyn stood up slowly. Her legs were stiff. If Sheila was interviewing Nathan in the street, that meant the house was empty. She felt around for the light switch. Once again, the gleam of trophies behind glass was blinding. The cardboard Nathan was gone. So was *A Cavalier*. Of course it was—her question at the rally had warned him. She snapped a picture of the blank space on the wall.

In a daze, she wandered through the quiet house until she found the kitchen. She turned off the lights and looked out the window. With the driveway gate still open, she could see people walking back and forth between parked cars. The neighborhood was mostly shadows, but the street was aglow, flooded in light. It looked like a movie set.

Crying again, she stumbled through the dining room and the art gallery. She didn't know where she was going. She didn't care. Charles was dead and it was her fault and nothing else mattered now.

She opened the door to the studio where he would have raped her. The smell of paint thinner triggered a flash of memory. *You want to be queen?* She spied a palette knife, squeezed it tightly, and fingered the metal point. She wanted to scream in pain. She wanted to bleed. Then his hands were on her ribs, tearing at her skin. *Gouge his eyes out!* She swung wildly, slashing air, shouted, "No means no," and fell against an easel. Naked breasts, pink and pale, mocked her from every angle. *I'd make you my queen.* She lunged forward again, stabbing at nipples. "I wasn't flirting, I wasn't flirting," she jabbered, "no way," as she punctured and tore through stiff fabric. "I'm here for the interview. Only that." When the knife blade snapped off, she continued her onslaught with the broken stem until she ran out of steam. Unable to stand upright, she braced herself against a table. It took a few moments for the room to stop swirling. The wounded women stared at her, eyes wide with lust. Paint tubes littered the tabletop. She twisted one open, dabbed her finger black, and wandered the maze of easels, tracing charcoal tears down rosy cheeks. "Cry it out, girls. We all have bad days." She dropped the paint tube and gripped the doorknob for balance. Her mind was blinking awake, like from a bad dream. She took one last look at the ragged, ravaged canvases, the stunned and weeping women, and gasped at the damage.

Back in the kitchen, she unplugged the cappuccino maker but found it too heavy to lift. She settled instead on a copper saucepan—she'd always wanted one—only to leave it lying on the living room couch. She retraced her steps, out the sliding glass door, across the patio, and around the side of the house to the front lawn. Sheila's car was still there. Maitlyn crouched behind it. She knew where she was and felt completely lost.

"Act like you belong here," Maitlyn's tennis coach used to say before a match. "Walk onto the court like you own it." *I belong here, I belong here.* Maitlyn repeated the mantra in her mind as she placed one foot in front of the other. *I belong here. This is my driveway.* Nearing the gate, she saw little red cones marking the spot where Charles had fallen. He was gone. His hat rested near the rear tire—Don't Mess With Texas. A policeman was rolling a measuring wheel down the middle of the street. He glanced up at her, then resumed his task. *I belong here, I belong here.*

To Maitlyn's right, a little ways up the street, Scott had his back toward her. His camera was pointed at Sheila and Nathan. A miniature spotlight atop his camera shone in their faces. A second cop was standing beside Scott, watching the interview. A third was talking on his phone and scuffing his feet against the blacktop.

Maitlyn kept moving forward, neither cautious nor hurried. *Just you and the ball.* She passed through the gateway, and no one seemed to notice. She heard Nathan's loud voice: "Just goes to show you." She turned left, ducked under the yellow crime-scene tape, and kept walking, on automatic. Scott had parked the Four-mobile a little ways down the road. The side door slid open. Maitlyn climbed inside and pulled it shut.

Maybe he's still alive. People survive gunshot wounds all the time. The ambulance arrived pretty quickly. They could have saved him. If anyone could pull through, it would be Charles. Maitlyn could see him falling, arms flailing, the hat tumbling to the ground. She summoned up the deep echo of his voice—"Two hands on the ball, motherfucker." She could hear him insisting that "Texas ain't the South, Texas is Texas." That was from the last time they met in the Botanical Building, when she had mentioned him being called The Mouth from the South, and he had objected. "In Texas," he had explained, "we got Mexicans and cattle. The South is just too much white trash. When you cross over into Louisiana, it gets real spooky real fast."

"What about California?" she had asked.

"Paradise," he had replied, "just paradise. Course, back home, the rednecks are in plain sight." He had cautiously scanned the garden walkways. "Out here in Cali, you never do know."

Maitlyn gradually noticed the familiar smell of Scott—cigarette smoke and oniony grease—and remembered where she was: the backseat of a Channel Four news van, surrounded by electronic equipment. And who she was: *A name you can trust.* And what she needed to do: *Start thinking!*

Looking up the street through the windshield, she could see the lawmen come and go. She knew the drill—locating empty shells, measuring distances, taking prints off the car, knocking on neighbors' doors. She saw Scott swing the heavy camera off his shoulder, signaling the end of the interview. She saw Nathan lean toward Sheila, like he was whispering in her ear. He patted her shoulder, then headed up the driveway. Scott and Sheila remained in the street, chatting with one of the officers. After a few minutes, Sheila shook the cop's hand and, like Nathan before her, disappeared through the open gateway.

Seeing Scott headed toward the van, Maitlyn climbed out—she didn't want him sliding the door open and freaking out at the sight of her. Still, he was taken aback. "Maitlyn, what the fuck? What are you doing here? What happened to your face?"

She wiped her hand across her cheek. It came away black. "It's paint." A charcoal tear—she had given herself one too.

"First Pendleton, now this." He shook his head in disapproval while loading his camera into the van. "He's not your assignment, Maitlyn."

"Did they release the victim's name?"

"You're gonna get yourself in trouble. Seriously. Let it go."

"Did they?"

"No. A black male. Neighbor saw him trying to climb the fence. When a deputy rolled up, he pulled a piece."

"A gun? Did they find it?"

"I assume so." He slammed the door shut. "How did you get here so fast?"

"Did they say where they took him?"

"Jesus, Maitlyn. Nathan is Sheila's gig—get over it. Just go home. Where's your car?" He looked down the street.

"Could you go ask where they took him?"

He looked back at her in disbelief, not understanding her desperate tone. "Keep me out of this."

Maitlyn watched him stomp around to the driver's door. She didn't want to explain how she happened to be there without Ciela. She also didn't want to be left stranded forty miles from home. When he started the engine, she opened the passenger door. "Aren't you forgetting Sheila?"

"She drove here herself. She didn't want to wait for me."

"Oh. So could you, uh, drop me at my car?" She gestured toward the officer taking photos of Charles's Jetta, the trunk still open. "They wouldn't let me park up here."

Scott wheeled the van carefully past several cop cars. They were county deputies, Maitlyn noticed, not local police. To keep Scott from asking questions, Maitlyn asked her own. "What did Nathan have to say?"

"What they always say. 'The sheriff's department is doing a great job.' 'Thank goodness they got here when they did.' Then he went off on illegals."

"Did he see the shooting?"

"He heard the shots. He thought it was a car backfiring until his security service called and told him to open the gate. How far am I taking you, anyways?" They had gone about a mile.

"You can let me out at that convenience store."

"The local stop-n-rob." He pulled into the parking lot. "I don't see your Vee-Dub."

"It's around the corner." She was surprised how easily the lie came out. "But I need to use the bathroom." She pointed to the glass storefront. Her stomach felt weird.

"You want me to wait?"

"No, I'm good. Thanks for the ride." She opened the door. She wanted to get away.

"You walked from here all the way to Nathan's house?"

"Yeah." She stepped out of the van.

He raised an eyebrow. "Just happened to be in the neighborhood?"

"Wait, hold on." She opened the sliding door and grabbed something from behind the seat.

"What's that?"

"Nothing. My purse." She kept it away from the open door so he couldn't see it.

"You're acting weird, Maitlyn. I don't know what's going on, but if Cooper finds out you're shadowing Sheila, he's gonna be pissed."

Maitlyn washed her hands and face and browsed the magazine rack. The store clerk kept looking her way but didn't say anything about her lengthy stay. Finally, a late-model sedan pulled up by the front door of the store. *Can't afford kids, but he drives a BMW.*

He greeted her with a grin. "Your chauffer has arrived."

"Thank you, Hassan. I really appreciate this."

"No prob." He was still wearing the tuxedo.

"Have you been out all night?"

"Pretty much. Can't stop, won't stop. Where to? Denny's? I'd be up for a Grand Slam." He glanced down at the framed painting she had placed by her feet.

"The hospital in Encinitas." The closest one, according to her phone.

"Are you sick?" His eyes narrowed with concern. "You look like shit."

"I'm fine. Let's go. We're covering a shooting."

"For reals?" His eyes widened. "Like a murder?"

"Yeah, like a murder."

He drove too fast, but this time Maitlyn didn't complain. It was almost 3 a.m. when they got to the hospital. Near the emergency entrance, two black-and-white patrol cars were parked together, driver's side to driver's side. The lettering on the cars announced "SHERIFF" and "KEEPING THE PEACE SINCE 1850." Two deputies were chatting through their open windows.

Maitlyn approached them with a friendly wave. "I'm with Channel Four News." They weren't impressed. They didn't get out of their cars. "Can you tell me why you guys are sitting outside this hospital?"

"Donut shop's closed," one replied. He had a round, pink face and fat cheeks. His service radio was attached to the collar of his sand-colored uniform. His thick arm, like a freckled snake, rested in his open window.

"Can you tell me the name of the officer who shot a man tonight?"

"Don't know anything about it," Fat Face told her, playing dumb.

"How about you?" Maitlyn asked the other deputy.

"You mean up in Rancho?" he responded.

"I can tell you one thing," Fat Face interrupted, not wanting his partner to win Maitlyn's favor, "the perp had a gun." He gave her a smarmy wink, which she did her best to ignore. Cops, sheriff's deputies, military police—all of them, she had decided long ago, were worse even than lawyers.

Inside the emergency room, a receptionist behind a plexiglass window told her flatly, "I can't give out that kind of information," then returned to her Sudoku puzzle.

The waiting room was empty—just a television set running infomercials—until a man in a white coat came out to greet her. "I'm Dr. Landon."

"Can you tell me the status of the shooting victim, Doctor?" Maitlyn asked.

"Are you family?" He had a surfer's tan and irrepressible dimples, but there was fatigue in his voice.

"He's a friend of mine," Maitlyn pleaded. "Charles Lockett. We work together at Channel Four."

"Oh, right." A slight smile suggested he recognized her, still he shook his head. "I'm sorry."

"Can you just tell me—is he alive?"

"I'm very sorry," he said quietly, "very sorry." He looked her straight in the eye to be sure she understood.

Mr. Cooper was already at the station. He sounded caffeinated. "Maitlyn, I'm glad you phoned in. Did you see our live cut-in?"

"No."

"Turn on your TV. We've got an officer-involved shooting in—you're not going to believe this—Nathan's front yard. Sheila's already on it. That girl is really something. And I want you to cover the black reaction."

"The what?"

"The African-American community. Talk to some people. Ministers. Students at SDSU. Maybe some football players. See what they have to say about the cops shooting another black man. Because, listen, Maitlyn, according to Sheila, the sheriff's department is acting a little hinky, like they're circling the wagons on this one."

Maitlyn looked across the parking lot. The two deputies were still sitting in their cars. "I want to cover the victim," she said into the phone.

Mr. Cooper paused. Maitlyn could hear him sucking his teeth. "No, I'm giving that to Sheila," he decided. "She takes the shooting up in Rancho. You take the response down here in the city. That might be the better assignment, by the way. If it turns out the shooting wasn't righteous, we might see protests, especially if the guy dies. Your packages could go national."

Maitlyn hesitated. How much should she say? And how was she going to explain her fingerprints being all over Nathan's kitchen, never mind the vandalized canvases. *I was researching a story about a stolen painting. He told me, Feel free to snoop. Those nudes were already destroyed, I swear. Maybe Nathan's wife did it. I drew the tear streaks because—I don't know—damaged women need to cry.* Fingerprints in black oil paint—you might as well just leave your business card.

"Are you there?" Mr. Cooper asked. "Hello?"

Back at the convenience store, Maitlyn had thought about running away. *Call a cab and be in Mexico before the sun comes up.*

"Maitlyn, can you hear me?"

But I have work to do, she had reminded herself. *Maitlyn Flutters—a name you can trust.* And she owed it to him. "It was Charles." It came out as a whisper.

"Did you say something? I'm having trouble—."

"It was Charles. He's dead. I'm at the hospital. I'm covering it."

10

Maitlyn had been up all night. She had seen her car confiscated and her friend shot dead. She wanted to go home and burrow under the covers and make it all go away. Instead, she walked back across the parking lot. "He's dead," she informed the two deputies. "The shooting victim." She could feel anger rising. "His name is Charles Lockett."

"That's too bad," Fat Face replied indifferently.

"Can you tell me what crime he allegedly committed?" Maitlyn asked. Fat Face stared at her blankly. His friend looked away. Neither spoke. "Maybe you could do me a favor then. My car got towed. I need help finding it."

Fat Face shrugged. "Call the department."

Maitlyn remembered asking Charles why he had refused to cooperate with the San Diego P.D. "They don't protect and serve no more," he had explained. "Your car stalls out, they give you a ticket but won't give you a lift. Back home, we call 'em law dogs. They see everyone as the enemy. Even white folk."

"So you won't assist me, deputy?" she asked, already knowing the answer but hoping to shame him.

"I bet you could assist *me*, sweetheart." He grinned at the deputy in the opposite car. "Maybe we could work something out." Another wink.

"What's the license plate?" the other deputy asked coldly. Maitlyn turned away from Fat Face and recited her plate number. The deputy tapped at his computer keyboard, still not looking at her. "Where was your car parked?"

"Rancho Santa Fe." She heard Fat Face start his engine. She wanted to ask the helpful deputy if his partner was always a jerk, but figured it wouldn't advance her cause.

"Okay, hold on." Ignoring the screech of Fat Face's cruiser swerving out of the parking lot, the deputy made a call on his cell phone, then gave Maitlyn the address of an impound lot in Carlsbad. "Probably set you back two hundred bucks." He saw her wince. "Maybe your employer will pay for it," he offered. With Fat Face gone, his tone was more sympathetic. "You were reporting on the shooting, right? In Rancho."

"Yeah." She noted his name tag. "Thank you, Deputy Wilson." She started walking away.

"Hey."

She turned to face him. *Here it comes — he asks me out.*

"Thomas Cunningham," he said. "That's the name of the deputy involved. It's not like it's a secret or nothing. But don't say I told you."

She called Channel Four again. They wanted her to do a live phone-in piece with the morning news anchor. "Go ahead, Maitlyn," a technician instructed.

"I'm at Scripps Hospital in Encinitas," she said into the phone. "While the sheriff's department has yet to make an official announcement, I've been told the shooting victim died at the scene. He has been identified as Charles Lockett, formerly an employee of Channel Four."

"Maitlyn," the anchor injected, "is this the same Charles Lockett who assaulted Congressman Nathan Saltenstall?" He knew, of course. He was just punching up the drama.

"Yes, that's right."

"We've all seen that video. Any idea what Mr. Lockett was doing at Congressman Saltenstall's house in the middle of the night — the site of the assault four weeks ago?"

Maitlyn squeezed her eyes shut and saw Charles walking away from the house with Nathan in angry pursuit. *Just you and the ball.* "That's a good question. The sheriff's department is investigating, but it may be a while before we get solid answers. I can tell you that I've been told the name of the officer involved — Thomas Cunningham."

The anchor wasn't impressed. He was pushing for a different kind of story. "I know this may be sensitive, but you worked with Mr. Lockett, right?"

"He was a technician at Channel Four." She was speaking for a television audience, but her closed eyes were watching Nathan shove Charles to the grass.

"Do we know anything about his state of mind since the earlier incident at the Saltenstall residence? The one on the video."

"Hard to say." Now it was Charles throwing his infamous punch in grainy slow motion. "He's no longer employed by Channel Four." Mr. Cooper had told her to emphasize this — Channel Four is not connected in any way to the shooting, Channel Four does not have a horse in this race. "But he's always...he's a very positive person." When she opened her eyes, tears were forming.

"Thank you, Maitlyn. I'm sure this is a difficult Sunday morning for you. We go now to Sheila Patterson, standing by at the —."

"Okay, Maitlyn," the technician came back on the line, "you're off. You okay?"

"Glad I wasn't on camera."

"You were fine. This isn't easy. Charles was one of us. He was a good guy." The technician was already using the past tense. "So, uh, what do you think he was doing up there?"

"In Rancho?" What was she supposed to say? "Probably trying to help someone. That's how he is, right?"

Yes, it *was* a difficult Sunday morning for her. She had no appetite, not even for coffee, and she ached to go home and bawl her head off. Still, she suggested that Hassan get that Grand Slam breakfast before the long drive down the freeway. She sat in the greasy booth, pushing back a tide of sadness and hints of panic, while Hassan mopped up his eggs. "I can bring you back up here tomorrow," he offered. The impound lot, they had discovered, was closed on Sundays.

"Thanks." There was no affect in her voice. Her car problems seemed trivial now.

"So, how long did you know Charles?" Hassan, too — the past tense.

She brought her hands together and cupped them over her nose and mouth. She took a deep breath and exhaled before answering. "He was already at Channel Four when I started. But he—." Choosing verbs was suddenly awkward. "We haven't worked together that much."

"Yeah, I didn't know him that well either. But whenever I had a question, I'd go to him first. He was a chill dude."

They sat in silence, out of respect for the deceased. Maitlyn could still see him flailing and falling and losing his hat. She had never before seen someone shot. Charles hadn't screamed or anything, just collapsed to the ground. *Why did the deputy say the perp had a gun? There was no gun. Charles wasn't a perp.* "Can a person post a video on the web without anyone knowing who did it?" She had broken the heavy silence, almost unaware she was speaking aloud.

"Uh, sure," Hassan answered. "I think so. You can just use a fake name or whatever. Definitely. I've seen that on Youtube — posted by Anonymous."

"And no one can trace you?"

"They can always trace you — your email address, your URL. I mean, like, you could probably encrypt it, but they could still determine the source. I think. Like the FBI. I don't know. Why?"

"Just wondering. I mean, what if a person had a video of a police shooting and wanted to make it public."

"Like from a cell phone? Like an eyewitness?"

"Yeah. But what if the eyewitness is scared or...." She waited while Hassan chewed his food.

"He could take it to, like, Wikileaks and let them post it. I think they do that. Or to a reporter. I mean, if somebody brought it to *you*, wouldn't you protect your source?"

The waitress came with the check. "I'll get this," Maitlyn offered. It was the least she could do. "But can you loan me ten bucks?" Her purse was in Ciela.

"Deputy Cunningham responded to the burglary call and confronted the suspect, a Mr. Charles Lockett." The speaker looked pleasant, but her manner was severe. "He ordered the suspect to drop his weapon, which we have determined was a large wrench. The suspect charged him, and Deputy Cunningham fired twice in self-defense." Maitlyn had turned on the television as soon she got back to her condo. Channel Four was airing the press conference live. "Deputy Cunningham tried to administer first aid but was unable to save Mr. Lockett. Also, we have reason to believe there may be other suspects involved. The 911 caller reported seeing two individuals. But an extensive search of the neighborhood, including Congressman Saltenstall's property, didn't find anyone. That's all I have for you at this time. Thank you."

Maitlyn stared at the screen. *Two individuals*. They were talking about her.

The camera held steady on the empty podium with limp flags in the background until the feed cut back to the anchorman in the studio. "That was the sheriff's spokeswoman addressing reporters at the county administrative center in Clairemont Mesa," the anchor intoned. "The spokeswoman declined to take any questions, but the important thing is that we now know the officer fired in self-defense. A large wrench can be quite heavy. It has sharp edges. You definitely would not want to be hit with one."

Maitlyn clicked it off. *Did searching the property mean just his yard or inside his house too?* By now, Nathan had certainly discovered the damaged paintings, or the deputies had. Either way, it was only a matter of time until they came knocking at her door. *I'm going to lose my job. Cooper's going to call me in, and that dweeby lawyer will be sitting there.*

She went into the bathroom, looking for her Ativan pills, then remembered that they, too, were in Ciela. "God help me." She splashed water on her face. Hassan was right—she looked like shit. The water didn't help. *I'm going to prison.* A cold sweat enveloped her.

Hide! She could buy a ticket at the airport and fly somewhere. Sweden. She had a former college roommate in Stockholm. Or she could take a taxi to the border and walk over to Tijuana. *And then what?* She shoved her phone cord into her pocket—she was going to need it—and found her passport and a back-up credit card in a bedroom drawer. She stared out the window. *I can't stay here. They'll arrest me. They'll confiscate everything — my laptop, my cell.* She could go headfirst off the balcony.

The taxi took thirty minutes to arrive. The drive went by quickly. Maitlyn got out at a stop sign and walked the rest of the way. The front door was unlocked. "Hello? Anyone home?" She removed her sunglasses. It was a foggy morning. She had only worn them so the taxi driver wouldn't get a good look at her.

"Mattie, what a nice surprise," her grandmother cooed. "Do you have the flu? You look drawn."

"I had a bad night. Hi, Sugar." The dog was yipping and jumping for joy at her arrival.

"I'm sorry. Poor you." Grandma gave her a hug. "What's this? What have you brought me?" She took the small painting from Maitlyn's hands. "Oh, he's delightful." She held the frame away from her for a better look at the old fisherman. "I love pastels. Where did you find him?"

"I just...don't ask."

Her grandmother could see she was upset and didn't push it. "He looks Greek. Where should we put him, Sugar?" The Sheltie padded after her as she carried the painting into the dining room and then the kitchen, looking for vacant space on her crowded walls. "This frame has seen better days. But I like it."

Maitlyn felt numb, same as a few hours earlier when she had walked down Nathan's driveway with the small painting held close to her side. *Why did I take it?* The last twelve hours were a blur. *And why bring it here?* She hadn't planned for her grandmother to think it was a gift, she just couldn't have it in her apartment where the cops were sure to discover it. The best thing would be to bury it in a box in Grandma's garage. *The best thing would be to burn it.* But it was too late for that.

"I'll find a good spot, Mattie." Grandma came back into the living room. "He deserves a place of prominence. I might have to move some things around." She noticed how Maitlyn was staring straight ahead at nothing. "Are you sure you feel okay? Tell the truth, love."

The truth? The truth was she had broken into Nathan's house and vandalized his studio and stolen a painting off his wall. *What was I thinking?* She shook her head. "I just need a nap."

Maitlyn went into her old bedroom and shut the door. She couldn't sleep—not without her pills. While her phone was recharging, she lay on the bed and stared at the ceiling. *They'll find the trophy room photos in my data. They'll find the shooting video.* Her hands were shaking and her stomach was in knots. *They'll kill me to eliminate the eyewitness.* She had seen that in so many movies. *I'll turn the key and Ciela will explode.* She stood up. She lay back down. She wanted to jump out of her skin. *I shouldn't have gone beyond the kitchen. I shouldn't have flirted.* She rolled onto her stomach and pounded the bed with her fist. "I'm so stupid!" she moaned into a pillow.

When she had calmed down a little and her phone was fully charged, Maitlyn went out to the living room. Grandma and Sugar had gone for a walk. She quietly opened the door to the sewing room. One of her cousins had convinced Grandma to buy a desktop computer, not anticipating that Grandma would have little use for it and zero aptitude. It was a good machine, though, and easily accepted the downloads from Maitlyn's phone. The video was dark and jerky. When the deputy and Charles shouted back and forth, it was hard to know what they were saying. The vicious kick though—you could see that. You could hear the gunshots. You could see Charles fall. He appeared to be grabbing for his cap. It was so Charles. *He loved his hats.*

Maitlyn wiped away her tears and watched the short video again, and again, until she was convinced—the deputy had taken something from the trunk. That had to be the wrench. He had dropped it next to Charles.

The computer was powered down and Maitlyn was back in the living room when Grandma returned from her walk. "Did you sleep, sweetheart?" Grandma asked.

"No. Maybe a little."

"I'm going to make you something to eat." Grandma headed for the kitchen, then stopped. "Whatever's bothering you, Mattie, you know I can keep a secret."

Maitlyn's phone vibrated in her hand. She retreated to the bedroom to answer it. "Yeah?"

"This is Dr. Landon. I just got your voicemail."

"Thanks for returning my call." Maitlyn had left the message just five minutes earlier. He had given her a contact number back at the E.R.

"I'm really sorry about your friend. We did everything we could."

Maitlyn paused to take this in. "You mean he was still alive?" She could hear him hesitate. "Dr. Landon?"

"I'm not supposed to—."

"Did he still have a pulse?"

"You know what—I'm just getting off work. You want to meet for coffee?"

Like a date? "Well, I don't really have a car right now. I just have a few questions."

"I'll come to where you are. Are you in Encinitas? I know a cool little place—."

"I'm way down in Coronado." She immediately regretted divulging her location. She had assumed the distance would discourage him.

"Give me an address. I'll be there in half an hour."

Shit.

It was a long walk to Hotel Del, but Maitlyn had energy to burn. Her head was hung over from lack of sleep, her nerves were on edge, still she felt like she could run a marathon. When a police car drove past, she turned her face away. *Am I a criminal now?* She didn't know *what* she was. She thought back to her second meeting with Charles in the Botanical Building. She had suggested they hold future meetings in Coronado, and he had responded with a laugh. "That's whiteopia down there. Soon as I crossed that bridge, they'd arrest me. Island-hopping while black."

She could still hear his deep laugh as she walked past the tall masts in Glorietta Bay. White boats and white sails. When she was little, she had imagined she would marry a man with a yacht and they would sail around the world. *Do dreams ever come true?* She stopped walking and studied a sleek vessel christened *Laughin' All the Way*. She wondered what it would sell for. *If I had a sailboat, I could slip down the coast to Baja, live on fish tacos, write a book, call it* Nathan and Me. *Until I got abducted by a drug cartel.*

"Call me Mel." He was waiting for her in the hotel lobby. "Feel like getting brunch?" Dimples like deep commas. "My treat."

The Sunday brunch at the Hotel del Coronado was legendary. Maitlyn, though, was in no mood to stuff herself with prime rib and crab legs, even after the walk. She just wanted to ask her questions and get away.

"All the champagne you can drink," he tempted.

She looked up at the elaborate chandelier. *I should have opened the Chardonnay last night. Then I would have stayed home and watched a movie and Charles would still be alive.* She counted the light bulbs to keep from screaming.

"Are you okay?"

"I just want coffee."

They found a table on the sun deck. The fog was lifting. "I was supposed to surf this morning," Dr. Dimples said, looking out at the breaking waves. "There's a ripping southwest swell. But I couldn't pass up meeting a beautiful woman."

Maitlyn managed a perfunctory smile. Her hands fidgeted under the table. *I'm an investigative journalist.* "How did Charles die?" she blurted. It came out almost accusatory.

"I'm really not supposed to give out that information."

So why did you come? She leaned forward. "We'll keep it off the record."

"You really say that? That's cool."

"It means no one will know you spoke to me." *Believe me.* "Were there two bullet wounds?"

"Actually, yes. One near the left clavicle. The other pierced the heart. Off the record, right?" When she nodded yes, he continued. He was happy to spill his story. "The left coronary artery was shredded. That supplies blood to the heart, so there wasn't much we could do—even though I'm a trained surgeon."

"What about his back?"

"The bullets didn't go through. That's typical of hollow points. Cop bullets. They mushroomed and tore up tissue and lodged in the thoracic cavity."

She pushed away the thought of Charles suffering. "I mean, if you were kicked in your lower back, what would that do?"

"If it was hard enough, it could damage your spinal column. I worked on a guy one time got kicked by a horse." He smiled. "You know, I see you on the news all the time." His eyes strayed briefly to her chest. "Is it fun being on television?"

"It's a job. Was there spinal damage?"

"I couldn't say."

"What about the angle of the bullets?"

"That stuff's really for the coroner. I was just trying to save the patient."

"Charles. His name is Charles." She felt suddenly irritated. "He was—is—my friend." Should she even be talking about him like this? It all felt so ugly.

"I know," Dr. Dimples smiled. "It totally sucks. We did our best."

"Did he say anything? Was he in pain?"

"He wasn't conscious. He wasn't like your boyfriend or anything, was he?"

She looked away. Despite her misery, she almost laughed— the trained surgeon was so inappropriate. *Do I walk back to Grandma's or ask this creep for a ride?*

"Do you surf?" he asked, gesturing toward the whitewater. "This is a good spot for beginners. Further up the beach, by the base, it gets tricky. It's called Outlet. Good place to break your neck."

Not a bad idea, she thought.

"Hey," he continued, "you feel like taking a drive?" He was relentless. "There's an old shipwreck down the strand. I could show it to you."

Like she hadn't seen it before. "Do you have a sailboat?"

"No. Why? Do you like to sail? I could get one. We could learn together."

She opted to walk. To avoid an awkward goodbye, she excused herself to the bathroom and kept going, long strides, brisk pace, out a side door, across the parking lot, and down the sidewalk. She saw another police cruiser and quickly turned off Orange Avenue. *Why are there so many cops around here?* Her pulse was racing. *Is it always like this?* Her hands were shaking. The coffee had been a mistake. Agreeing to meet Dr. Dimples had been a mistake. *How does a person get so much confidence, just inviting himself into my life?* She hadn't made a good decision in weeks. *Am I losing my mind?*

Keeping to side streets, she ended up at Tidelands Park, where energetic young men were playing soccer and shouting in Spanish. Maitlyn remembered her mother saying, "Mexicans love parks," as if that was a bad thing. Her mother's house in Phoenix — she could hide out there. *No, that's the first place they'd look.*

When one of the soccer players whistled at her, Maitlyn hurried away, down to a little sandy beach on the bay. In the distance, she could see the gray hulks lined up at the navy docks. *Hassan was right — those ships don't keep us safe.* She looked up at the bridge soaring over the water. She wanted to be up there, driving Ciela with the top down and the radio turned up loud. *I need to make good decisions. Starting now.*

11

But how do you know if a decision is a good one? *Listen to your inner voice*—Maitlyn had read that often enough—*cultivate your intuition.* But her mind was going a mile a minute and drowning out any intuitive whispers. *If I hadn't gone beyond the kitchen, he wouldn't have attacked me in the studio, and maybe we would have become friends, Nathan and me, it would have been me instead of Sheila.* She shook her head. *Where do these thoughts come from?*

She tried sitting on a park bench and closing her eyes, only to jump up and start walking. She couldn't make up her mind. Everything was hanging in the balance—her career, her freedom, everything. "When you get in trouble," her father once told her, "you can come to us—that's what family is for." He had said *when*, not *if*—Maitlyn was sure of it. *He must have known about bad decisions.*

She hurried along the waterfront, then found herself turning around, not ready to face her grandmother's patient understanding. How do you explain to someone else what you don't understand yourself—like why even go back to Rancho, why mutilate the nudes? *What kind of person am I?* She was afraid if she started confessing, she might discover the answer and not like it. And for all she knew, two sheriff's deputies were waiting in her grandmother's living room, helping themselves to a plate of peanut butter cookies.

When Maitlyn got back to the park, she turned around again. It was either head for Grandma's or drown herself in the bay. As she walked, she phoned Scott, who answered by saying that he'd been about to call her because, "What the fuck? I mean, what the *fuck?*"

"I know," Maitlyn replied. It was the simplest thing to say.

"I mean, what was it, four weeks ago that we were taping the interview in Nathan's living room? Remember he kept asking me, 'You got it in the can, Scott? Tell me you got it in the can.' And then that meeting with Cooper. He's got his hat on backwards and 'two hands on the ball' and all that. And now he's dead?"

"I know."

"I don't get it. I mean, what was he doing going back there? Was he going after Nathan?"

"No, he —." She caught herself. "I don't know."

"Did you know something was up?" His disbelief became suspicion. "Is that how you got there so fast?"

"You told me where you were," she replied, proving nothing.

"Yeah, and you somehow drove up to Rancho and parked your car and walked up to —."

"I drove ninety, Sherlock. How did *you* get there so fast?" The best defense is a good offense. "I mean, how did you even know there was a shooting?"

"Sheila called me, and I went right to the station and grabbed the van." He sounded pleased with himself. "I knew it was gonna be big."

"How did Sheila find out?"

"I don't know. Maybe she got a tip. Maybe from the sheriff's department."

"Come on, Scott. They don't want reporters on the scene of a shooting."

"Maybe Nathan called her. There's a shooting outside his house, and he sees an opportunity for more free air time. That sounds like him, doesn't it?"

"Yeah, it does. But how come you parked the van away from his house?"

"Because there was a fucking crime scene in the way. Du-uh. They wouldn't even let *you* park in the neighborhood."

"But they let Sheila drive through the crime scene? They let her park in Nathan's driveway, where they were supposedly searching for another suspect? Have you wondered about that?"

"This is why you called me?"

"Sheila was already there, Scott."

"What are you saying?"

"Don't be dense. She knew about the shooting because she was at Nathan's house when it happened."

He paused before changing tack. "You're spying on her, aren't you? You're trying to get her fired?"

"No. But so what if I am? I'm a reporter, and if she's" — *How to put it?* — "having an affair with him, that just might be news."

"Aw, shit." He had lost the argument. "Have you told Cooper?"

"I'm thinking about it."

"I'm just a cameraman, right?" He sounded worried. "I just point and shoot."

"Did you already know about them?"

"No. I don't know. I thought it was possible. They have, like, a familiarity. She sometimes refers to him as Nate. But...."

"Have you talked to her this morning?"

"Yeah, we're going back up there this afternoon. They want her to do a spot in front of the gate, maybe talk to some neighbors."

"Did she say anything new?"

"Like what?"

"I don't know. Like, did the cops search Nathan's house?" *That* was why she had called Scott. *Did Nathan find the vandalism? Did detectives collect fingerprints? That* was what she wanted to know. "I mean, she was still there when we left."

"All she told me is Nathan is flying to Washington today. Shit." Scott was finally allowing himself to see the obvious. "That's another thing — she always knows his schedule."

Maitlyn didn't say anything to her grandmother, just fled to her bedroom, curled up in a ball, and let herself cry. Even when the tears stopped, she felt like she couldn't get out of bed. She had been up all night, and trying to manage all her emotions, not to mention maneuvering through a gauntlet of men — Scott, Mr. Cooper, Dr. Dimples, Hassan, the deputies — was crushing her. She was tired of gauging every word. She didn't want to manipulate any more conversations. Now that her mind had stopped racing, she mostly felt scared. She lay in bed, shivering, pushing back panic. *Breathe*, she reminded herself, *in and out*. Her breathing reminded her of the next step. "Okay, I'm scared," she acknowledged quietly. "Of course, I'm scared. Who wouldn't be?"

How many crimes had she committed? Theft, vandalism, maybe lying to a law officer, maybe obstruction of justice. They would arrest her at work and perp-walk her to the parking lot. *Damaged goods*. She would be in court wearing an orange jumpsuit, her hair unwashed. She would never become a news anchor, never have her own show. She would never see her grandmother again. *Breathing in, breathing out. Breathing in* — but what good is observing your breath when you are tumbling off a cliff? She rolled back and forth on the bed. She caught herself panicking. "The danger is gone, I'm safe." Maybe it wasn't true, but she kept saying it, hugging her pillow and saying it — "The danger is gone, I'm safe."

Then, all over again, it was Charles, grabbing for his hat. It hadn't happened like in a movie — no slow motion, no dramatic music, no spurting blood, just the cop yelling and then *bang!* And no cut to commercial, no scrolling credits. Charles had fallen...and nothing had changed. It was still night, she was still hiding in the bushes, the world hadn't shifted. Everything had remained the same. She had never imagined that a shooting could be so normal. Charles was dead, just like that. *Men always die.*

A heart attack had taken her grandfather, and that was just the beginning. A few years later, her father's motorcycle had run a red light, and a minivan had launched him fifty yards through the air. That was the police determination—the minivan driver was not at fault—but it made no sense. Her father had no alcohol in his blood. He was always careful on the road. Afterwards, her mother spent a lot of time standing at the intersection, watching the lights blink red and green, waiting for them to fail, to prove her theory, but they never did. "The city must have fixed them right after the accident," she insisted.

Thinking about her father was a comfort for Maitlyn—not his death, but before, when everything was right, when he came home from work in his VW Bug, his pants white with chalk dust. He had gone to UCSD to become an engineer but ended up a math teacher. The bedroom in Grandma's house had been his before it was hers. Lying there, she felt close to him, closer than to her mother, who she only saw once or twice a year anymore. Her grandmother, the house on Coronado, Sugar—this was her family. If she kept her mind on her father, she told herself, everything would be okay.

When Maitlyn finally emerged from her room, her grandmother was in the dining room, admiring the old fisherman. "He's a delight. But you shouldn't spend money on me." She had taken down her new La Jolla seascape to make room for the pastel painting.

"I stole it from Nathan's house," Maitlyn answered groggily. She was sick of secrets. Her stomach was in knots.

But her grandmother only laughed. "Sure you did. Did you learn anything more about his fake?"

"Not yet. But he knows I know about it." She had questioned him at the rally, and then the little painting had disappeared from the trophy room. That wasn't a coincidence. "He knows everything," she muttered to herself. The slashed canvases, the second suspect—he had to know. And if the video comes out, he will guess who filmed it—the same person who had swiped the old fisherman—*that bitch from Channel Four.* She had heard him spit that ugly phrase into his phone while he stood beside his pool—"That bitch from Channel Four, the blonde one." *Did I dream that?* She tugged at her hair. She couldn't do this alone—she was in over her head. "Grandma, I think I might be in trouble."

"This is about the shooting on the news, isn't it?" her grandmother asked. "I had football on while you were gone, and they kept talking about it. He was your friend—the black guy."

"Charles." She wanted to shout but stayed calm. "Charles Lockett." She collapsed into a chair at the dining room table and buried her face into her hands. "I don't know what to do."

"What do you *want* to do?"

"I want...." She saw the red lettering on his hat—Don't Mess With Texas. "I want people to know he wasn't...a perp. He was there because he was helping me."

"That sounds reasonable. You're a reporter. Report the truth."

Sure, and go straight to jail, do not pass Go. I'd have to tell everyone I was there, I was the other one. Maitlyn sighed. "The truth is...I really did steal that painting from Nathan."

"Oh." Her grandmother saw that she was serious. "And he—Charles Lockett—he helped you steal it?"

"No. He wasn't a thief." *The past tense.* "That was later. I mean, the painting came later." *And I didn't even want it.* Maitlyn was having trouble recalling the sequence of events. "It's a long story." *I wanted the copper pot. But I took the painting instead. I'm the thief.* "I'm going to give it back, Grandma, I promise."

"Don't you dare," Grandma replied sharply.

"But...." Maitlyn shook her head and stretched her eyelids, trying to make sense of her crumbling moral universe.

"He'd want me to have this painting. A token of appreciation. For loyalty. I'm one of the original Saltenstalwarts, you know." Grandma waved her hands and sang, "Nathan, Nathan, he's our guy, throwing touchdowns on the fly." She paused, trying to recall the jingle. "Spins his balls like no one can, Nathan, Nathan, he's our man." She laughed. "Something like that. I was a cheerleader, you know, way back when."

"I know." Maitlyn hated cheerleaders. No, she hated the *mention* of cheerleaders, hated being reminded of trying out for the squad several times in high school and ending up, instead, on the tennis team. No one paid attention to the tennis team. She stood up. "I have to go make a phone call."

As Maitlyn left the room, her grandmother was polishing the splintered wood that framed Nathan's painting. "I still can't believe his line let him get blindsided," Maitlyn heard her say. "The fumble was their fault."

Maitlyn had to make a phone call because she knew how the story would run. Charles Lockett was an angry, confused, dangerous man. He assaulted Nathan Saltenstall, and it cost him his job. He became obsessed, took to stalking the congressman. He was outside Nathan's residence, preparing to break in, when the deputy arrived. Rather than submit to arrest, he threatened the officer with a heavy wrench. An unstable black man in a white community late at night—the deputy *had* to open fire. That would be the dominant narrative. Charles was the perp, and Nathan, the man who would have raped her, was the intended victim. And back in Texas, or wherever they lived, Charles's family—his parents, the three brothers, the ex-wife—would wonder what happened to him, how he had turned bad. And they deserved to know the truth. Charles deserved that they knew the truth. He'd only been trying to help. He was the hero. If her life was over anyway, she might as well do the right thing.

"Maitlyn," Mr. Cooper answered her call abruptly, "talk to me. Have you got a story? Are black people upset?" He sounded normal, thank goodness—he hadn't yet been informed that his irresponsible news chick was wanted for breaking and entering.

"Is this phone secure?"

"Secure? What kind of question is that? Is *your* phone secure, Maitlyn? Is anybody's?" Charles had said the same thing. That's why he had always wanted to talk in person.

"Could you meet me somewhere? I think I've got something big."

"What is this—Deep Throat?" Mr. Cooper chuckled at the reference.

Maitlyn ignored it. "I'll be at that park right after you cross the Coronado Bridge."

"You're serious, aren't you? What's this about? Is it the rising sea level again? Maitlyn, it's probably just high tide. Check a chart."

While her boss was being dismissive, Maitlyn was imagining Agent Hansen, with her hair in a bun, listening to a recording of this phone conversation. The FBI, Maitlyn assumed, would try to uncover the source of the mysterious video that implicated Deputy Cunningham for murder. She had to be careful. "A navy ship sunk in the harbor," she told Mr. Cooper, already back to lying—*Maitlyn Flutters, a name you can't trust*—but she didn't know how else to do this.

"That's it?" He sounded amused. "I'll send a camera."

"No, I, uh, something weird is going on. I think they're trying to cover it up. But I've got an eyewitness."

"Seriously? Fucking A. Channel Four is kicking some ass this weekend. That reminds me, I've got a bone to pick with you. How did you find out the name of that deputy?"

"Uh," Maitlyn hesitated, "one of his colleagues."

"Did you get verification?"

"It was the right name. We got it first, right?"

"You lucked out. *We* lucked out. Unverified disclosures are how we get sued. You're a professional, Maitlyn. Do it by the book."

"Okay. You're right. Which is why I need you to see this sunken ship." Mr. Cooper loved to be needed. "If the navy invokes national security, I'm going to need guidance."

Maitlyn headed back to the park, feeling on autopilot again. She had always loved the wide view along the bay, reaching north to the airport and south past the navy piers and straight east to the downtown skyline. Now, the world was closing in on her. She could only see straight ahead, and not very far. When her phone vibrated in her pocket, she dug it out quickly and checked the caller ID before answering. "Hi, Sunny."

"I just heard," Sunny said quietly. "This is so sad. Just awful. I miss him already. That deep voice. And think of his poor daughter."

"Charles has a daughter?"

"Yeah. She must be like twenty by now. I should call her. But what would I say?"

"Yeah, that's tough." She wondered what else she didn't know about Charles. "Say you're sorry, I guess."

"It's so weird. What do you think he was doing back at Nathan's house?"

"Sunny, I've got another call." *Thank goodness.* "I've got to take it. I'll call you later."

It was Scott. "Maybe Charles knew about Sheila and Nathan," he said excitedly. "Maybe he was trying to expose them."

"Charles wasn't like that. He was straightforward." *Not a snoop like me.* "Hey, I've got Cooper calling me." *Thank goodness.* "I better take it."

Mr. Cooper was phoning from the parking lot. "I'm here. Where are you? Where's the *Titanic*?"

Maitlyn met him near the soccer field and didn't mince words. "This isn't about a sunken ship. I'm sorry. But it's still a cover up. They aren't telling the truth."

Confusion delayed his anger. "What are you talking about?"

"Someone sent me a video." She pointed to her phone. "It shows Charles getting shot."

He looked at her as the news sunk in. "Let me see it."

"I deleted it." That was the truth. "After I downloaded it."

"Where is it—on your laptop?"

Actually, it was a short walk away, on the hard drive of her grandmother's dusty computer, but Maitlyn wasn't ready to share it just yet. She didn't trust herself to make hasty decisions. *One step at a time*, she had told herself.

It took Cooper a moment to realize that she wasn't going to answer. He scratched at one of his coyote ears. "Okay, who sent it to you?"

"A privileged source."

"Right. Are you sure you want to do it this way, Maitlyn? It gets tricky. Maybe the video's not even legit."

"It's definitely Charles. And he didn't have a weapon."

"Oh, Christ. Are you sure?"

"Charles wasn't resisting." She could see the deputy's brutal kick. *Deputy Thomas Cunningham*. "He had his hands in the air."

Mr. Cooper turned away, toward the soccer players, taking a moment to consider the implications of what she was telling him. Then, suddenly, he came alive. "Okay, number one, I need to see that video—before we do anything. But if it's what you say, we'll have to bring in legal. We'll have to bring in everybody. Have our tech guys check it out. This is going to explode." He had his phone out and was making a call. "Yeah, get me Jerry," he said into the phone, then promptly changed his mind. "No, wait. Just tell him to be in my office in twenty minutes." He grinned at Maitlyn. "Tell him it's about a shipwreck."

12

On Monday morning, Maitlyn was feeling better thanks to five glorious milligrams of Ambien. While sneaking the pill from her grandmother's medicine cabinet the night before, she had caught a glimpse of herself in the mirror and frowned at what she saw — *I'm the thief* — but asking for the sleeping aid would have only given Grandma more cause for worry. *Sometimes you have to lie.*

After breakfast, they headed north, opposite rush hour traffic, Grandma driving and venting. "She passes and then discovers a hidden card," she grumbled, expecting Maitlyn to understand her exasperation. "Invariably, it's an ace." She kept both hands tight on the steering wheel and her eyes straight ahead. "But how can I tell her I want to play with someone else? It's like being married."

Maitlyn half-listened while fiddling with the internet on her phone. Grandma had been complaining about her bridge partner for years, and nothing was going to change. When the phone rang, it was Mr. Cooper, wondering why Maitlyn wasn't at work, they needed her right away. "My car got towed," she told him simply. "I'm on my way to Carlsbad."

With the phone to her right ear, Maitlyn heard Cooper say, "We're dotting all our i's today." Her left ear took in Grandma's continued griping: "We play three no when slam is cold." Maitlyn had no idea what either one was talking about and felt no inclination to ask.

The impound yard was tucked between business parks near the Palomar airport and hidden behind a tall fence topped with spiraling barbed wire. Two shiny tow trucks sat out front. In the office, a short man with grease-blackened fingernails took a bill from a hook on the wall. "Here you go, ma'am," he said, placing the invoice on the counter. "Blue Beetle." No wedding ring, and the tip of one of his thumbs was missing. "We take credit cards with I.D."

Maitlyn read the total. "Are you kidding? Three hundred dollars?"

"Long drive out to Rancho," he explained matter-of-factly, "plus storage." He looked to be about sixty. Dandruff flecked his gray sideburns. Duct tape reinforced his smudged glasses.

"I need to get a purchase order from work. They'll send you a check."

"Sure." He wiped his mouth with the back of his hand. "But you want your vehicle now, it's a card or cash." With his index fingers, he tapped at a computer keyboard covered by a plastic dirt guard.

"I'm not paying this today." Maitlyn had no intention of telling Channel Four where and why her car was confiscated, and they probably wouldn't let her expense it anyway, but she didn't want this grubby mechanic thinking he could demand whatever he wanted from her.

Still pecking at the keyboard, he said to her, "Ma'am, just so you know, every day you wait is forty bucks more for storage."

"That's extortion. You have to open the gate and let me have my car." She was beginning to hate fences. "You have to give me my car." Just that quickly, the tears started flowing.

"Jesus God almighty," the man snorted. He shook his head in disbelief but appeared unsure of himself. "Ma'am," he said, sounding almost sympathetic, "maybe your mother can help."

"What?"

He nodded toward the parking lot, where Grandma was waiting. "Just go ask her. That way she doesn't have to bring you here again tomorrow."

Maitlyn wiped her eyes. It wasn't the bill she was crying about, not entirely. She was just so tired of all these arrogant men having their way, with their grubby hands and their presumption and their gates and their guns. Her father hadn't been like this.

No longer crying, she pulled out her phone and summoned up the website she had saved. "Do you own this place?" she asked.

"Probably longer than you've been alive," the man answered, glancing up at a clock on the wall.

"Then you should know that under California Vehicle Code section 22658 and section 22953, my car was towed illegally."

"Yeah," he laughed through his nose, "you can save that for the judge."

"It also says this." She began reading aloud from her phone. "A person who charges a vehicle owner a towing, service, or storage charge at an excessive rate is civilly liable to the vehicle owner for—."

"Four times the amount charged. It's posted right there." He pointed to a laminated document of fine print tacked to the wall.

"Good," Maitlyn sputtered, trying to maintain her thrust, "so you can't plead ignorance." But she could see that her appeal to the law wasn't going to work. "Do you watch the local news?"

"Are you paying your bill or not?" he huffed, dropping any last pretense of civility.

"My name is Maitlyn Flutters. I work for Channel Four."

"I don't have time for this." He returned the invoice to the hook on the wall and folded his glasses into his shirt pocket.

"I'm an investigative journalist. I'm going to start looking into your towing practices."

"Is that a fact?" He turned to a younger man, who had just entered the office from an internal door. "Can you believe this bitch?"

The younger man eyed Maitlyn. "I seen her on TV." He had dark hair and a slight Mexican accent. He stuck his head back out the door and whistled to someone.

This bitch. Maitlyn's face was burning with anger. "You think I'm kidding? I'm going to talk to my friends in the sheriff's department, like Deputy Wilson. I'm going to call the Better Business Bureau. I'm going to post on Angie's List." She pointed an index finger at the owner. "I'm going to call Agent Hansen down at the FBI."

The owner stood back from the counter, folded his dirty arms across his chest, and looked out a window, trying to show both indifference and disdain. Another dark-haired man came in, curious to see what was happening or perhaps to ogle the furious woman. The two employees exchanged a few grinning comments in Spanish. The only word Maitlyn recognized was *pinche*.

"And maybe," Maitlyn continued, "I'll talk to I.C.E. about your workforce." She kept her eyes on the owner, matching his suddenly seething stare. She could hear the two employees exit the office. She knew she had scored. "Do you know the penalty for hiring illegals?"

"Okay, lady," he groused loudly, breaking eye contact and reaching for the invoice, "I'll release your vehicle. Just so you stop your crying." He slammed the bill on the counter, unfolded his glasses, and found a pen. "But I need to see your driver's license and your social security card."

"Sure."

"And I want your cell number and your work phone."

She would give him fake contact numbers. She had done that with men before. "My purse is in the Blue Beetle."

"Wait here." He took her car keys from a hook and opened the door to leave, then stopped. "I don't get full payment in thirty days," he sneered, "my collection agency is coming after you. And they will ruin your credit score, I guarangoddamtee it, Marilyn."

"Thirty days. No problem." She had won the battle of wills — that's what mattered. "And it's Maitlyn."

It's Maitlyn — the words lingered in her mind as she drove her car out of the impound yard. She popped an Ativan under her tongue and waved goodbye to Grandma. The yard owner offered his own goodbye salute with a single finger, and it wasn't the playful kind. "Idiot," Maitlyn mouthed, then patted the dashboard the way a rider soothes a horse. "I'm sorry you had to go through this, Ciela. I'm sorry I let them touch you. I know what it's like, believe me."

It felt good, though — not just recovering her vehicle, but having fought back. She didn't know where it had come from — the courage to bluff the owner, or even the idea. She had never before threatened anyone like that. The words had tumbled out on their own momentum. "I'm the hero," she said aloud, as she steered onto the freeway. She pursed her lips and nodded her head in triumph. Twenty minutes later, the anti-anxiety drug kicked in. She could feel her whole body relax — the first time in two days. "Gonna stand my ground," she sang along to the radio, "and I won't back down."

Still feeling empowered, she strode down the hallway to see Mr. Cooper. "It's Maitlyn," she announced, as she knocked on his office door and pushed it open.

"Did you bring it?" were the first words out of Mr. Cooper's mouth.

"I didn't have a memory stick. And no way I'm sending it over the web." She looked over at the dweeby lawyer, who was sitting in the corner fondling a Starbucks cup. *And I'm not playing my trump card just yet*, she might have added.

"Here." Mr. Cooper found a flash drive in his desk drawer and tossed it to her. "We need to move on this."

"We're going to have a lot of questions," the dweeby lawyer interjected, "starting with provenance."

"Once it's out there," Mr. Cooper continued, "I want you to go record a spot with a"—he pulled up something on his phone—"Reverend Hutchings. He contacted us, asking about Charles. He's local NAACP. Should be good for some righteous indignation." He tapped at his phone. "I'm forwarding you the details."

"First, I want to do some background on Cunningham," Maitlyn said.

"Who?"

"The officer involved. Like, does he have a record of complaints? Have there been other shootings?"

"Maitlyn." Cooper shook his head.

"Basic investigative journalism. He falsified his report, you know."

"No," Cooper fired back, "I don't know. How could I know if I haven't seen that video?"

"At this point," the dweeb added, "we don't even know the video exists."

"And another thing," Cooper continued, "you are *not* an investigative journalist." He had run out of patience. "You're not an investigative anything. That includes that sea level business. You're the face of the news, not the source, okay?" He softened his tone slightly. "The face. You're good at that, Maitlyn." Then his impatience returned. "I need you on breaking news. I need you, right now, on the black community. I told you before, Sheila takes the shooting. So anything we find on this Officer Cunningham, we give to her."

"Sheila's on Nathan," Maitlyn blurted.

"That's right."

"Sheila's all over Nathan. In fact, Sheila is…." She couldn't do it. Another trump card she couldn't play.

"Please, Maitlyn, go do whatever you have to do so that we can have a look at that video." Mr. Cooper pointed to the door. "ASAP. The video." Another grubby man giving orders. "If it's really what you say it is."

Maitlyn drove to Balboa Park and sat in Ciela, regretting that she hadn't fought back. *Your new hot news chick,* she should have told Mr. Cooper, *is sleeping with her assignment.* But ratting out Sheila — that didn't feel right, and it was dangerous ground for someone equally vulnerable to exposure, someone who had left black fingerprints all over Nathan's house. So she had balked.

You're the face of the news, not the source. Maitlyn looked out the windshield. Two squirrels were chasing each other up and down a tree. Maitlyn didn't notice. She was staring at a chessboard, unsure of her next move, and only the Ativan in her system kept her from panicking as she realized the extent of her problem: she didn't know the rules, didn't know how each piece moved, wasn't even sure of her objective. Yes, she wanted to expose the killer cop and redeem Charles's good name. But there was also her own good name to protect, and with it her career. What would happen when the video was made public? And what about those fingerprints? How come she hadn't been arrested yet? Did she dare go back to her apartment?

She checked her phone for text messages. The only thing interesting was from Tina, an old college roommate: OMG U knew that guy they shot? Maitlyn hadn't heard from her in over a year, but Tina always did love scandal. She would be wanting dirty details, Maitlyn guessed, and Tina's second text confirmed it: Lunch next week?

Maitlyn put the phone aside. If only she could send Charles a text message and, one last time, meet him in the Botanical Building. "What should I do, Charles?" she asked aloud. "You promised you would help me." She pressed her forehead against the steering wheel and exhaled heavily. "Fuck."

Finally climbing out of her car, Maitlyn walked across a patchy lawn to the Redwood Club, where the midday bridge game was just getting started. A few players glanced up at her. She could see recognition in their expressions. These were the people who watched the evening news — the middle-class elderly, white and gray and trifocaled. This was her audience. And Nathan's. If the media polls were correct, these were the folks who still believed what the news anchors told them and the one demographic that always turned out on election day.

"My granddaughter, Maitlyn," Grandma said proudly to the three others at her table.

The thief, Maitlyn added in her mind.

"Good to see you again, Mattie," Grandma's partner said, peering up with her one good eye.

"Just leave it unlocked, honey," Grandma instructed, as she handed over her house key.

Then, serious and silent, they all turned back to their cards. The face of the news was in their midst, and she might as well have been invisible.

For a few minutes, Maitlyn watched them play, understanding none of it. "The game is dying," Grandma had told her more than once. "Ours is the last generation." *Maybe I'm in the wrong business*, Maitlyn thought as she tiptoed out. *Funeral planning — that's the future.*

Maitlyn sat at her grandmother's computer, watching Charles raise his hands and fall to the ground. To the outside world, his life had been reduced to three brief digital recordings: punching Nathan in the front walkway, knocked over by Nathan on the front lawn, getting shot down in Nathan's street. Three violent acts — that would be his online presence for eternity, that *was* Charles Lockett, that was all you needed to know.

But with the touch of a button, Maitlyn could eliminate the third. She could hear the dweeb's nasally voice: *At this point, we don't even know the video exists.* It wasn't *out there* yet. Just thinking about it made her stomach twist. If your universe is daily shaped and reshaped by electronic flashes, if a few megabytes of memory either way are the difference between fact and fiction, then a few keystrokes could change reality forever. Hit the delete key, and Deputy Cunningham's version of events would go unchallenged, his lies would become truth. A cold-blooded murder would become courageous public service, and the septuagenarians at the bridge club would never know the difference.

But, at least, maybe I can have my life back. Maitlyn could erase the file — it was that simple — unhitch herself from tragedy and go back to presenting traffic backups and other local fascinations with a pleasant tone and winning smile, like Mr. Cooper demanded. That was sounding pretty good right now. She wasn't cut out for all this drama. She was an island girl. *And anyways*, she told herself, *it won't bring him back.* Her little surreptitious recording wasn't going to resurrect Charles, no matter how many viewers it might draw on YouTube. She tapped DEL, and the computer asked her if she really wanted to send this file to trash. She opted for CANCEL. *I'll go take another Ativan,* she thought, *then I'll do it.* She wasn't quite ready to be the hand of God.

Sugar was curled up on the living room couch, her usual spot while waiting for Grandma to return. "What would *you* do, Su-su?" Maitlyn asked, flopping down at her side. The fluffy dog responded by hopping into her lap and licking her face. "That's what I thought," Maitlyn said, "love is the answer." She smoothed the dog's coat. "I haven't been kissed in a long time."

Then her phone rang. "Now what, Cooper?" she asked aloud, but the incoming number was a 202 area code, something from back east, probably telemarketing. She let it go until the caller finished leaving a voice message.

"Maitlyn," the recording began, and immediately she recognized the strong male voice—not the slow rhythm of Charles's comforting bass, more like a strident, confident tenor. There was no hesitation, no irony, no self-deprecation. "This is Nathan. I think we have some things to talk about. Call me back at this number." A voice of entitlement. "Sooner is better than later."

"Oh, shit." Maitlyn paced around the living room. "Oh, shit." She ended up in the dining room, looking at the old fisherman. "Fuck." The f-word used to make her uncomfortable. *Shit* had always been her limit. But the harsher expletive was coming more easily these days. She was finding it useful. "I'm fucked."

13

"We are all saddened by this tragedy," the minister said solemnly, "but we must resist the urge to rush to judgment. About Mr. Lockett and also about Deputy Cunningham. We pray for them both and their families."

"Are you concerned," Maitlyn asked him, "about relations between law enforcement and the black community?"

"Yes, of course. Always." He was comfortable speaking for a television camera. He had a powerful presence, even with his hands folded, even seated behind a desk. He had done this before. "We support our brothers and sisters wearing the badge. We rely on them to keep our neighborhoods safe. But we also expect them to extend to people of color the same dignity and respect they would want extended to them."

"Have you reached out to the sheriff's department regarding this incident?"

"No, I have not."

"Are you planning to?"

"I talk to law enforcement officials all the time. I suspect it will come up at some point."

"So this isn't a big issue for you?" Maitlyn was running out of things to ask.

"It's *an* issue, yes. One of many. Community outreach is an essential part of our ministry. That's who we are. Prison ministry, hospital ministry, homeless ministry, family crisis intervention." The list rolled off his tongue with a practiced familiarity. "We feed shut-ins. We minister to our sisters trapped in prostitution. We do the Lord's work wherever and whenever possible."

"Thank you, Reverend Hutchings."

"My pleasure. God bless." He waited a moment for the camera to stop recording, then came around the desk to shake Maitlyn's hand.

"That was super," she said to him. *And pointless.* The interview would never make the air. No news is no news. Thankfully, too, because her hair and makeup were not at their best.

Earlier, after hearing Nathan's ominous message, Maitlyn had rushed to Ciela. She didn't know where she was going, she only knew she had to keep moving. *Don't sit still.* Something had to be done, she just wasn't sure what. Leaving Coronado, she had driven like Grandma — white-knuckling the steering wheel, eyes blindered, looking only forward. That way she wouldn't get any bad ideas on the bridge. *I think we have some things to talk about.* Nathan had said *things*. Plural. *How many things?* she wondered.

When she found herself heading up Banker's Hill, her heart began pounding. *They'll be waiting.* Sweat beaded on her forehead. *They'll lock me in jail.* She turned off Juniper Street and parked in front of the community garden, a safe distance from her apartment building. *Is it too soon for another Ativan?* She got out of her car and walked among the garden plots. She had the feeling she was being watched, even with no one in sight. She stopped behind an avocado tree. *Now what?* This was like hiding in the hedges at Nathan's house. Should she call him? She could still hear his words — "Sooner is better than later" — and wondered, *Was that a threat?* She pictured herself riding a tiger, like the lady in the limerick — doomed once she dismounted. *Do something!*

She made a phone call — to Reverend Hutchings, to set up the interview. "How about today?" she suggested, not considering the state of her appearance. "I could come right now."

"If we're finished here, Ms. Flutters, there's someone I'd like you to meet." The firm hand on her upper back gave Maitlyn a start, but she stifled her unease. The minister was a big teddy bear, broader at the shoulders even than Nathan, but with a manner more gentle. She wanted to lean into him. *I could use a hug,* she realized. When Hassan made to follow them, Reverend Hutchings stopped him. "Please, son, no camera. My apologies."

"It's all good," Hassan assured him. "This church is off the hook, by the way. I hear your choir is fly. Like tight."

"That it is, my man, that it is."

"Right on," Hassan concluded, pleased to be pleased. "Epic." He turned to Maitlyn. "I'll just chillax outside."

"Sometimes," Hutchings chuckled after Hassan was out of earshot, "I don't know *what* these young brothers are saying." Then he ushered Maitlyn down a hallway to a quiet room, where a delicate young woman was seated, reading a Bible. "This is Capucine," the minister said, by way of introduction. "Capucine, this is Maitlyn."

"Hello," the young woman said shyly as she stood up. She appeared confused by the meeting.

"Nice to meet you, Capucine," Maitlyn said, extending her hand. The woman's grip was feeble. "You have a lovely name." Capucine was beautiful, despite her downcast and troubled mien. *Trapped in prostitution?*

"Capucine works in our day care program," the minister explained. "The children love her. We all do. She's a blessing."

"That's terrific," Maitlyn said, feeling relief for the woman. Still, she couldn't place her. The kinky hair and dark eyebrows didn't fit with the pale skin and narrow nose. *Maybe Middle Eastern,* Maitlyn thought, *or Colombian.* But how to explain those blue irises peeking out from heavy eyelids?

"Maitlyn's with Channel Four News."

Capucine's eyes lifted slightly. "Did you know him?"

It took a moment, but it was there—the cheekbones for sure, maybe the curve of the lips. When Maitlyn wobbled, the good minister rescued her. "Capucine is Charles Lockett's daughter."

"But you're so...." Maitlyn said stupidly, before catching herself.

"Her mother is white," the minister explained, rescuing her again.

"She's from France," Capucine added in a near whisper.

"Oh, okay," Maitlyn stammered. Black Texan, white French—the pairing didn't make sense to her. *Did Charles once live in Europe? Was he in the military?*

"Why don't we sit down," Hutchings said warmly, offering Maitlyn a folding chair.

This gave Maitlyn a moment to steady herself. "He was a good man—your father. I'm very sorry."

"Thank you," Capucine nodded. If she started to cry, Maitlyn would too.

"You were there, right," Hutchings asked Maitlyn, his palms together at his chin, "at the Saltenstall residence?"

"What? No!" *How does he know?* If she hadn't been seated, she might have bolted for the door.

"I mean when Mr. Lockett and Mr. Saltenstall had their altercation. I thought you—."

"Oh, that. Yes." Her temples were pounding. "I had just interviewed Nath—the congressman. But I didn't really...."

"Capucine is trying to understand why her father went back there. On his last night. I thought maybe you could bring some truth."

"He...." *Shit.* Maitlyn fidgeted, unsure of where to rest her hands. *How do I do this?*

"You said he was a good man," Capucine said

"He was," Maitlyn said. Then she had to break eye contact. In a framed print on the wall, Jesus was calming a stormy sea. His skin was dark. Maitlyn could hear Charles: *Just looking out for the talent. You'd do the same for me.* They were both waiting for her— the gentle minister and the pleading daughter. *Fuck it.* "He was there—Charles, your father, at Nathan's house—because I needed help. It's my fault." She couldn't withhold tears any longer. "I'm sorry."

"Cat girl, dat girl, so what she a fat girl?" Hassan was sitting in the driver's seat of the news van, window down, dancing from the waist up, and rapping too loudly. "Gonna make my heart flip, gonna make the scales tip, ohhhhh-ver." He spotted Maitlyn coming toward him from the church and slipped his headphones down around his neck. "We outta here?" He noticed her strange expression. "You okay?"

"I need you to do me a favor."

"That's me — the favor alligator. Chop chop."

"When you get back to the station, give this to Mr. Cooper." She handed Hassan the flash drive. "He's waiting for it."

"Heard, understood, acknowledged." Hassan saluted. "Where are *you* going?"

"To see Whatshisface." It just came out. It was news to her.

"MVP?"

"No, my lawyer."

He worked on the fifth floor of a downtown tower, with a bird's eye view of the endless flow of traffic on the 5. "Makes it easier to spot ambulances," he liked to joke, though his work was mostly corporate litigation. "When I make partner, I'll get the bay side of the building," he had told her. "When I'm senior partner, I'm installing a hot tub." His receptionist did her best to cover her surprise at seeing Maitlyn again, then sent her back to the familiar office. Too familiar.

"Don't get up," Maitlyn said quickly, before he could mistake this for a conjugal visit. It had happened before — even after their breakup. "I need you to represent me."

"You know I don't handle DUI's," he smirked.

"If only," she replied, not rising to his bait. A drunk-driving citation would be a relief compared to what she was facing. "I

need you to make a phone call for me. I'll pay your normal rate."
One phone call, fifteen minutes—she guessed—one hundred
dollars. Cheaper than a towing bill. When he didn't respond, she
pressed on. "I mean, right now."

He checked his watch. "Maitlyn, I—."

"Just take a minute," she insisted. "And don't ask me any
questions."

That made him laugh. "A client I can't question. That's a new
one. Can I at least ask who I'm calling? You look great, by the
way."

"No, I look like shit. I'm a complete mess. But thanks. You're
calling Nathan Saltenstall."

"Seriously? You're going your separate ways already?"

"What?"

"You think I don't hear things? It's a small town, darling."

"What things?"

He laughed and looked away, grinning. "O-kay," he
conceded, when he noticed her waiting for an answer. "Nathan-
banging-a-reporter kind of things. Sorry, but you asked."

She shook her head. "Wrong reporter." Then she had an idea.
"Try Sheila Patterson." Let San Diego's legal eagles spread the
word. "I thought everybody knew."

"Oh."

He had tightened his face to hide any feelings, but Maitlyn
recognized the tell. He was relieved his ex-mistress hadn't landed
with the superstar. She hated that word—*mistress*. Her phone was
buzzing. "I have to take this," she said.

"Let me guess. Your little buddy, Scott." Whatshisface hated
Scott, though they'd never met.

She ignored him and answered Mr. Cooper's call. "Did
Hassan find you?" she asked.

"It's blank," Mr. Cooper said. "There's nothing on it."

"You're kidding."

"Are you playing games, Maitlyn?"

"Maybe it was corrupted. It was *your* flash drive."

Whatshisface chuckled. "The ol' corrupted flash drive trick," he said, then grinned when Maitlyn raised her middle finger.

"Listen," Mr. Cooper continued, "I want to send a technician over to your place, let him copy it."

"No. No way. I can figure it out."

"Then do it," he ordered, "figure it out. Today, Maitlyn. I'm not kidding."

"Okay, I gotta go."

"And what were you doing interviewing that pastor before it came out?"

"I called him, like you said. He insisted on doing it today." *Sometimes you have to lie.*

"Wasn't exactly breathing fire, was he?"

"That's coming, don't worry. I told him about the video."

"You're kidding." He sounded exasperated. "Are you kidding?"

"Seriously, I gotta go. I'm at my lawyer's." That would give him something to think about.

But he wasn't listening. "Do you realize what you've done? You've scooped yourself."

She hung up. "Station politics," she explained to Whatshisface, who had migrated over to the window.

"Yeah," he said. "You know what, this might not be a good idea, me being your lawyer."

"No," she agreed, "it's a terrible idea. I wouldn't be here if I wasn't desperate, obviously. But I need someone I can trust to keep a secret." Her tone was becoming sarcastic. "You're good at secrets."

"Right." He looked out the window, his mind wandering off, as it often did.

Is he thinking about me, Maitlyn wondered, *or his wife?* Part of her was hoping it wasn't the wife, and the rest of her was trying to banish that thought from her head. *He's the jealous one*, she insisted to herself, *not me*.

"Did I ever tell you," he asked, "if you squint you can see Mexico from here? Not that you'd want to." Turning away from the window, he put his hands in his pockets—another tell: nonaggression. "You do look good."

"No," she replied, shaking her head. No, don't charm me. No, I won't fall for it. No, I'm sorry. She felt sad—about everything. She loved him and hated him. And she hated that. "Actually, I've been thinking about going to Mexico." She had to stay spiteful to resist his pull. "There's this surgeon who wants to take me."

"Haven't you had enough surgery?" Again, the smirk—his own defenses.

"He's helping me clear up recent scars," the bitch from Channel Four smirked right back. "He has remarkable technique."

14

In fact, Maitlyn had known the flash drive was blank. She had given the device to Hassan to deliver to Mr. Cooper to buy time. Nathan's message had confused her. She didn't know what it meant, didn't know what it portended, didn't know her next move. And then she had looked into Capucine Lockett's sad eyes and, without knowing why, told her the truth—beginning with the phone call to Charles for help when she was trapped in Nathan's yard, and ending with the cop planting the wrench next to Charles's fallen body.

"My father wasn't assaulting him?" Capucine asked.

"He was trying to open the gate for me. That's it." Maitlyn wiped at her eyes. "He was being a good Samaritan."

"Lord, have mercy," Reverend Hutchings said quietly.

Capucine hadn't shed a tear. Her heavy grief seemed to keep her calm. "Can I see the video?"

Maitlyn nodded a yes. "It's painful to watch. But I'll bring it." There was no way to say no.

Later that day, when Maitlyn returned to the church, she carried with her a new flash drive, one bearing a video downloaded from a seldom-used computer in an inconspicuous house on Coronado Island. The church doors were standing open, the parking lot was full. Maitlyn had to park down the street in front of a dumpy Mexican restaurant that smelled like a butcher shop. She looked around cautiously before exiting Ciela. The foreignness of the southeast part of the city always unsettled her—all concrete and iron bars, no greenery, no neon—so far from the verdancy of Balboa Park and the sea breezes of Coronado, so close to Tijuana, or so she imagined. Outside the church, a grizzled man pushed a shopping cart. Inside, the hallways were teeming with women who hushed when Maitlyn entered. She tried to look relaxed and friendly without smiling. A smile seemed inappropriate. "Reverend Hutchings is waiting in his office," one woman said loudly. "You just go in."

Hutchings plugged the flash drive into his computer, and the solemn parade began. Two or three people huddled around the computer screen, watching Deputy Cunningham confront Charles. Then they left the office, making room for the next folks to file in. Maitlyn sat in a chair in the corner of the office, listening to their anguished responses. One elderly man shouted, "That's murder—straight up!" A few women exclaimed, "That ain't right!" The others just moaned and groaned. Capucine was seated at the desk, in the minister's large chair, saying nothing, her face frozen, just watching the video over and over.

When Maitlyn stepped out of the room to get some air, a white woman confronted her. "Tell me," she said, "how this photography came to you."

"I took it with my phone," Maitlyn replied. "I was there." When you start telling the truth, it's hard to stop.

"But you have not presented it to the police?"

"No."

"Because it's worth money, no?" The heavy accent did not obscure the accusing tone. "He was my husband. I am Monique Lockett." She gestured toward the minister's office. "That should belong to me."

Maitlyn didn't know what to say. "I'm very sorry. I thought…." She looked around for help, but no one was paying attention to them. "Charles said—he told me you were divorced."

"You were his lover?"

"No. We just—we worked together."

"Hmmph," the woman snorted, and walked away.

Maitlyn circled the block twice, checking for police cars, before steering Ciela into the parking garage. It was late Monday afternoon, her first time back home since Sunday morning. She half expected her apartment to be in shambles, the shelves emptied, the pillows ripped open, but nothing appeared out of place. The note was still posted in the kitchen. She read it aloud: "The danger is gone. I'm safe." *Was there ever any danger*, she wondered, *or am I just paranoid?*

She looked inside the refrigerator. Not much to eat. Alone on the top shelf, the expensive Chardonnay was aglow, like a golden icon. *I should have opened it on Saturday, gotten tipsy, and stayed home.* She shut the refrigerator door, shaking her head. *How much trouble can one girl get into?* She opened it again. "No point making the same mistake twice."

Wine glass in hand, she collapsed onto the couch. *What a day!* She had finally unloaded her oppressive secret—part of it anyway—telling Capucine and Reverend Hutchings about hiding in the hedge and watching Charles get shot. *Did I say too much?* She felt like she was losing control of what came out of her mouth. She had told Hassan that she was going to see Whatshisface. *What was I thinking?* She had told Mr. Cooper she was at her lawyer's office. *Divulging secrets, left and right.* And when the lopsided clerk at the office supply store rang up the flash drive and asked, "How is your day going?" Maitlyn had replied, "I witnessed a murder, got threatened by a congressman, my car got towed, and just now I had to beg my ex-married boyfriend for help."

"You should totally tweet that," the clerk suggested.

Then, driving back to the church, through unfamiliar and disorienting neighborhoods, Maitlyn had called Hassan. "Are you free again on Saturday?"

"For you, madam, free," he answered in a strange accent. "Everyone else pay cash."

"You're weird, you know that?" She didn't mean it in a bad way.

"True that."

The Ativan bottle warned, "Do not take with alcohol." But that was just the drug company being overcautious. Maitlyn tossed the little white pill to the back of her throat and washed it down with a big gulp of wine. "May cause drowsiness," the bottle also advised.

"True that," Maitlyn said aloud.

Before Maitlyn left the church the second time, Hutchings had thanked her with the hug she craved. "You're the bearer of truth," he said. "Truth shall set us free." The minister wanted the video made public right away, and Capucine had nodded in agreement. Fortunately, the girl's mother had disappeared from the scene. *More than a few holes in her screen door*, Charles had once explained.

"True that," Maitlyn said again, lifting her glass in an ironic salute to Monique Lockett. "French toast."

Then her mind replayed her brief stop at Channel Four later that afternoon after she'd left the church. "It's on here," she had told Mr. Cooper, "I hope," and handed over the new flash drive, not mentioning the screening session she had held for Hutchings's congregation. Cooper had responded with a skeptical look, like *this better be good*. He ran the video, then watched it again, and again, maintaining a sober face throughout. But when he looked up, his voice betrayed a muffled delight. "Now we've got something," he said, reaching for his phone. "I mean, it's awful what happened to him. Terrible. But we've got to play the cards we're dealt, and this—it could go big. I hope it vets out." He couldn't resist a sly grin. "Who was the source again?"

The drowsiness was slow arriving, so Maitlyn poured another glass of Chardonnay—"buttery without being oaky," the label promised, "and hints of pear, going down smooth." It had been in her refrigerator for several months—a birthday present, from whom she couldn't remember. "Happy birthday," she saluted herself. She also swallowed another pill. She didn't just want to relieve her anxiety. She wanted to forget everything and sleep for twenty hours because tomorrow might be crazier yet when the video became breaking news: *Yes, ladies and gentlemen, an anonymous home video proving a white deputy lied about shooting an unarmed black man outside the upscale residence of football hero, congressman, and Senate candidate Nathan Saltenstall, who had earlier exchanged fisticuffs with the same, now deceased, black man.*

"The only thing missing is a sex scandal," Cooper had said in wonderment, and had ignored it as a joke when Maitlyn—still helplessly telling the truth—had blurted out, "If you want, I can get you that too."

With every sip of Chardonnay, Maitlyn let go of the day's drama, starting with Reverend Hutchings. Maitlyn could still smell a hint of his cologne on her blouse. "We will be sweating the sheriff's department," he had assured her. "We will demand prosecution. This cannot stand unanswered."

And Whatshisface: "If Sheila Patterson is banging Saltenstall, what's she doing reporting on his campaign? You might want to give her my card, because someone's gonna get sued before this is over."

And the man with the shopping cart who had asked for spare change as Maitlyn strode toward the church: "I'm so poor, I can't pay attention." Maitlyn had laughed out loud but hadn't stopped walking.

And Grandma, who had left a phone message when she got home from bridge: "Mattie, you left the front door standing wide open. I found Sugar over at the park barking at the *Fort Worth*. I'm worried about you. I think you need to slow down."

The buzz was starting to hit Maitlyn—*hints of pear, going down smooth.* Or was it her phone buzzing? Fortunately, she had it within arm's reach and didn't have to peel herself off the couch. "Hello?"

"Just a heads up," Mr. Cooper began, "legal has already signed off. Tech says it looks legit. We'll start breaking into our regular programming in ten minutes. Then we'll lead with it at six. The sheriff's department has refused comment. They're demanding we hand over the original file. Don't be surprised if they want to talk to you about your source, who they seem to suspect was Charles's accomplice. But we'll back you." He waited for her to respond. "Maitlyn?"

"Okay." She was too sleepy to take it all in.

"Reach out to that minister again. That's where the action's gonna be — like I told you."

"Roger, dodger." That sounded like something Hassan would say.

"Keep me informed."

"Roger Ramjet." She smiled lazily. *I'm drunk.* But she was too droopy to laugh.

After Cooper hung up, Maitlyn thought about turning on Channel Four, but the remote control was too far away. Instead, she thumbed through old messages on her phone. Seeing Charles's number, she dialed it. "Y'all got my voicemail," his deep voice announced from the dead, bringing tears to her eyes. She hung up quickly. It was too weird.

Who else could she call? She dialed up long-lost Tina, who had proposed lunch. "Sorry I missed your call," Tina's voice answered. "Leave a message and I'll respond as soon as I am able. God be with you." *Tina got religion?* Speechless, Maitlyn hung up without leaving a message. "Don't judge," Tina used to say, coming back to the dorm hung over after another Saturday night with another strange guy, "everyone needs a slutty friend."

Maitlyn noticed that she had missed a call from Dr. Dimples. She started to call back, but caught herself just in time. "Psyche," she said, as if she had fooled him. She wished Sugar was with her on the couch.

When she closed her eyes, she again saw the homeless man outside the church. She assumed he was homeless—his cart appeared to contain his earthly belongings. He, too, like Charles, must have a story, a biography. Like was there an ex-wife? Did he have children? Meeting Capucine had transformed Charles in Maitlyn's mind. The man who had rushed out to Rancho in the middle of the night to rescue her was more than just a fired tech guy with time on his hands, more than just a scrapper who gave Nathan what he deserved. He was a father. He had relationships and responsibilities. His daughter was real. And more than that, beautiful. The best cosmetic surgeon in the world could never make Maitlyn as pretty as the blue-eyed, dark-haired, reed-thin Capucine. Beautiful without even trying. In Maitlyn's mind, that made Capucine somehow more significant, her misery all the more tragic. Indeed, all of the women in that church seemed so real, so alive in their anger and sadness, so different from the cynicism and emotional deadness Maitlyn regularly encountered at Channel Four. *Am I dead too?*

A bird slammed into the glass of the balcony door. Then it banged again. It couldn't be a bird—it was coming from the front door. "Now what, Cooper?" Maitlyn crawled to her feet, knocking over the empty wine bottle on her way to the kitchen. *Cooper wouldn't come here.* Another knock, insistent. *What did he warn me about the sheriff's department?* She traced her hand along the wall of the hallway for balance. "Who's there?" She checked that the door chain was in place.

"FBI, ma'am." A male voice. "Agent Rudner with Agent Cruz. We're looking for Maitlyn Flutters."

Oh, shit. "Do you have a search warrant?" *That's what you're supposed to say, right?*

"No, ma'am. We're not conducting a search. We'd just like to speak with you."

"I'd like that." She leaned against the door. "A gal gets lonely."

"Ma'am, I believe you contacted us about a stolen painting. We're from the art crime team."

Shit, shit, shit. "I'm real tired." She'd been on the verge of sleep or already under—she wasn't sure which.

"Just take a minute, Miss Flutters." Another male voice. "Could we come in?"

"I have to call Whatshisface." She wondered if he was still at work.

"Sorry?"

"Do you know what time is it?" She wondered where her phone was. Her head felt fogged in.

"Uh, a little after 5 p.m., ma'am."

"I need to frenchen up." She noticed that her words were slipping.

"Ma'am, are you okay?"

She splashed water on her face, rinsed her mouth with toothpaste, and unlocked the door for the two men, polite and stern in their suits and ties. "Welcome to Pill Hill," she said. That was the other name for Banker's Hill—a reference to all the physicians' offices. She directed them to the couch. Taking the armchair, she tried to match their tall postures. Keeping her head upright was a chore.

"Where exactly did you see this painting?" one of the agents asked.

"What painting?" She gripped the chair.

"Van Mieris's stolen *Cavalier*," the second agent said.

"I believe you said it was in Congressman Saltenstall's house," Agent Number One continued. "Is that correct?"

"I didn't steal a painting. Look around." She noticed the agents exchanging glances. "You guys are cute."

"Forgive me, Maitlyn, are you drunk?" Number Two glanced at the empty bottle lying in the middle of the room.

"Only a couple of swallows. Better than going out and going shot. Getting." Her eyes refused to stay open. "I need to lie down, sheriff." She stood up, trying to remember the way to her bedroom.

"That seems like a good idea. We can talk about the painting another time." The men were standing to leave.

"Besides, Nathan has enough paintings," Maitlyn slurred. Then the walls moved. "Was that an earthquake?"

"Whoa. Why don't you sit right here." Someone was helping her to the couch. "Nice and easy."

She braced herself against the cushions. "Two hands on the ball."

"There you go. We'll be sure the door is locked."

"Two hands. That's what he did to me."

15

Maitlyn leaned her head back to soak up the sun's rays. The radiant heat on her face countered the chill ocean breeze. Hot and cold. That had been her week — cold fear laced with hot anger, panic interrupting shame, despair mixed with the exhilaration of a whirlwind. A blur. A nightmare. A rollercoaster without safety harnesses. Feeling the stretch in her neck, she imagined her head falling off and tumbling into the water. *Which part would be you — the sinking head or the torso left behind? Where, exactly, is your self located?* She didn't want to follow that thought too far.

A rollercoaster week, Saturday to Saturday, begun with an ill-advised query — "Congressman, do you have a painting by Frans van Mieris?" — and ending with, well, no end in sight, just one more unanswered question: *How much trouble can one girl get into?*

She had moaned herself awake late Tuesday morning. Her head throbbed. She hugged her shoulders to stop the shakes. The cushions were damp with sweat. She tried to work out why she had slept on the couch. Her recall ended at opening the birthday Chardonnay. *Must have been quite a party*, she thought, when she spied the empty bottle, a sentry dead at his post. The shivering wouldn't stop. *I need Ativan*, but that would require standing up, and she wasn't yet ready to take on that challenge.

Slowly, Monday came back to her — the church, the flash drive, Whatshisface. *What time is it? I need to call the station.* She struggled to a seated position. *Where's my phone?* She felt queasy. *I'm never drinking wine again. Just smoothies.* Even a smoothie sounded repulsive. She staggered to the bathroom and vomited into the toilet. What she saw in the mirror was disheartening — *the face of the news...if it's all bad.* She located her phone but felt too weak to talk. She folded herself into bed. An hour later, she was still there, shivering and aching. *I'm dying.* Panic sweat moistened her face and underarms. *I have to call someone.*

"Maitlyn," he answered, before she could speak. "Thanks for calling me back. How are you?"

"What?" she mumbled. *When did he call?*

"I've been thinking about you ever since the Hotel Del. Fun morning, hunh?"

"I need some medical advice."

"Sure. What's up? You sound tired."

"I think I tried to kill myself last night."

Dr. Dimples went silent for a moment. "Seriously? Like...."

"No. I just...." She described her symptoms and what she could remember about her evening — wine and pills.

"Sounds like possibly a couple of things. Hangover, for sure. And maybe rebound effect from the lorazepam. Have you taken any this morning? That's the Ativan."

"I can't find the bottle."

"I see. How long have you been on it?"

"I don't know. A few weeks." She had to think about this. "Ever since...." *Ever since he tried to rape me.*

"Okay. Here's what I suggest. Lots of fluids and Tylenol. Vitamin C if you've got it. And you're going to have to taper off the meds. That means taking some now, and then slowly reducing over the next few weeks. You should probably talk to the prescribing doc."

This was irritating. "How do I take it if I can't find the bottle?" she whined. *Not to mention, can't get out of bed.*

"Right." He paused. "Okay, I don't normally do this, but I could bring you some samples from the hospital."

No. No way. She didn't want him knowing where she lived. "Yeah, okay," she conceded, "could you?" What choice did she have?

When she hung up with Dr. Dimples, whose real name she couldn't recall and didn't really care to, the phone rang.

"This is Agent Rudner."

"Who?"

"From yesterday. Just calling to make sure you're okay."

"Oh." *Yesterday?*

"I apologize for coming by so late in the day. You were a little out of it."

"I'm sorry—who is this?"

When shadow cooled her face, Maitlyn opened her eyes. A passing cloud was blocking the sun. She recognized its shape—a cotton-ball albertosaurus. Her father, she remembered, had taken her to the natural history museum, and afterwards, walking around the park, he had pretended to be "Alberto," tucking his elbows into his t-shirt so that only two fingers on each hand were visible in the sleeves, swaying his head heavily back and forth, and roaring, "Te quiero comer." She would give anything to return to that day, back when dinosaurs spoke Spanish and she was safe and decisions weren't so crucial.

What would her father think of her now, the girl who got so wasted by herself on a Monday night that she had blacked out? She could conjure up a twenty-year-old memory of laughing in the park, yet she still had no recollection of the visit from the FBI five days earlier. On Tuesday morning, when she had finally caught on to what Agent Rudner was telling her, she had started to panic until she was sure her clothes were all on correctly. If two federal agents really had been in her house, she concluded, at least they hadn't taken advantage of her. But one of them, she was convinced, had stolen her pills.

A seagull squawked loudly a few yards away from Maitlyn, demanding to be fed. For the fifth time, or maybe the hundredth, she checked her phone, as if a message had arrived without her hearing the ringer, which was turned up high. Her stomach was in knots. The clock said he was fifteen minutes late. There was no activity on the docks except the noisy bird which, after a few minutes without satisfaction, flew off. *Time for an Ativan.*

Dr. Dimples had delivered the pills, as promised, on Tuesday afternoon. By then, Maitlyn had been able to climb out of bed and answer the door. But she kept the security chain in place and didn't let him in. "Sorry," she told him, "I'm not fit for company. But thank you so much. You're a saint." Then she closed the door in his face, feeling ashamed of blatantly using him and embarrassed for looking like an addict. And not long later, she found her original bottle of pills between the couch cushions. "Could I be more pathetic?" she asked aloud.

Another seagull flew overhead as Maitlyn snapped the tiny pill in half and slipped one piece under her tongue. Dr. Dimples had warned her to reduce her usage if she could. When she looked skyward again, the albertosaurus was now a dolphin rimmed with gold where the sun was breaking through. If she couldn't go back twenty years to simpler times, she would happily trade her arms and legs for flippers, slip below the Pacific's surface, and glide away from it all. But the dolphin didn't last either. It dispersed into an altocumulus archipelago, which soon gave way to brilliant light and endless blue, providing her, at last, with an answer: *How much trouble can one girl get into? Sky's the limit.*

"Congressman, I represent Maitlyn Flutters," Whatshisface had said into the phone. "I understand you'd like to speak with her."

The conference in Whatshisface's office—that's one thing she *wanted* to forget from Monday. She had committed herself to never speaking to him again—*him*, the lion cheetah, her former married boyfriend or whatever he was—but there she was, sitting across from his desk, hat in hand as it were, realizing how much she hated depending on men. They always had an ulterior motive.

"No, Congressman, she wants to meet in person. Just you and her. No aides, no security guards, no tape recorders." Whatshisface paused to listen. "Sure, I can wait." He swung the phone away from his mouth and asked Maitlyn. "So where's this hush-hush meeting going to be?"

"The *Lipschitz*," she said.

"Funny." He hated when she purposely mangled the name of the yacht. "How about a hotel suite?"

"Your boat. I'm serious." Her tone was firm. She wasn't asking permission.

"No way." He was perturbed. "I can't have you—."

"Let's call your wife and see what she thinks." That was a trump card she'd been holding for a while.

"Yeah, I'm here," Whatshisface said to the phone, then listened to Nathan for a moment. "Saturday should be fine, Congressman." He looked to Maitlyn for a nod of approval. "No, your house is out of the question. How about my office?" He gave Maitlyn a look of calculated confusion.

"The boat," she commanded, and held her phone out so that he could see his wife's number ready for dialing.

"Hold on, Congressman." He swung his phone away again. "Maitlyn, the boat's a mess. And I'm going to be out of town."

"Perfect." She wasn't ceding an inch. "Tell him."

A brief stare-down, then he gave in. "Congressman, she wants to meet you, I gather"—he rubbed his forehead in one last hesitation—"on a Van de Stadt 55 on Shelter Island." He picked up a framed photograph from his bookshelf. "It's a sailboat, sir. Steel hull. Oregon pine mast. An impressive vessel, I assure you, nothing seedy." He replaced the sailing photo. "How about you call us when you're back from D.C.? We'll give you the details then." A few more polite words, and then he hung up. "Maitlyn, what the—?"

"No questions," she interrupted, "remember?"

"So I'm your pimp now?"

"You always were," she snapped back, not quite sure what she meant.

He ignored her spite. "You're going to owe me for this. Big time."

"Yeah, right." That was laughable. "Just send me a bill. And make sure he understands—just him and me."

The actual name of the sailboat was *List Wish*. "It's a racing joke," Whatshisface had told her, but never bothered to explain. Sitting in the stern, watching the clouds disintegrate, Maitlyn tried to breathe away her nervousness. Then she heard his voice.

"Maitlyn?" He was striding down the dock, his famous face hidden behind sunglasses and beneath a white baseball cap. "Permission to come aboard?"

"No. Stay there." She squinted at him and exhaled slowly to hold back a wave of panic that had her pulse rising. He was dressed for the occasion in deck shoes, belted twill shorts, and a blue polo shirt—the picture of a weekend sailor, the sporty man who would have raped her. "Are you wearing a recording device?" She had rehearsed all of this in her mind.

"No." He held his arms wide, as if that proved something. "I've come alone, as requested."

She hesitated. Could she trust him? Her hands were shaking. "Pull up your shirt."

"Wow. Not even a little flirtation first?" He lifted the shirt slowly, like it pained him. "See. Nothing. No wires." His stomach looked firm, his chest powerful. "I don't suppose there will be a mutual level of disclosure."

"Turn around."

The skin on his back was pocked. "Are you going to spank me too?"

"Where's your phone?"

"In my pocket."

"Get rid of it."

He laughed dismissively. "I'm not tossing it in the water, if that's what you mean." He pulled the phone from his shorts. "There." He held it up. "I've turned it off, okay? I won't call the White House. I could, you know. The Oval Office."

"So you can grope his wife?"

"What? We play golf."

"Sit down on the dock."

"Is this really necessary?"

"I don't want you attacking me again," Maitlyn snarled, and then her anger came out, "asshole."

"Hey, get a grip. I told you, that was a misunderstanding."

"Bullshit. You tried to…." She couldn't say it.

"I'm sorry about that. I really am, I swear." He looked sincere. "Maitlyn, I swear."

"So sit down then, asshole." The anger helped. It was crowding out her fear.

"My knees," he explained. "How about I just stand?"

She noticed ugly scars on both legs. "Here." She picked up a large plastic bucket. "Use this." There was violence in her toss, but he caught it with ease. "And this." She flung over a flotation cushion—again, easily handled. "Now what did you want to talk to me about?"

He flipped the bucket upside down and stacked the cushion on top. For some reason, she had expected to see him in his campaign trail outfit—blue suit and red tie—but the yachtsman getup made perfect sense. No one looking their way would guess that the man seated on the bucket was "presidential material," as the media trope now had it, and no one would suspect he was discussing criminal activity.

"Did you send your friend to thrash my studio?"

"No. What?" She had come prepared to lie, but her surprise was genuine. She hadn't anticipated this angle.

"We're going to have to do this the hard way, is that it?"

"I honestly—I don't know what you're talking about." She tried not to look away as she feigned total ignorance. "What friend?"

Nathan put a hand to his chin and tilted his head, as if unsure of how to proceed. "How do I know that *you* aren't recording this? Or that you don't have the FBI hiding in the cabin there?"

"The FBI? I thought we were here to discuss Sheila." That was Maitlyn's plan—keep him on the defensive—and it worked.

"Sheila? Who's Sheila? You mean Sheila Patterson, the reporter?" His confusion was unconvincing.

"I hope you're prepared to pay her rent, because she could lose her job. Conflict of interest." He tried to object, but she cut him off. "Don't say you don't know what I'm talking about. And we both know what it could do to your family-values campaign if word gets out." A week ago she had never threatened anyone in her entire life, and now the list included the man at the impound yard, Whatshisface, and Nathan Saltenstall. It didn't feel good.

After a moment of thought, Nathan started his own prepared speech. "Let me tell you what *I* know, Maitlyn. Last Saturday night—a week ago—your friend Charles, before he got shot, broke into my house and tore the shit out of my studio. All this business now about that video and him being unarmed and innocent—he was breaking and entering and probably deranged. He was mad at me because I kicked his ass on national television, and so he vandalized my home. My *home*." Now *his* anger was coming out. "My *paintings*." His face was reddening. He pointed an accusing finger. "And I think you had something to do with it. Maybe you sent him because you misunderstood my behavior in the studio that day, for which I have apologized on several occasions. Am I getting warm? I mean, why else would he destroy my studio? You *sent* him and whoever was with him—the mysterious accomplice who got away with one of my favorite pieces. *That's* what I want to talk about. Because if word gets out about all that, losing your job will be the least of it."

Slow down, Maitlyn told herself. *Choose your words with care.* But her mind was racing, trying to sort through what she had just heard. Danger and opportunity arise together—someone had told her that. "First of all," Maitlyn began, trying to appear calm next to Nathan's furor and not yet knowing what would be her second point, "I didn't send Charles anywhere, least of all to destroy your studio or whatever you say he did."

"Sure you didn't."

"And second," she continued blindly, and then it came to her, "why hasn't the sheriff's department said anything about this breaking and entering?"

"Because I didn't tell them. Because I—." He caught himself. "This has to be off the record, okay? I mean it, this whole conversation. This is not a media op."

"Off the record," she agreed. *Like I would make this known.*

"Good. Here it is. I couldn't let the cops into my house to examine a crime scene because of you." He pointed a finger and spit out the accusation. "Because you told the FBI, not to mention the whole world out at Pendleton, that I have a stolen painting."

Feeling the satisfaction of having been right all along, Maitlyn finished his thought. "And you don't want law enforcement to find where you've hidden it now."

"You could have come to me in private. That's what a serious reporter would do—not ambush me at a rally."

"I met you once in private. That was enough."

"I didn't know it was stolen. Allegedly stolen. That's the truth, I swear." He held up his right hand, as if taking an oath. "I have a friend—former friend—who acquires art for me. You saw my collection. Some of it. He never told me that little painting might be hot."

"Then how come it was locked away in your trophy room?"

"It wasn't locked. You got in there, right? That's where you saw it. There's no lock on that door. I take people in there all the time. They want to see the trophies. Think about it—I'm a public figure. Do you think I'm so stupid that I'd knowingly buy stolen art?"

"You're stupid enough to attack a reporter in your home."

"Jesus, are we still on that?" He stood up in frustration and took a step towards the boat. "You need to let that go. I'm sick of it. Sick of it!" Malevolence shrouded his face.

"Don't come on this boat." Maitlyn looked around for something sharp.

"No?"

"Don't come near me."

"What if I do?" He looked left and right—no eyewitnesses in view. She grabbed her phone, her lifeline, ready to speed dial. After a dangerous moment, Nathan took a step backward. "Okay, here's what I want—my offer. I'm going to turn that painting over to the FBI, let them determine its origin, and then I'm going to sue my art agent. The man's crooked. I started looking into it this week. He's probably been skimming off my purchases for years. Maybe selling me fakes. But I need to wait with the feds until after the election. I can't have it coming out now. And I also need you to not say anything about my friendship with Sheila."

"Friendship?" Maitlyn snorted.

"That's right—we're friends—big deal. But people will assume things."

"You want *me* to do *you* a favor?" she asked incredulously.

"No. Not a favor. Call it," he almost smiled, "an arrangement. You keep quiet on this, and I won't expose your friend Lockett for the criminal that he was. Deal? I'll even sweeten the pot. Once I'm elected, I'll give you the exclusive on the stolen painting and how I maybe got duped."

Maitlyn watched Nathan walk away. When he disappeared behind the patchwork of hulls and masts, she exhaled and took stock. *I didn't commit to anything*, she told herself, *my options are still open*. She had nodded a yes, but that was only to acknowledge his offer. She hadn't said "It's a deal" or "I accept" or even "Mum's the word." Then she realized why the phony yachtsman had not waited around for her to promise silence. *If I talk, Nathan talks, and if Nathan talks, Charles loses all public sympathy.* The release of her video had changed the narrative. In one news cycle, the black man who had threatened a dutiful sheriff's deputy on a dark street had become a professional network technician shot down in cold blood by a lying, racist cop. In just seventy-two hours, the footage of "Killer Cop in San Diego" had received three million views on YouTube. Tomorrow at mid-day, Reverend Hutchings would be leading a protest march from North Park to Balboa Park, concluding with a rally against police brutality. Just as quickly, though, Nathan could upend the narrative again — *Shooting Victim Involved in Saltenstall Break-in* — and Maitlyn knew that Nathan knew that she wouldn't want that.

Maitlyn tried to construct a balance sheet in her mind — the pros and cons of keeping her mouth shut. The cons were two: The man who would have raped her probably becomes a U.S. senator and the new hot news chick who had compromised all professionalism continues on her soaring career trajectory. San Diego's hush-hush power duo would escape their just deserts — indeed, be rewarded for bad behavior. They would vacation on tropical islands and be seen at the best restaurants in New York — while Maitlyn returned to local interest feel-goods. On the pro side of staying silent: Nathan keeps the studio rampage to himself, and the potential jurors of San Diego County, not to mention the beautiful, fragile Capucine Lockett, don't hear on the evening news that Charles Lockett had been up to no good. For Charles to receive justice, Nathan and Sheila had to escape it. That's how

Maitlyn saw it, anyway—until her own great liability muddled the ledger.

"How did you know the painting was hidden?"

Maitlyn let out a frightened gasp. "Geez, you scared me." She hadn't seen him returning down the dock.

"You said that the cops would find where I hid the painting *now*."

"I just—." This part she hadn't rehearsed.

"It was you, wasn't it? *You* ruined my studio."

"What?" A simple denial was called for, but she couldn't do it, she couldn't let Charles keep taking the blame.

"You were in my house that night. That's how you know I moved the painting. It wasn't him. It was you."

She sat silent, frozen almost, and her failure to protest spurred him to further realization.

"You're the accomplice my neighbor saw. Holy shit, Maitlyn, you're fucked. When I call in the detectives...." He shook his head in a kind of amazed joy. "Fingerprints, hair DNA, the whole kit and caboodle. Tell me it won't match yours." When she still couldn't find words, his mood suddenly blackened. "You fuckin' bitch," he seethed. "Those were my paintings. My work. You ruined my art." His voice rose to a shout. "You fuckin' cunt!" In a single, powerful motion, he grabbed the flotation cushion, like taking a football snap from center, and rifled it at her. His all-pro arm was on target. The cushion slammed into her chest and chin, knocking her backward. He followed, taking care with his creaky knees as he hoisted himself onto the boat deck. Then something halted his advance.

"M-V-P. M-V-P." It was Hassan, motoring up in an inflatable dinghy, the one normally tethered to Whatshisface's yacht. "Saltenstall all up in the heazy," he called out, "fo sheazy." His left hand steered the little outboard motor. "How about a smile, Greatness?" His right hand clicked photos with a camera which was strapped to his neck.

One look at the long-focus lens, and Nathan reversed course. He clambered off *List Wish*, a hand covering his face. Regaining the dock, he turned to face Maitlyn with a pointed finger. "I want the old man back. And it better not be fuckin' damaged. It's worth more than this boat." He kicked the bucket, sending it flying over the water and landing just short of the dinghy.

"Gooooooooal!" Hassan cheered, as Nathan hurried away.

16

Goooooooal! The word echoed in Maitlyn's ear for two days, even as Nathan's demand for silence left her floundering. *What's the goal here,* she asked herself, *what am I trying to accomplish?*

At first she meant *right now, at this protest march,* as she scurried around on Sunday morning, lining up quickie interviews. *Sure, just tell the story* — that was the direction Mr. Cooper had given her when he made her a reporter — *but which story, from whose perspective?* The protestors had a story. "We're sick of being presumed guilty," one told her. "Whose streets? Our streets!" they chanted as they stopped traffic on University Avenue before turning south on Sixth. A sign pleaded, "Stop killing us!"

The bemused hipsters at the sidewalk restaurants had stories too, finding their brunch interrupted by a sea of brown faces. They shouted encouragement, raised their thumbs and coffee cups in approval, and clicked their cell phone cameras to prove they'd been there. "I couldn't agree more," a pale woman with pink hair and tattooed arms raved for Maitlyn's microphone. "All this shooting has got to stop. On both sides." Her dining companion remarked on the beauty of Hillcrest's diverse community: "We've got Gay Pride Parade and now this. I mean, it's sad. But at least they're doing it, right?"

The Latino busboys probably had a story too, but Maitlyn promptly dismissed that angle because it would never make the air. She went, instead, for the good-news approach. "The sun is out, the marchers have remained peaceful," she explained to the camera, "and the onlookers have been respectful. The feeling down here this afternoon is festive — just more proof that San Diego is, indeed, America's finest city."

Later, the question gnawed deeper. *What's my goal in life? To be evening anchor? To be happy? To be the best me I can be?* With the familiar answers starting to appear incompatible and unhelpful, the doubt seeped to her core. How could she decide which compromises to make if she didn't know what mattered most? Staring into the side view mirror of the news van, she heard herself murmur, "I don't even know what I am." Disquieted, she made the mistake of asking her cameraman for his view of human existence.

"That's too real," he answered. "I'm just living the life till the presidents roll in."

"What?"

"When my photography drops, I'ma score *lettuce*. The next Yousuf Karsh."

"Speak English, Hassan."

"Money." He took his hands off the steering wheel and scissored them in the air. "Must be the money."

To call or not to call? Maitlyn sat in her office on Monday, staring at the phone. Indecision had her paralyzed. Then Capucine Lockett came to mind — the hooded eyelids and silky brown skin of her sad, striking face. *Café au lait — that's her color. Texas black sweetened with French cream.* Capucine had stood next to Reverend Hutchings on the stage during the rally in Balboa Park, a silent witness to her father's memory. The minister had wrapped her in a mighty hug as the crowd chanted, "Justice for Charles!" Justice — that seemed as good a goal as any.

Sitting up straight in her chair, Maitlyn dialed the number. "We need to talk," she began.

"Is this the rapist?"

"What?" *What?!*

"That's what you did," he sneered. "You raped my paintings."

Maitlyn hung up. *I used to be a decent person.* She stared at her dark computer screen. *If they fire me, I probably deserve it.*

Mr. Cooper had summoned her first thing that morning, before she had even logged in and checked her work messages. "Those feeds from the protest yesterday," he said as she sat down, "you didn't look your best. Are you getting enough sleep?"

"I'm fine. Nothing wrong with the reporting, right?"

"A few broken windows would have helped."

"Yeah, I know," she agreed, recalling in her mind the scene at the Sunday rally, where Hutchings had addressed a crowd of tired marchers surrounded by sunbathers on the lawn and curious dog-walkers on the nearby sidewalk. "This isn't exactly L.A."

"What about the video? Have you called them back?"

"Not yet." The sheriff's department had left several messages for her at Channel Four the previous week, adding to her misery.

"You don't have to give up your source, but talk to them. They say they need your help. Do this one right, Maitlyn. No funny stuff."

"Okay," she answered blankly, wondering when she had ever engaged in "funny stuff." Maybe he meant when she invaded Sheila's turf at Camp Pendleton. Or the business with the blank flash drive. *He doesn't know the half of it,* she reminded herself.

"Next topic," Mr. Cooper said abruptly. "There's a rumor going around. I want you to be straight with me."

Maitlyn shrugged, expressed surprise and skepticism at the scenario he described, said she hadn't heard anything—back to being a liar—then hurried to her office, where she popped an Ativan, not bothering to break it in half.

If they fire me, I probably deserve it. The sweet little pill was finally kicking in when she redialed Nathan's number. "Seriously, we need to talk," she began again.

"Then don't hang up on me," he said sourly. "And don't piss me off. If I decide to show them what happened to my studio, they're going to subpoena your ass—your phone, all your calls and texts. They can do that now. And then they'll find out who filmed the shooting, won't they?" He had put it all together. "Placing you at the scene of the crime."

Maitlyn felt a tightening in her throat. Charles had warned her that phone calls weren't safe, that the government was collecting everything.

"I want my pastel painting back," Nathan commanded. "It was a gift, you know. From Valerie. On our anniversary."

"Word is getting out," Maitlyn managed to croak.

"What word?"

"About you and…that person we discussed. Your *friendship*." *Keep it vague*, she decided, *in case they're listening*. "My boss just asked me if it's true."

"And you said…?"

"I said I had no idea."

"What you need to say is that it's absolutely not true."

Need! How she hated men telling her what she *needed* to do. "What *you* need," she fired back, anger again topping fear, "is to be seen with your wife. I mean—." She caught herself. *What the fuck? Am I helping him now?*

"What about our other issue? Should I expect a call from your friends in blue windbreakers?"

"Don't worry about them. They think I'm a freak-job."

When Agent Rudner called her on the previous Tuesday, when he told her they'd been in her apartment the previous night inquiring about the missing van Mieris, Maitlyn had suffered two waves of panic. The first eased when she found no evidence of having been undressed. The second arose when he explained that her answers had been confused, that she had been "somewhat babbling about stolen paintings," and they wanted to clarify what she had meant.

Paintings – plural – what did I tell them? Shivers sent Maitlyn stumbling again to the bathroom.

"Are you okay, Miss Flutters?" the polite voice asked, when she finally returned to the phone.

"No. I don't know. I just puked." Each word was an effort. "I should call you back. Maybe tomorrow."

But so far she hadn't. She couldn't face him, not after having made a total fool of herself. She imagined a flurry of mocking emails about the dumb blonde news chick, the entire FBI having a good laugh at her expense. She also worried that she might have let slip something about the pastel fisherman with the splintering frame that now hung on her grandmother's wall. For three days, she cringed at the sound of her phone. It was never Agent Rudner, *thank God*. Then came Saturday and the showdown with Nathan on the boat dock. After that, talking to federal agents had become completely out of the question, and her drunken performance had become fortuitous. If Agent Rudner ever did call back, she would stay in character: the babbling, unreliable, alcoholic airhead – just another false lead and a waste of time.

"Freak-job," Nathan echoed her, "that sounds about right."

"I have photos," she said, trying to put him back on the defensive. "From Shelter Island. Just so you know."

From his hiding spot in the boat slips, Hassan had captured the clandestine meeting on the dock. When Nathan, seething with recrimination, approached Maitlyn the second time, he hadn't noticed Hassan motoring the dinghy back toward the *List Wish* until it was too late. The final photographs showed the candidate slinging the cushion at Maitlyn and pointing an accusatory finger.

"Clever," Nathan growled. "I ought to make you my press secretary." The growl softened to a chuckle. "Actually, that might solve a lot of problems."

Maitlyn wasn't sure, but he sounded like he might be serious.

When she finally did speak with the sheriff's department, a stern voice informed her that whoever had filmed the shooting was a "person of interest" and "essential to a criminal investigation" and "if you don't identify your source, Miss Flutters, you could be, yourself, up on charges."

Faced with yet another domineering male, Maitlyn remained calm. "I'm not a rookie reporter, Detective, I know how this works." Don't let them intimidate you — that was like rule number one for dealing with law enforcement. "I'm returning your call as a courtesy, not an obligation." She had prepared that line in advance.

"Naturally, we appreciate the consideration on your part," he replied, sounding momentarily amiable. Then the sternness returned. "We might be more understanding of your, shall we say, professional restraints if you simply tell us how you came into possession of the video file."

"Not a chance."

"It was an email, right, with a media attachment?"

"I'm familiar with the First Amendment. I hope you are too."

No more threats followed — the detective had blinked. "Could you do this then? Could you contact the source and tell him we might be able to arrange immunity?"

"Immunity from what?"

"Yeah, good question. From whatever is preventing him from coming forward. Like, the video looks like it was shot from the Saltenstall property. We'd probably be able to drop any trespassing charges. In exchange for cooperation, of course. The district attorney's office would have to work out the conditions. Could you pass along that message?"

"I'm not sure, actually. What kind of cooperation?"

"He—whoever he is—he's eyewitness to a shooting. We need to know what he saw. Not just what's on the video, but before and after. We want to make sure justice gets done."

Justice. What the sheriff's department really wanted, Maitlyn guessed, was somehow to discredit the eyewitness's video, show a sinister motive, make it inadmissible evidence, to protect Deputy Cunningham from prosecution. They always looked after their own, and she could see through their machinations. *I'm an investigative journalist,* she reminded herself, *no matter what Cooper says.*

She could also see, finally, a way out. *I've passed on the message,* she would inform the detective, *and my source is willing to make a deal.* With legal immunity, she could tell the world how Charles had been trying to free her from behind a locked gate, and how Cunningham had shot him down for no good reason, and that Nathan "family values" Saltenstall possessed stolen art and was having an affair and how he had attacked her in the studio and that's why she had avenged herself on his paintings. She could throw off the burden of secrecy and deception and come clean. She could stop threatening people and using them and calculating every move. She could go back to being honest.

And then get fired—for any number of reasons, but mostly as damaged goods.

"Ahhhhh!" Maitlyn dropped her elbows onto her desk and pressed her face into her hands. With her fingers, she clawed at her skull. "Why didn't I just stay home? Jesus! Just stay home and take a bath and Charles would still be alive, and none of this—." She tugged at her hair. It was all too much. She stood up and stared at her office door. She had told her secret to Reverend Hutchings and Capucine Lockett and Capucine's strange mother. Word was bound to spread. She almost wished it would. She sat back down, placed her forehead on her desk, and tried to keep her sobbing quiet.

17

Sometimes, the best thing to do is nothing. Don't rat out Sheila. Don't negotiate for immunity with the district attorney. Don't resume discussions with the FBI. Just let go. Step out of the drama. *Give yourself a break*, Maitlyn told herself. Or maybe it was a justification. She had weighed her options over and over and, finding none of them satisfactory, framed her indecision as wisdom. *Let the world spin without you.*

In other words, back to local interest stories. Two teenagers stumbled across live ordnance along a popular hiking trail. The wild animal park announced the birth of tiger cubs. New bike lanes opened on Rosencrans. "News you can snooze," Hassan snarked.

But Maitlyn wasn't complaining. She did the spots, went home, and forgot about them. She went to the gym. She made time for meditation, sometimes sitting for over an hour. She even went to lunch with her old college roommate, whose first question, once they got past the How-have-you-been?'s, was "What's it like knowing someone who got killed?"

"Surreal," Maitlyn answered, her mind replaying the scene in a flash. As usual, Charles was crumpling to the ground. "Frightening." Sometimes it happened in her dreams—the hat flying off. Don't Mess With Texas.

"That must be hard. It's in your face every day."

"I've tried to stop thinking about it." *Thanks for bringing it up.* "What about you? How's work?"

"Same ol', same ol'." She sipped her iced tea. "Real glad I got that psychology degree." She was a cashier at an auto dealership.

"You know, it seems like they make such a big deal out of it when a black person gets shot."

Maitlyn bit her lip. *Same ol' Tina — talking before she thinks.* She looked around the restaurant for a waiter until Tina's comment had trailed off, then changed the subject. "Are you seeing anyone?"

Tina blushed. "So, his name is Greg. I never thought I'd be with a *Greg*. And a plumbing contractor?" She laughed. "Tall, dark, and handy." The line sounded tired. "But he's amazing. I met him at worship. He totally wants to meet you, get the lowdown. He thinks that video of the shooting might be a fake."

"It's not a fake." *Tall, dark, and dumb.*

"That's what I said. But he's all, like, it's a big conspiracy to make Nathan Saltenstall look bad. He wanted me to ask why you wouldn't say where it came from." Tina paused, waiting for an answer.

"Confidentiality. It's standard practice. Maybe we should order." *That way I can eat and get out of here.*

Another week, another story. A man in a business suit parked his car at Sunset Cliffs, walked to the precipice, and fell sixty feet to the unforgiving rocks below. The Channel Four team arrived minutes ahead of the competition and rushed to set up, placing Maitlyn with her back to the Pacific blue. "He accidentally slipped," an eager eyewitness recounted for the camera. "It was crazy. He was looking at his phone or something. Then he just dropped, and I'm all, 'No way. No friggin' way.' I still can't believe I saw it. This will be on television, right?"

Hassan had a different perspective. "I don't blame the guy," he volunteered, as they drove back to the station. "Everyone says getting old sucks. Like Wild."

"Like what?"

"Wildabeast," Hassan clarified. "Stone cold MC." He broke into a rhythmic chant. "Not what I hoped, but Grandma's stoked, Granddad's doped, yo, wearing diapers. Heed your —."

"You think the guy *jumped*?" Maitlyn asked, cutting off the rap performance.

"Yeah. But Sunset Cliffs? Come on." Hassan emitted a scornful puff. "I mean, go out bad-ass, like get a wingsuit and fly off Yosemite. That's me. When I'm fifty." He resumed rapping. "Heed your horror-scope. Hit da wipers. All y'all gotta pay the piper." He raised his hands from the steering wheel and waggled his index fingers. "Wocka, wocka, wocka, gonna char this town." He honked the van's horn. "It's goin' down."

Drivers in nearby cars looked over. Maitlyn studied the sun visor. *Is this how Barbara Walters got started?* she wondered.

The station was buzzing. The world *had* been spinning. Sheila had quit. Or was fired. The rumors about her were true. Or she had told Mr. Cooper to go fuck himself. Or a network affiliate in Chicago had offered her a job. "All of the above, actually," Sunny told Maitlyn. "Nathan's been pulling strings."

Maitlyn had to sit down to process this news. "I guess he wants her out of the picture."

"Literally," Sunny agreed. "Did you see the footage of him at that rally in Fresno? Doting wife at his side."

"Valerie?"

"He's such a prick."

Valerie is her own woman — that's what Nathan had said. In the kitchen. Before guiding the hot news chick toward his studio. *Want to see what's behind door number three?* Maitlyn felt anxious all over again. She gripped the chair to keep from running out of Sunny's office.

"You know what this means, don't you?" Sunny asked.

"He wins the election." Maitlyn shook her head in dismay. "And Sheila gets airtime in a prime market."

"I mean, for you."

"You're back on Nathan," Mr. Cooper announced buoyantly, clearly pleased to be playing the beneficent boss. "What's wrong?" Maitlyn's lack of elation disappointed him. "I thought it's what you wanted. You practically ambushed him out at Pendleton."

"What I want," Maitlyn replied, struggling to emit words from a suddenly dry throat, "is to cover Charles's murder." She noticed her pulse thumping at her temples. She thought about her purse back in her office. She had tapered off of the pills but carried a supply for reassurance.

"Nothing there to cover. The internal investigation will take weeks. They've probably got the NSA digging through your online activity to identify your source." The rabid coyote grinned. "I hope you haven't been looking at porn."

"What?"

"Just kidding. Women don't really go for that stuff, right?"

Maitlyn wanted to protest, but what was she supposed to say?

"If the D.A. brings charges against that deputy," Mr. Cooper continued, "Jeffrey covers the trial, which will probably get delayed for months. If the D.A. says the shooting was legit, then we might have something. We'll send you back to that black church. You can report on the outrage. But for now, you're our dedicated Saltenstall correspondent." He leaned back in his chair, contented. "You should be happy. If he wins in November, this is like the biggest story to hit San Diego since...I don't know...the fumble, maybe." He sat forward again. "How did it go again? Keep your hands on the ball, Saltenstall? And think if he runs for president in two years."

Maitlyn finally managed to speak: "No." For the sake of her sanity. "No way." So she didn't end up at Sunset Cliffs herself. "I'm fine with what I'm doing."

But Mr. Cooper had stopped listening. His cell phone was buzzing. "I have to take this," he said. "Don't leave."

Maitlyn turned to her own phone and found one new text message—from Sheila. It read simply: Best wishes! For Maitlyn, though, the subtext was clear: *I'm taking my cute little nose to the third-largest media market in the country, stepping stone to network headquarters in New York, while you're stuck as the local yokel in market number 28, so please respond with congratulations, and have a nice life, bitch!* Maitlyn closed her eyes, exhaled a little too loudly, and didn't text back.

"I almost forgot," Mr. Cooper resumed, once his phone call had ended, "Nathan's scheduled some big speech up north, and right afterwards he's giving us an exclusive interview." Mr. Cooper hadn't *almost forgot*—he was playing for drama. "Giving *you*. Nathan specifically asked for you. So pack your bags. You and Scott. It's all arranged."

Maitlyn stared at the coyote, her face blank, not agreeing to the assignment, but also, she noticed, not objecting.

Her boss pointed a scolding finger. "And stay on the script you're given. You can ask about the rumors—they're okay with that—the elephant in the room, no pun intended." He paused for laughter, but his audience was cold. "Republican elephant," he explained, and celebrated his cleverness with a snort. "But don't mention Sheila specifically. She's off-limits. And don't go pulling Iran out of your sleeve again. Or stolen paintings, for God's sake. You're a professional—remember that. Keep the Saltenstall camp happy. We want to maintain access."

Maitlyn sat motionless, still stuck in neutral, still saying nothing.

"And, please, Maitlyn, don't *you* go hooking up with him."

As soon as she got home, Maitlyn changed into shorts and jogged around the park. Without intending it, she found herself headed toward the Botanical Building. She hadn't gone to his funeral. She didn't know where he was buried. The bench where they had met, among the ferns in the lath-striped light—maybe she could feel close to him there. Hassan had casually inquired, "Do you miss him?" In a rare moment of vulnerability with the dippy cameraman, she had admitted, "Sometimes I catch myself asking him for advice." *Him*—the ghost of Charles Lockett.

When she reached the indoor garden, it was already closed for the evening. She walked to the nearby lily pond and gazed at the coins carpeting the algaed bottom. "People think tossing pennies in there is good luck," Charles had told her, "but it's only quarters that work. You've got to be willing to invest."

Right now she wanted *him* to tell her it was okay to do the interview. If she sat down again with Nathan, no one would ever believe he had assaulted her. But what did she want to be, the face of the news or the face of a victim? She needed to invest.

"So he's like your magic Negro?" Hassan had continued the conversation. "That's cool. Mine's Tupac." Blocking out that particular echo, Maitlyn scanned the sidewalk, hoping for a stray coin but finding only bits of trash.

"Are you going to be okay with this?" Scott asked, as they set up for the interview in a hotel ballroom. "I mean, after what happened. At his house."

"I'm over it," Maitlyn assured him, while wondering what had taken him so long to express concern. "I'll be fine," she added, still trying to convince herself. On the flight up to San Jose, she had held a silent pep talk: *I faced him at Camp Pendleton. I survived the encounter on the boat dock.* She would have preferred to stay home, but this was about her career now. *The danger is gone, I'm safe.* She refused to be damaged goods. *And I'll take an Ativan.*

"Good, cuz they're here," Scott alerted her, nodding toward the door.

Nathan and Valerie were holding hands as they followed a handful of campaign aides into the ballroom. "Ms. Flutters,"

Nathan boomed, for all to hear, "always a pleasure." He released his wife's hand and headed Maitlyn's way.

It was him all over again—the creep in the kitchen, the monster at the marina. *He would have raped me.* Maitlyn set her jaw. *I'm a professional.* She shook his meaty hand. *He would have beaten me to death on the boat.* She avoided his eyes. *He can't hurt me here. I'm safe.* She turned away and popped a second pill.

"We'll need one more chair," Nathan commanded, eyeing the set-up. "Valerie and I will be doing this together."

He can't hurt me, Maitlyn repeated to herself, *his wife is here.* She took slow breaths to avoid hyperventilating.

"Valerie, have you met Maitlyn Flutters?" Nathan was oozing bonhomie. "Fantastic reporter."

"A pleasure," Valerie lied, offering a grim smile and weak handshake. She had the drawn face of a pretty woman who had lost her soft looks to the stresses of business meetings, political calculations, and competing adulteries. First lady material.

"We need to be in the parking lot in twenty minutes," an aide announced.

Maitlyn looked over in surprise. "I thought—."

"Yeah," the aide said, "change of plans."

"I was told—."

He looked at his watch. "Eighteen minutes, actually. Sorry." There was no regret in his voice.

"Let's do this," Nathan ordered, taking a seat and waving Valerie over. "Ms. Flutters, start with our marriage." He grasped his wife's hand. "Right, Hon?"

Scott gave the signal—cameras rolling, microphones hot— and Maitlyn prodded herself into action. She had rehearsed the intro: "Republican congressman and Senate candidate Nathan Saltenstall and his wife, Valerie Saltenstall, are sitting down with me here in San Jose. Just moments ago, the congressman finished delivering a major address." Channel Four had insisted she call it that. Nathan's people had demanded it: *major address.* "Congressman, you touched on numerous issues." She focused her gaze above his brow. "But I'd like to begin by asking you about some rumors regarding—." She had intended to say "alleged marital infidelities," but was tripped up when a different phrase—*Nathan-banging-a-reporter kind of things*—came to mind. She couldn't remember who had said that.

Nathan saved her. "I think I know what you're referring to. I'm supposedly having an affair. Or multiple affairs. With who, I have no idea. I've been hearing those things forever—in football *and* politics. People will say anything without any proof whatsoever. It's not true. It's simply not true. Valerie and I—."

Valerie came to life. "I think a lot of it comes because I have my own career." She nodded her head, expecting solidarity from Maitlyn. "It's sexist, really, you know, like a successful woman can't also have a strong marriage."

"Is that why you've joined him on the campaign trail?" Maitlyn asked.

"I'm here—."

"She's always been part of my campaign," Nathan interrupted.

"I'm here," Valerie repeated, her voice steely, eyes unblinking, "because this is historic. My husband's going to be elected to the U.S. Senate. I want voters to know he has my full support. I can't imagine anyone better suited to represent the great people of California."

"Really, she's the one who should be running," Nathan said, expertly finding the fine line between generous and patronizing. "I'm not afraid to say that. Now, let's move on."

Maitlyn checked the notes on her lap. In his big speech, Nathan had proclaimed, "The climate science is unclear. The jury is still out, and we can't let the gloom-and-doom crowd hold our economy hostage, not when we have the greatest technology in the world." That had brought a couple of questions to mind. *Do you know something the science community doesn't know? Do you disagree with the U.S. Navy, which is very concerned about rising sea levels?*

"Congressman," Maitlyn began, "I want to ask you about global warming."

The aide suddenly stepped into her sightline, held up both hands, fingers wide, and mouthed, "Ten minutes."

"No, ask me about Wyoming," Nathan instructed.

Maitlyn wasn't sure what to do with that. *I'll ask what I want,* she wanted to say, but she knew it wasn't true.

And Nathan didn't give her the chance. "We haven't really had a U.S. senator from southern California since 1992," he said. "Think about that. Wyoming has half a million people and gets two senators. I love Wyoming, but it's time the twenty-two million people in southern Cal got some representation. Nothing against the Bay Area either."

"We've had too much of San Francisco values," Valerie said flatly. "We need balance."

"Bring a little guacamole to their sourdough," Nathan explained quickly, trying to compensate for his humorless wife. "We're all about diversity."

Interview over, the campaign entourage was hurrying out when Nathan turned back. "Ms. Flutters, can I speak with you a moment?" He gave Scott a look, indicating this would be a private conversation. "Unplug those mics, would you?"

"You got it," Scott answered. "Great speech, by the way."

When Scott stepped away, Nathan lowered his voice to a hiss. "I want my little painting back." The bonhomie was gone. "No more games." It was malice now. The elephant was astomp. He glanced toward the door, where Valerie had just exited. "She thinks I took it off the wall to spite her."

Maitlyn answered by finally meeting his eyes. With enough hate, she remembered from the boat dock, she could stare daggers into him and not flinch. "I don't know what you're talking about." Stare daggers and lie with ease.

He ignored the denial. "I want it back this week. That way she stays happy, and then I stay happy, and then you...." He jabbed his index finger into Maitlyn's sternum, a move so quick and unexpected that no one else in the room would have seen it, yet so powerful it knocked Maitlyn back a step. "You stay out of jail."

Gouge his eyes out! She brought her hands up to her chest to defend herself and looked around for help. Scott was bent over his equipment. The pushy aide was reentering the room to corral his candidate.

"Congressman," the aide called, "we really need to move out."

"Funny story," Nathan said, no longer muffling his voice, "Valerie keeps asking why my studio is locked. I told her I'm working on a surprise for her." His campaign smile was relit. "I think she'll be *more* than surprised when I finally show it to her." He looked pointedly at Maitlyn. "I think everyone will be." Talk about subtext: *The crime scene is sealed. I've still got your fingerprints.*

"Long trip for that," Scott said, then noticed Maitlyn's discomfort. "Hey, you okay? We'll do better next time."

Maitlyn was in tears and gasping for breath. Her chest hurt. Nathan was gone, but the air in the ballroom was still heavy with his malevolence.

18

"Hi, Grandma." No answer. No dog. "Hello?" The house was quiet. *Must be out for a walk.* Maitlyn was relieved to have the house to herself. She headed for the dining room, removed the painting from the wall, and held it at arm's length, studying the old fisherman. "Bad news, Zorba, you're headed back inland." She had to do it. "It's best for all involved."

All except Charles. Now that Maitlyn had done the second interview, now that she had again appeared on air with the congressman, looking relaxed and congenial—or mollified, anyway—the world would never know the real reason Charles had slugged Nate the Great. *You can't fix stupid.* Maitlyn grimaced. "See, I've lost all my bargaining chips, Zorba." Shameless Sheila was halfway across the continent. Valerie was back at Nathan's side. And Nathan was pinning the stolen van Mieris on his art buyer. *Asshole.* The man who would have raped her had won.

How to break the news? *Grandma, it's the right thing to do. I should never have brought it here. It was a big misunderstanding. Grandma, I'll bring you something better.* In search of a plastic trash bag, Maitlyn went to the garage and discovered it empty. *That's weird.* No Grandma, no dog, no car. *Must be at the grocery store.* She peeled a bag from a thick roll. *Except she doesn't take Sugar shopping.*

Back in the dining room, Maitlyn puzzled over her next step. Delivering the pastel painting in person would be incriminating. Fed Ex might work, with a fake return address. Or find a third person to hand it over. A small, mean voice arose: *Ruin it!* Maitlyn gripped a dinner fork in her fist and took aim: those glinting eyes, that sun-aged face—so humane, so unsuspecting. *I'm not a murderer.* Charles was falling again. Don't Mess With Texas. Maitlyn set aside the fork. *Deputy Cunningham — that's the murderer.* She cried quietly for a few minutes — cried for Charles, and for Capucine, and for herself — then wiped the cracked frame for fingerprints and slid it into the black bag.

Maitlyn was on her way out when she heard the garage door grinding open. *Might as well get this over with now.* She set the bag down and went to greet her grandmother. "Are you okay?"

Grandma was in tears. "Mattie, oh, Mattie." Her face looked old.

Maitlyn wrapped her in a hug. "What's wrong?" Then she knew.

"I've lost my best friend."

Grandma had opened the front door to speak with the mailman. Sugar had zipped past them. "She must have heard a ship." The driver of the car never slowed down. "A Volvo, I think. I don't know." Grandma had rushed the broken, whimpering dog to the vet, but nothing could be done. "How many times did I tell her to wait for me?"

They sat in the living room, crying and consoling. "I'm going to be so lonely," Grandma despaired.

"I'll come by more often," Maitlyn promised, and hoped she would.

"Everything you love, you lose. It's a terrible cliché. Just terrible." She was working Sugar's collar like worry beads. The metal I.D. tag was shaped like a heart. "Whatever will I do with this?"

When the afternoon light had faded, Grandma reached across the arm of the couch and switched on a lamp. "What's in the bag?" Her voice sounded tired.

"That? Oh, that's — you know that painting I gave you?"

"You're taking it back?" The alarm in her face was devastating. "My Greek fisherman?"

"No, no." Back to deceit. "I just—." This was not the time. "I wanted to see about having it…this coastal climate down here…like is there a way to protect it from the dampness?" Maitlyn's stomach was clenching. She knew her grandmother knew.

But Grandma let it go. "He'll be fine. I've never had a problem with any of my oils."

"Oh, okay." Maitlyn pulled the painting from the bag. "I can hang it back up then."

"Wait." Grandma took the frame gently into her hands. "You don't mind a little humidity, do you?" she asked the fisherman. "Did you know I've lost my little Sugar? She was such a good dog. You saw her." She started to cry again. "Such a good dog."

The next morning, Grandma was up early and dressed for bridge. "Today's game is sanctioned," she explained to Maitlyn, who had spent the night on the island to keep her company. "I need the masterpoints." She noticed Maitlyn's frown. "I'll be fine." She looked across the living room to Sugar's favorite spot on the couch and sighed. "Coming home, though, will be dreadful."

Maitlyn nodded. She knew too well the hollow feeling of a dark apartment and no warm greeting. It never seemed to get easier. "I'll try to come by after work. Unless we get a real shocker." That was the most unsettling thing about local interest reporting—you started hoping for tragedy.

"If my partner can count to thirteen—that will be a shocker."

Driving to work, Maitlyn thought about her one childhood pet, a Shubunkin goldfish named Tiger. The death of Tiger had felt cataclysmic and, even now, kept her from considering a cat for her condo—the inevitable ending would be unbearable.

Sifting through emails on her office computer, Maitlyn couldn't stop thinking about her grandmother and how she had gone off to play cards as if nothing had happened. *She's lost a husband and son*, Maitlyn reminded herself, *she knows how to cope*. That was a relief. The little pastel was back up on the dining room wall for now. *I'll give it a couple more days*.

Then came the shocker. "Maitlyn, do you want to take a phone call?" the Channel Four receptionist asked. "Some guy saying he has a tip."

"What about?" Maitlyn asked impatiently. Tips came in all the time. They usually went to the news director's office.

"He says he'll only tell *you*. Won't even leave a number. And caller I.D. is blocked."

"It's not legit." Hot news chicks develop special radar for detecting stalkers.

Twenty minutes later, Maitlyn's desk phone buzzed again. "Same guy," the receptionist explained, sounding apologetic. "He says it's regarding a painting."

Oh, shit.

"I want to discuss stolen art," the voice said, by way of introduction. He sounded calm, almost sleepy.

"Who is this?" Maitlyn asked.

"Let's say a concerned citizen."

Of course. "Concerned about what?"

"Satisfaction." Sleepy and creepy.

"Who do you work for?" But that was easy. "Saltenstall, right?"

He ignored the question. "We should meet. Old Town at noon." Then he hung up.

Danger and opportunity. Maitlyn had no idea what she was getting into. *I'm an investigative journalist*, she reminded herself, as she parked Ciela. *I'm following up on a tip — no crime in that*. In truth, she was hoping for opportunity—to return the Greek fisherman without admitting to theft, to close the episode and move on.

She got out of the car and looked around. Should she be conspicuous? She had her phone in hand, 911 on speed dial, and her thumb on the button. Was he already watching her? She took off her sunglasses and walked slowly. *Act like you belong here.* Out of habit, she headed toward the little tourist mall with the hot sauce shop. She loved perusing the possibilities—five hundred different types of bottled fire—even if she always went home with the same one.

"Proves you're still not a risk-taker," Whatshisface had informed her, upon observing her rigid shopping technique. He was always extolling the virtues of reckless behavior. "Turn deuces into aces if you dare—that's my mantra." He had shared this on their very first date. "Can't win big unless you're willing to lose." Only later did the impulse behind his evangelism become clear.

"Follow me." A short man stepped by her, heading across the parking lot toward Old Town's historic buildings.

"Wait!" she called out. He was moving slowly, but didn't stop or look back. Had she heard correctly? She trailed him at a distance until he disappeared into a big barn. *Danger and opportunity.* The sign over the door read "Seeley Stable Museum." *I'm an investigative journalist.* She followed him in.

Wood floor, spot lighting, free admission. Once her eyes had adjusted to the shadowy interior, Maitlyn spied him waiting toward the back. White face, brown jacket, wide around the middle. She guessed him for fiftyish.

"The nineteenth century had its charms," he suggested, indicating with a nod an old stagecoach.

She stopped ten feet short. "Do I know you?" She was keeping her distance and keeping to her pretence: *I know nothing about a stolen painting. Just following up on a tip.*

"We spoke on the phone." He looked past her. "I want to share some history with you."

She turned to follow his gaze but there was nothing to see. They had the dusty museum to themselves. "I thought this was about art."

"We have a mutual acquaintance." He paused, like he expected her to agree.

"Why all this mystery, Mr....?" When he still didn't divulge his name, she fiddled with her phone to indicate impatience and importance. "Look, I'm very busy."

"Off the record?"

"Yes." *Duh.* She didn't want the internet screaming CORONADO WIDOW CAUGHT WITH SALTENSTALL PAINTING!

"This goes back a few years," he said quietly. What had sounded like sleepiness on the phone looked, in person, like indifference. "I got an offer." Like every phrase came with a shrug. "The client wanted a serious reproduction."

"Nathan Saltenstall."

"The client wanted a van Mieris." Shrug. "Wanted it indistinguishable from the original."

"Wait. That's what this is about?" Maitlyn felt her stomach calming, like when Ativan kicked in.

"I thought, make a perfect repro from a photo?" He shook his head. "I'm a good painter, but—."

"Hold on. What Nathan has—the van Mieris—is fake?"

The man paused. There was commotion at the museum entrance. He lowered his voice even more. "Turns out, the client had the original."

"The one that was stolen?"

"Makes it a lot easier. You follow?"

"Yes." She imagined the man peering at old brushstrokes. "No. Why would he—?"

"Want a fake too?" He shrugged, then pointed to an old freight wagon. "Think that's authentic?"

"I have no idea." This was annoying. "Could we cut to the chase?"

"You return the forgery to the museum. You keep the original." He mimed wiping his hands clean. "And Bob's your uncle." He was about to say more, but stopped.

Two young boys, with mother in tow, were rushing toward the wagon. "Horses pulled it," the taller boy proudly explained. "They didn't have trucks in the oldy-timey days."

The man brushed past Maitlyn. "Let's go outside."

Deuces into aces if you dare. Maitlyn used the phrase to embolden herself, but kept her phone ready as she followed the man around the outside of the barn.

"I'm pretty sure *that* is the genuine article," he said, as they approached a donkey standing behind a barnyard fence. The pen smelled real enough. "Come here, donkey." The man banged a large gold ring against the aluminum crossbar. The donkey remained motionless. "But you can never be entirely sure." He risked a sidelong glance at Maitlyn's chest. "The world is full of fakes."

Maitlyn pretended not to notice. "I haven't seen anything about *A Cavalier* being returned."

"Deal went south." The man dug into his jacket for cigarettes and offered one to Maitlyn. When she declined, he poked one into his mouth. "The guy's worth millions and he won't cough up a hundred grand, which I thought was a bargain of an insurance policy on his little treasure. Tried to jew me down to thirty. It's a question of respect, really." He patted at his pockets, feeling for his lighter. "How did you know to ask him about it?"

Maitlyn hesitated. *Because he tried to rape me in his studio, and I hid in his trophy room, and my grandmother had taught me a little about art.* "I can't reveal my sources."

"Good. That's a good answer."

"How did you know I asked him?" The Pendleton ambush had never made the air.

Rather than explain, he lit his cigarette. "Suddenly, he's willing to pay full price. Wants it done yesterday." He turned to blow his smoke away from Maitlyn. "Wants me to live at his house and work nonstop, like I'm Rumpelfuckinstiltskin or something." Shrug. "Like I don't work fast enough already."

"So why tell me? I mean, if it's off the record, I can't—."

"I want you to ask him about it again." Without warning, the man jumped away from the fence. "Ow! Sonofabitch!" The donkey had come up behind him. "The damn thing bit me." He rubbed his hipbone. "Listen, I'll make it worth your while. Just get it on the news."

19

"Jesus H. Criminy, Maitlyn. Don't you get it? We are not asking Nathan about stolen paintings."

"This is for real," Maitlyn insisted. Mr. Cooper was the one not getting it. "My source said—."

"Your source said," he echoed sarcastically. Maitlyn had told him what the man at the museum had claimed about being hired to duplicate *A Cavalier*. "Does he have it in writing?"

"No, but—."

"Do you have any corroboration at all?"

"We would be asking Nathan to confirm or deny—that's all."

"You already tried that, remember?" He tilted his head downward to glare over his glasses. "And then I had to go do damage control with his campaign director, who's a real jerk-off, by the way."

"So we just sit on this?"

"Sit on what? An anonymous call-in with a goofy story? There's nothing to sit on."

It *was* a goofy story—that was partially why she believed it. "What if it's true? What if the guy goes to Seven, gives *them* the scoop?"

"Yeah, or what if we break the story—Nathan buying art on the black market or whatever it is—and suddenly his campaign produces the receipts and proves us wrong? Think Nathan might find that useful? First, he's attacked by a black man. Now it's the so-called liberal media out to get him. Think a sharp campaign strategist couldn't cook that up?" Mr. Cooper wasn't asking for Maitlyn's opinion. He never did. "I mean, after everything—

Sheila, Lockett, your routine out at Pendleton—you think Nathan wouldn't love to make us look like a bunch of dipshits?"

They both turned their attention to the muted television. CNN was frantically reporting the crash of a small commuter jet back east. NO SURVIVORS, the subtitle scrolled out beneath the blurry image of an empty field, STAY TUNED FOR MORE BREAKING NEWS.

"Look, Maitlyn," Mr. Cooper resumed, "I know you have ambitions." He gestured toward a CNN reporter decked out in designer rainwear. "I know you want to be an A-lister. And then Sheila goes catapulting up to Chicago. Of all people." He shook his head in mock sympathy and disbelief. "Your time will come, okay? Right now, you've got a front-row seat to the hottest political show in the country. You can ride this horse a long ways. Just play it by the book."

The book. What does "the book" say do when your assignment is the Senate campaign of the creep who would have raped you? Maitlyn's eyes went to Mr. Cooper's office shelf: industry awards, photos with local celebrities, not a single book.

Mr. Cooper unmuted the television. "…to us live from the crash site," the anchorwoman with the perfect face was saying, with the proper mixture of perkiness and sorrow. "Again, we believe all onboard Flight 427 are deceased." Maitlyn had heard she had fat ankles. "We'll be keeping you updated as events unfold."

"Events don't *unfold*," Maitlyn informed the anchorwoman.

"Sorry?" Mr. Cooper frowned at her.

"This is all bullshit," she let out, "you know that? Just total bullshit."

Before accelerating out of the Channel Four parking lot, Maitlyn lowered the convertible top. She was feeling light, feeling free. *This is all bullshit*. Just saying it aloud had been cathartic. News you can use, a name you can trust—*just total bullshit*.

Motoring across the bridge, Ciela soared through the sky, blue on blue, another perfect San Diego afternoon. An old favorite came on the radio. Maitlyn cranked the volume and sang along: "Watch out, you might get what you're after." She hadn't told anyone she was going home early. She put one hand up in the air and belted out the chorus, "Burning down the house." She was way over the speed limit. *Fuck it.* She wanted to be there when her grandmother arrived home. She was too late.

"In here," Grandma called from the dining room table.

Maitlyn bent over to hug her. "How was your bridge game?"

Grandma shook her head. "Let's not talk about it. How was *your* day?"

"Uneventful." *Unless you count my boss ordering me not to do my job.* "Nothing worth mentioning." *Except, perhaps, the donkey biting the forgery artist who was trying to bribe me.* "How come you're sitting in here?"

"I was just talking with him." She pointed to the wall. "We were saying how much we miss Sugar." The fisherman's twinkling eyes looked moist.

"Oh." Maitlyn's voice betrayed her dismay. This was going to be difficult.

"Mattie, if you have to take him back to wherever he came from…."

"No." The perfect opportunity, but she couldn't do it, her grandmother had lost enough.

"It's just a painting." Grandma stood up. "Here." She reached for the worn frame.

"Grandma, it's okay." Maitlyn put out a gentle hand to stop her. "What if we take a walk?"

At the water's edge, Grandma pointed to a small combat ship. "That's *Freedom*. You can tell by the camouflage paint. Sugar would have been barking like crazy. She loved the navy."

Maitlyn allowed the reminiscence to linger in silence before she changed the subject. "I'm thinking about quitting Channel Four."

"And do what?"

"I don't know." She hadn't gotten that far yet. "Take a long, long nap." Across the harbor, a ribbon of black smoke ascended from Banker's Hill. She hoped it was her apartment building.

"I thought you liked being on television."

"I do." Her phone buzzed in her pocket. She checked the incoming number and let it go to voicemail. "It's just that, it's like, I can't keep my head above water." That was really how it felt. "The harder I swim, the deeper I get. There's no winning." Another buzz. This time a text: Nathan @ 6pm. "Grandma, one sec. I need to call in."

Scott picked up immediately. "He's holding a press conference. Can you meet me here in fifteen?"

"Make it twenty." She knew it would be closer to thirty minutes by the time she drove across the bridge and up to Channel Four. "Where's he gonna be?"

"You don't want to know."

When they got back to the house, the absence of the dog hung heavily. Maitlyn found her car keys and hurried to the bathroom. When she emerged, her grandmother handed her a plastic trash bag. Maitlyn knew what was inside. "Grandma, no."

"He doesn't belong here." A quick hug, then Grandma disappeared behind her bedroom door, shutting off further argument.

They bucked afternoon northbound freeway traffic before following the winding roads into Rancho. Three cop cars were strategically stationed at Nathan's gate. Scott parked down the street, behind two other news vans, got out, and readied his camera. Seeing Maitlyn's inertia, he asked, "Are you coming?"

When she didn't respond, he told her, "I won't let you out of my sight, I promise."

Her hands were shaking. She was crying. She couldn't help it. "It happened right there," she said. She couldn't open the door.

Scott fussed with his gear. He didn't know what to do with her tears. After a polite interval, he said, "I have to go set up."

Maitlyn hardly heard him. She was watching a deputy cross the street. He was kicking Charles in the back. *Why?* She shook her purse and found the pills. *Why did I come here?* She looked up the street again. Charles was falling and falling. Don't Mess With Texas. She put her forehead on her knees and cried until she felt the Ativan rescuing her.

Eyes dried and makeup redone, Maitlyn climbed out of the Four-mobile and started up the familiar lane. *One step at a time*, she reminded herself. She pushed back the memory of being trapped behind the fence. And the image of Ciela atop the tow truck. And Charles pulling himself over the gate. *All my fault*, she knew, and pushed that away too.

Act like you own the place. A female deputy glanced at the press pass hanging from Maitlyn's neck and indifferently waved her up the driveway. They both pretended not to notice the indiscreet leering of another deputy. "Yeah, *I'll* send you a video," he said, as Maitlyn passed. "Cuz you like that sort of thing, don't you?"

Keep breathing. On the lawn where Nathan had once shoved Charles, reporters and camera crews were gathered, waiting for the great man to emerge from his house. Maitlyn joined the vigil and asked around, but no one seemed to know the reason for the press conference.

"The usual free air grab," the reporter next to her suggested.

"He's announcing his new girlfriend," someone behind them gibed.

"And she's a lesbian," another added, "to get the San Fran vote."

Maitlyn was thinking about how to pop the question. *Fuck Cooper*, she had decided. The forgery artist wanted her to ask about the stolen van Mieris on camera, had even offered to pay her, so that he could squeeze Nathan. "When he feels the heat," the man had explained outside the museum, "my fee goes up. I'll give you half the difference." He had shrugged like it was no big deal. He was keeping his eyes on the sneaky donkey. "I don't want your money," she had informed him. "Name your price," he had insisted, and scribbled out a phone number.

My price? What she wanted was justice. And that, she admitted to herself, standing in front of the house where it all began, meant vengeance. She could agree with the forger on that — *make the bastard pay*. And the less she cared about her job, her career, the easier it was to contemplate.

A campaign aide appeared in the front walkway. Somewhere back there, just out of view, Charles had punched Nathan. *Because he would have raped me.* Just that quickly, Maitlyn was ready to flee to the van. But she'd have to pass that slimy deputy. She looked around for Scott, for reassurance. He gave her a thumbs up from behind his camera.

Then Nathan came striding out. "Good afternoon," he said into a bouquet of microphones. "Thanks for coming out here today." He was all smiles. "I just wanted to let you all know my cholesterol tests came back good." His audience chuckled. "No, you're here because I am pleased to announce this afternoon that my campaign has now received endorsements from every one of my Republican colleagues in the House. Every single one. They all agree I'll make a great senator. Or maybe they just want me out of their hair." More chuckles.

But Maitlyn wasn't laughing. She felt a rising nausea. The man who would have raped her had the local press corps in his greasy palms, and she could barely stand to be in her own skin. She hated this yard. She hated the house. She hated him.

"What this means for California voters is I'm a uniter. I'll be able to push legislation through the Senate." The polls had him edging ahead of his Democratic opponent, and it showed in his relaxed confidence. "I'll reach across the aisle. I'll get things done."

After few more banalities, Nathan invited questions, to which he provided ebullient and vacuous answers. *The usual free air grab.* When he spotted Maitlyn's raised hand, he grinned. "Miss Flutters, let me guess, you want to know if I abducted the Mona Lisa." When the joke fell flat, he tried to explain it. "She asked me something like that out at the Marine base. I mean, Miss Flutters did, not the Mona Lisa." That got the laugh he was seeking. "Their smiles are similar."

With heads turning her way, Maitlyn maintained tunnel vision. *By the book,* Mr. Cooper was admonishing her. *You're a professional.* "Congressman, could you tell us why some of your House colleagues didn't endorse you till now?" *Blah, blah, blah.* The question bored even her.

"Actually," Nathan continued, ignoring her query, "I'd be happy to discuss missing artwork with you." His tone was jovial. His eyes were saying something else.

"Yes, well," Maitlyn sputtered. *You think he wouldn't love to make us look like a bunch of dipshits?* She took a deep breath and ignored Mr. Cooper. "Okay, could—." Her voice cracked. *Just you and the mic.* "Could you comment on rumors that your personal art collection contains at least one very valuable stolen painting?"

"Yes, that's true," he replied, without hesitation, "one of my paintings *was* stolen. I have people looking into it. I hope to get it back soon."

"Have you spoken to the FBI?"

Viciousness flickered across his face, there and then gone—you had to be looking for it to see it. "But to answer your earlier question about my colleagues—as you all know, we've been on summer recess." The campaign smile beamed anew. "They've been busy endorsing ice cream and cherry pie."

As soon as Nathan pronounced the press conference finished, Maitlyn hurried over to Scott. "Let's get our intro," she said. The man who would have raped her was gone, and she was feeling better about things.

"Why bother?" Scott was busy with a cigarette. "There's no story here. And, holy shit, Cooper's gonna be pissed at you."

"Nathan brought up the painting, not me." She was already preparing her defense. "And we can make this a feel-good." *We leave you this evening with Congressman Saltenstall entertaining reporters, reminding us that politics can still be fun.* "We'll cut everything but his jokes. Cooper will like that." *No news is good news.* She indicated that she wanted the house in the background. "Let's get this. Live from Rancho, the Saltenstall comedy tour."

"Mrs. Flutters." One of Nathan's young lackeys was approaching—angular and pale, a buzz cut in a dark suit. "The congressman would like a word. I'll take you to him." He extended an arm to usher her along.

"No thanks," Maitlyn replied.

The aide blanched. "Congressman Saltenstall, I mean. He—."

"Not interested." She almost felt sorry for the boy. He looked disoriented.

"You're turning down face-time with—?"

"Exactly." She saw his type at every Nathan event, strutting behind their red ties and lapel flags—little jerks who squeaked through adolescence without catching a clue.

"Everyone else here would die for this kind of access." He was almost imploring her.

She surveyed the news crews fanned out on the lawn, shooting their spots. "Let them."

"I'll go with you," Scott offered, meeting Maitlyn's eyes with a knowing look.

The aide held up a hand. "Private meeting. Off the record. Just her." He felt confident keeping people out but clearly struggled with how to lure Maitlyn in. "You know, it's totally casual."

"I'm sure it totally is."

"He's waiting by the pool."

"Oh, in that case," she snickered. "In that case, tell him..." She wasn't sure what to say. "Tell him we're reframing the issue."

"What issue?"

"Tell him it's damage control."

I think he just wants —."

"I know what he wants," Maitlyn snapped. "Just tell him what I said. Reframing the issue. He'll understand."

20

When they did finally meet, several weeks later, it was afterhours in a downtown law firm. "Congressman Saltenstall, a real pleasure," Whatshisface said, unlocking the lobby door for him. "I apologize for all this cloak-and-dagger."

"You've got a wacky client, counselor," Nathan half-whispered.

"Occupational hazard."

"I hear ya," Nathan said. He had come alone. That was the agreement. "I bet you've got some stories."

"Oh, yeah. Every clown's got a claim in court."

"Some real gold diggers, huh?" Nathan knew he was on safe turf. They were a couple of dudes, immediately comfortable shooting the shit. "You handle divorces?"

"Not if I can avoid it," Whatshisface joked, then saw an opportunity. "Only in elite cases."

"Sure. Makes sense."

"I hope you're not in need of counsel," Whatshisface added, hopefully. "Congratulations on the campaign, by the way. We're in here, Congressman."

They entered Whatshisface's private office. He had refused to participate at first—he was still pissed about being strong-armed the last time—but the thought of meeting his childhood idol in person had proven irresistible. "You know Maitlyn Flutters, of course."

For her part, Maitlyn hated the whole idea of it. She was here only because she couldn't think up a better solution. She remained seated near the window, as far as possible from the door.

"Congressman," she said flatly. Eavesdropping on their mutual backslapping had darkened her already dismal mood.

"Miss Flutters." Nathan noted her coolness and didn't approach her. "I hope we can finally put this entire business behind us."

"I hope so too," she agreed. *Asshole.*

"And, again, I apologize for any misunderstanding. Truly."

Maitlyn nodded. His good humor, she knew, was for the other asshole in the room, the one who had just called her a clown.

"I believe this is the item in question," Whatshisface said, lifting the small pastel from the shelf behind his desk.

Nathan took it into his large hands. "The frame is different," he observed with displeasure.

"I understand there was some damage," Whatshisface explained. That's what Maitlyn had told him—the frame had required replacement. "Not to the canvas, though."

"For a change," Nathan sneered, holding it up for a closer view. When he examined the backside, the old fisherman winked at Maitlyn. The twinkle seemed diminished.

"It's a great painting," Whatshisface offered. "I've been enjoying it, actually. That new frame is one hundred percent black walnut. Hand carved. Probably better than the original."

Like you would know, Maitlyn thought to herself, but she had to appreciate the way her former married boyfriend was laying it on thick. *Can't win big unless you're willing to lose.*

"I'll be having an expert evaluate it," Nathan grumbled.

"You should, absolutely," Whatshisface agreed. "Now, just so we're clear, Congressman, my client is not asking for a finder's fee. She's just pleased to see the piece reunited with the proper owner."

"How magnanimous," Nathan scoffed. "I don't suppose she'd like to explain just how she happened to *find* it."

Maitlyn kept her face blank and let Whatshisface do the talking.

"That's correct, Congressman. She's taken a bit of a risk getting it back to you and would rather not say anything more. No harm, no foul kinda thing." Maitlyn had only told him that it was complicated and that Nathan wouldn't press the matter—he had too much to lose. "Or offsetting penalties, right? Replay the down."

Nathan ignored the football reference. "So, we're done with it—all of it?"

"My understanding—."

Nathan cut him off. "I want to hear it from her." He glared hard. "Drop the whole thing." It was an order.

Fuck you, Maitlyn wanted to say, but merely conceded, "Yes. Fine." *Fuck you.*

"Good," Nathan said. "You're getting off easy, you know."

"And you know all about dropping things." It just came out.

Nathan's eyes narrowed. "Just for the record," he parried, "that little Dutch painting you asked about—definitely a fake. Modern pigments. I had it tested."

"Glad to hear it," Maitlyn said. *I hope you're paying the forgery artist what he asks.*

"If we're finished," Whatshisface interjected to ease the tension, "Congressman, forgive me, but would it be too much to ask you to autograph this?" He reached for an old sports magazine. "I've had it since I was a teenager."

Nathan took the magazine and admired the cover photo. "Jesus, I was young back then."

"Your rookie season. I was just getting into sports." Whatshisface was finally allowing himself to gush. "I remember I got your jersey for Christmas."

Nathan held the cover for Maitlyn to see. "Good-looking kid, huh?"

"Never did win that championship for us," Maitlyn replied. It was something Charles had said.

That was a Monday evening. On Tuesday morning, she went to see Mr. Cooper.

"Maitlyn, come in, come in. You look nice this morning." Ever since watching the footage from the press conference in Rancho, he had been extra full of himself. He had been proved right, he believed, about Nathan's camp pushing the forgery story to entrap gullible reporters. Nathan had raised the issue himself—why else would he have done that?

"Mr. Cooper, I...." Maitlyn had intended to sound bold and assured—*I quit*—but the word caught in her throat. Instead, she held out the envelope.

"What's this?"

"My...my resignation."

"Seriously?" When she nodded, he unfolded the letter. "Did you get a better offer? Let me guess—Los Angeles?"

She shook her head. "This just isn't right for me anymore."

He scanned a few lines. "Maitlyn, Maitlyn." His tone said *Don't be silly*. His half-smile said *I know better*.

"I want you to know I appreciate what you've done for me, giving me the chance. Really." She had a short speech prepared. "I just—." She was starting to cry.

"Now, now," Mr. Cooper said, not quite consoling, not quite chiding—probably the best he could do when faced with female tears.

She wiped her eyes. "I need a break."

Mr. Cooper sat up straight. "Here's what we're going to do." He turned to his keyboard—a show of resolve. "Take a leave of absence. Then come back refreshed. How's six months?" He was looking at a calendar on his computer screen. "The elections will be over. Things will be a lot calmer."

"I don't know." She hadn't expected this, didn't think temporary leave was an option.

"Unpaid, of course."

Then on Friday afternoon, when white-collar San Diego was tuning out the news and easing into another sporting weekend, the county district attorney announced that Deputy Cunningham had acted unprofessionally but not criminally in the shooting of Charles Lockett. No charges would be filed.

Maitlyn didn't hear about it until Sunday afternoon, when she stopped by her grandmother's house. No one from Channel Four had bothered to call. No one had texted a heads-up. She was already out of the loop, on leave and irrelevant.

She immediately left a voicemail for Mr. Cooper, offering to "cover the response in the community." She felt an obligation. She was thinking about how Capucine must feel to learn that the unprovoked killing of her father was not a crime. She could hear the women in Reverend Hutchings's office moaning, "That ain't right."

Mr. Cooper finally responded on Monday afternoon with a text: Thanks. We'll handle it.

On her morning run through the park, Maitlyn swung south toward the Air and Space Museum without even a glance at the Botanical Building. She didn't need to talk to Charles. She already knew what she had to do—publicly admit that she had recorded the video herself and testify to what she had seen and heard while cowering in Nathan's front hedge. *I've waited long enough.* She no longer needed to fear losing her job. She didn't even want her job.

She extended her stride as she passed the little United Nations building. Having made the decision to come forward, she felt energized. Nathan might feel threatened by her revelations— he had stood up for Deputy Cunningham, after all—but she would take her chances. *The danger is gone, I'm safe.* She noticed a smile forming. She laughed out loud. It could have been this easy all along. *Truth shall set us free*. Reverend Hutchings had tried to convince her of that.

Her phone was ringing when she got back to her apartment. She unlocked the door and hurried to answer. The caller I.D. stopped her: Dr. Dimples. He tried once a week. She was going to let it ring out, like usual, but changed her mind. *The truth*.

"Hey, how are you doing?" he began. "I just wanted to catch up."

"The truth is I'd rather you didn't call me. I'm sorry."

"Oh." He clearly hadn't expected frankness. "Okay. That's cool. Uh, see you around, I guess."

She hung up, tossed her phone on the sofa, and said aloud, "No, I guess not." Relieved of another burden, she danced across the living room to the sliding door. "The truth is I'm sick of all you." She stepped onto the balcony and looked toward downtown San Diego. "The truth is I want to do what *I* want to do." She extended her gaze across the harbor to Coronado Island. "The truth is I'm going to investigate rising sea levels." She laughed. It was an epiphany. "Global warming hits San Diego, and Maitlyn Flutters is on the job." It felt right. "The hot news chick is now the *hot news* chick." She straightened her posture to emphasize her bust. "The hot *hot news* chick."

She would shower first, she decided, then call the district attorney's office with her belated confession. Or maybe the FBI — they were less likely to protect Deputy Cunningham. But that would be embarrassing, calling them again, and would they even take her seriously? *It wouldn't be the same two agents. Still, they would know.* She was still debating as she toweled off. *I have to do this — for Charles. And they can't ignore an eyewitness to a police shooting.* She looked for her phone. *But they will type in my name and read my file.* And how much shame could she bear? *Flutters,*

Maitlyn — reporter for Channel Four, drunk and delusional. She decided to wait until the afternoon, see how she felt then.

Lunch was the house specialty: tuna salad and a slice of melted cheddar on a toasted English muffin. It felt like home, and good thing. "Grandma, you can say no," Maitlyn began cautiously, "but I might need a place to stay for a little while." Banker's Hill rent was too much for a rookie freelance journalist. "It would just be until — ."

Her grandmother smiled. "As long as you want. That room will always be your room — you know that."

"Thank you." More tears — all around.

"You'll have to put up with your old granny watching TV in the middle of the night." Grandma had trouble sleeping sometimes. "And *he'll* be here, of course." She looked up at the Greek fisherman, smiling down from his weathered frame. "I'm so glad you brought him back."

After lunch, they drove to the ocean side of the island to walk on Dog Beach at low tide. *I'll call the FBI when we get back*, Maitlyn promised herself. Admiring and slightly coveting the mansions lining Ocean Boulevard, she couldn't help but wonder how soon this would all be flooded. The big stone breakwater couldn't stop a swelling ocean.

On the wet sand, it was the usual tongue-lolling circus of retrievers and sheepdogs and spunky terriers. A brown Lab sporting a red bandana dropped a sopping tennis ball at Grandma's feet, and soon she was chatting with the dog's owner. "We come here every Wednesday," he volunteered. "I walk two miles. Hunter probably runs ten."

Watching man and dog continue down the beach, Grandma said, "No wedding ring. Maybe you should come back next week."

"Grandma," Maitlyn protested, but she had noticed too. Also, the relaxed way he smiled at her without ogling.

"Do you remember coming here on your sixth birthday? That's all you wanted to do—play with the dogs."

"What I remember is coming here in junior high and kissing Anthony…uh…I can't remember his last name." *And I can't remember the last time I kissed anybody. I'll probably end up like Grandma—no husband, no job, sitting in the dining room talking to a painting.*

When they reached the ugly fence of the naval station, they turned around and retraced their steps down the sand. The dark skin of a passing jogger reminded Maitlyn of Reverend Hutchings's church. *Are they planning another protest?* she wondered. *Maybe this time I should march.* She knew she probably wouldn't. She thought of Monique Lockett. *I should interview her about Charles—she has a story too—even if she's nuts.* Maitlyn reached for her phone but it wasn't there. She had purposefully left it behind. *Relax*, she urged herself, *enjoy the beach.* But without the reassuring weight in her pocket, she felt disconnected and anxious. *Who* isn't *nuts?*

"I'm glad you'll be staying with me, Mattie," her grandmother said. She hadn't stopped smiling since lunch. "This is where you belong."

After helping her grandmother bring in groceries, Maitlyn rushed to her phone. You have 7 new text messages, the little screen announced, triggering a pleasant feeling inside her. She still mattered. She still existed.

The texts were from Sunny and Scott, mostly saying WTF? Then one arrived from Tina: OMG. Something was going on, apparently. Something big.

Maitlyn clicked on the internet and found *BREAKING NEWS: SALTENSTALL IN AFFAIR.* Her grandmother called to her from the kitchen, but Maitlyn didn't hear. *NAUTICAL LOVE-NEST.*

MONKEY BUSINESS. The headlines flew past her. *VALERIE FURIOUS.* Maitlyn scrolled to a photo of a sailboat. She felt a cold sweat starting. Her temples were thumping.

In the next photo, Nathan was either grinning or grimacing. Maitlyn was trying to duck the flying cushion. "Congressman Saltenstall and reporter Maitlyn Flutters," the caption read, "enjoying pillow fight at San Diego marina."

"Maitlyn," her grandmother called again, "is someone at the door?"

Maitlyn looked out the window to the front yard. A news van was parked by the mailbox. A second one was pulling in behind it.

Timothy Braatz is a professor of history and nonviolence at Saddleback College in Mission Viejo, California. His historical writings include *Peace Lessons*, *Surviving Conquest: A History of the Yavapai Peoples*, and *From Ghetto to Death Camp: A Memoir of Privilege and Luck* (with Anatol Chari). He is also the author of numerous plays, including *The Devil and the Wedding Dress*, *Helena Handbasket*, *Paper Cuts*, and *One Was Assaulted*, and an earlier novel, *Grisham's Juror*.

To read the first chapter of *Grisham's Juror*, please turn the page.

GRISHAM'S JUROR is set in Laguna Beach, California. When a high school math teacher finds his summer vacation interrupted by unwanted jury duty, he turns to Grisham novels for guidance and soon is imagining a conspiracy at every turn. His search for the big money connection behind a gang-related murder and a mysterious defense attorney becomes a personal journey into the luxuries and laments of life in an Orange County beach town.

1

How does one avoid jury duty? I thought I had it figured out. You 1) write a letter explaining that while you'd love to fulfill your civic duty, one hundred fifty algebra students would lose their hard-won appreciation for least common denominators and seize the opportunity to terrorize some bewildered substitute instructor provided, at no small expense, by the school district taxpayers. If the jury assignment happens to hit during summer vacation, you 2) request a change of date due to serious, lingering, infectious illness and, when a new date is approved, refer back to 1. If 1 somehow fails to secure your release, you can always 3) simply ignore the summons—what are they going to do, send out the highway patrol?

Actually, what they're going to do is send out a nasty letter refusing further medical postponement without extensive documentation and threatening contempt of court and several hundred dollars in fines. Now what? Marissa suggested I consult her John Grisham novels.

-If you want to outsmart the judicial system, you should find out how it works.

Open a Grisham? Desperate times, desperate measures. The first book I looked at was about jury members being assassinated one by one. If that's how it works, just kill me now and spare me the time in court. The second suggested ways to get yourself on a jury and see justice served, not sidestep it altogether. Not real helpful, Marissa.

-I guess you're just going to have to go.

-A courtroom in July? I'll die.

-It's just one day.

-Unless I get selected.

-The odds are against it.

-With my luck—

-Be obnoxious. You're good at that.

My friend Pete seconded the motion.

-Dude, just ask the bailiff where you can score some weed.

In the third Grisham I attempted, this hotshot young attorney takes a position with a major partnership, works his butt off, gets lots of perks, then discovers the entire operation is corrupt, basically organized crime, only he can't quit, he's compromised, so he ends up taking it down single-handedly. The way he does it is pretty ingenious. Okay, I confess, I caught myself enjoying Grisham. Go ahead and laugh—I know I did, whenever Marissa brought home his latest bestseller. If the masses are buying it, how good can it be, right? Which is why I hadn't told her that I'd read number three cover to cover and then picked up a fourth, being the story of a tax lawyer who loses his job, apartment, girlfriend, and goes to work defending the poor and homeless. The pleasure, I discovered, comes in Grisham's everyman prevailing over corporate villains. Human decency triumphing over the power of money. The underdog on top at last.

I was over halfway through number four, the fired lawyer now sticking it to his evil ex-employer, when the bailiff called all rise and the judge came in. I had planned not to stand—surely that would get me home by lunch—but I popped up with the rest of them. A woman judge—short black hair going gray, half-moon reading glasses on a beaded chain, a friendly librarian smile, like a younger, taller version of that Supreme Court justice. She apologized for the long wait this morning, reminded us no cell phones in her courtroom, and went to work. A murder trial, she explained, and it might last a week or more. This is Mr. Sloan, the prosecutor. Meet the defense attorney, Mr. Lawson.

-They're going to ask you some questions, some of you will be excused, don't take it personally.

Not to worry, Your Honor, no hard feelings, I promise.

-Any reason why any of you can't serve?

She surveyed her kingdom—a few assorted court personnel and sixty attentive citizens in a dingy room, twelve of them seated in the jury box, the lucky winners of the court clerk's initial lottery.

-Any reason why you can't be fair and impartial?

That was my cue. Your Honor, I read about this case in the paper, I don't recall all the details, but I know he's guilty of something. Your Honor, the prosecutor and I once had a heated argument over a parking spot, he may not remember it, but I'll never forget his weaselly face, that haughty smirk, the dismissive tone: Tough luck, buddy. Your Honor, my best friend in high school was murdered, and I just…I just can't…I'm sorry, Your Honor.

A quiver full of arrows, and I couldn't let one fly. Some old guy got excused for a bad back, no doctor's note requested. A single mother of three couldn't afford childcare. Someone actually did know the prosecutor. Her Honor, Judge Silverson, was a soft touch. She released eight prospective jurors without arching an eyebrow, even the woman who claimed her mail-order business would suffer. Yet I remained silent. My palms were sweating, my throat was dry, I knew she would see right through me. Lying was never my strong suit. So much for Plan A.

Probably it didn't matter. I'd read on the internet that attorneys want jurors they can persuade—not too stubborn, not too sharp.

Lowest common denominators. That was Plan B, I'd play it smart, if it went that far. Most likely, though, they'd have a jury chosen before my number was called. Marissa was right, the odds were in my favor.

My cell phone vibrated in my pants pocket. From the bench, Judge Silverson was explaining peremptory challenges. Attorneys can excuse prospective jurors without cause, although according to my internet source, the Supreme Court has ruled they can't reject candidates solely on race, gender, or ethnicity. Of course, if anyone pressed the issue, a clever attorney could always find other, more acceptable explanations for having removed an unwanted demographic. Interesting, but Her Honor was holding forth on basic procedures, not case law, so I slid the phone out of my pocket and onto my lap and read the new text message: How is it going? Ignoring a scolding glance from the prospective juror to my right, I texted back: Murder. Guy named Jack. Home by 2.

-Have you ever made a big mistake, a serious mistake, that you immediately regretted?

Mr. Lawson, the defense attorney, was approaching the jury box. He was a large man with thick hands that he held open, palms up, a gesture of congeniality. Practiced, I'm sure. And that hitch in his step—wouldn't a slight limp make a big guy less intimidating, more human? It was all calculated, all theater, I knew that from the Grishams, and I was on to him. But what was he going for with his opening question? A big mistake, immediately regretted—wouldn't that include everyone, if they were honest? Of course it would. He wasn't looking for mistake makers, he was trying to identify sympathetic jurors who might understand that we're all just a bad decision or two away from a felony, jurors who might be inclined toward leniency. Except doesn't someone who readily admits to a mistake believe in owning up and taking responsibility, and wouldn't a defense attorney want to keep Mr. Stand-Up-And-Be-Counted off the jury? Quick, if I were in the box, would I raise my hand? No. Attorneys don't like stubborn jurors.

Juror Number Four, a heavy-set white woman, once agreed to a puppy, knowing full well she was allergic. Juror Seven, it turned out, told his wife don't be silly, went up on the roof to clear gutters during a rainstorm, and snapped his ankle in two places when he hit the ground. And Juror Two, with her straight brown hair and awkward slouch, what was her big mistake?

-I got married.

She said it quietly, and Mr. Lawson softened his voice to match hers.

-You regretted that?

-I was only eighteen. I wasn't ready.

-That must have been difficult.

-We got divorced. But I'm remarried. It's better now.

-Good. That's good. Now tell me, is there any reason why you can't give my client a fair hearing?

-No.

-Do you think it could be possible the police have arrested the wrong person? Is that possible?

-I guess so.

-Do you have any relatives who are policemen? Any friends?

-No.

-Do you believe that police can make mistakes, big mistakes, even when they're doing their best?

-Anyone can make mistakes.

Indeed. My mistake is I didn't get Sharon to marry me. I was probably too uptight, too critical of her dramatic personality. She had a great sense of humor, she was hysterical, she could be a bit much. If we had gotten married, life would certainly be more interesting. I should have found a way. Or maybe not. Pete says marriage is like cheese, it makes everything taste better, until it goes bad. Then it can kill you.

Somebody near me chuckled. Juror Five, the only African American in the box, was entertaining the court with his big mistake.

-I bought a hundred shares of my brother-in-law's company, and it tanked.

I was reminded of those education seminars where everyone states their name and tells us a little about themselves. Hi, I'm Joe, I teach chemistry, that's about it, oh and I enjoy sudoku. I'm Jane, A.P. English, two cats. And then there's always some oddball who enjoys sharing his foibles with strangers over bad coffee at eight in the morning.

-About a year later the stock came back up, way up, there was a buyout, and I'll be honest with you, I had to tell my wife that I'd sold it six months earlier. At a loss. A big loss.

The laughter was surprisingly loud—a roomful of strangers releasing tension. But Juror Five was no oddball. His beard was perfectly trimmed, his tie was powder blue and expensive—more expensive maybe than defense attorney Lawson's entire suit—his voice a rich baritone, a serious man by all appearances, yet still able to laugh about a failed investment. If we were making a movie here, he'd be the defense attorney, unfazed by some redneck prosecutor's insinuations. No, if we were making a movie, he'd be the judge. Mr. Lawson asked him about his business: home entertainment systems. Mr. Lawson asked him about his MBA: USC.

-No way they'll keep him.

Was the man to my left whispering to me or talking to himself? I turned to look. So far as I could tell, he was the only other African American in our jury pool. Two out of sixty. He noticed me looking and shook his head.

-Gonna make it all white if they can.

For a county population that's only two percent black, two out of sixty is significant overrepresentation, but I chose to point out a more obvious calculation.

-There's gonna have to be some Latinos.

The southern end of Orange County is rich and white, Reagan land. The rest of the county, once middle class and white, becomes browner and poorer by the day, and the jury pool appeared to reflect that. Lots of Latinos or Hispanics or whatever the proper term is, and also a number of Asians. An all-white jury was highly improbable. My new friend didn't agree.

-Wait and see, I'm telling you.

Mr. Lawson had finished getting acquainted with the twelve in the box, thanked them twice, a little too heartily if you ask me, and sat down, making way for Mr. Sloan, the prosecuting attorney, a much shorter and quicker man. No limp, no open palms, just a brief greeting and thank you for your attendance let me remind you, ladies and gentlemen, of a juror's obligation to the truth. Where's the charm, Mr. Sloan, the play for our sympathy?

-I have just one question for the twelve of you.

Oh, I get it, the efficient public servant, no unnecessary flourishes, no wasted tax dollars, a man with no pretense, a man you can trust.

-Do any of you believe it's okay to take the law into your own hands?

Come on, Mr. Sloan. What juror, sitting twenty feet from a black-robed judge, is saying yes to that? No one, see, no hands. Mr. Sloan didn't hesitate.

-What if you felt like you'd been cheated?

Juror One came to life. Dark hair slicked back, effortless mustache—Hispanic down to his *dedos*.

-Yeah, I would.

-You would what?

-If I'd been cheated I'd do something about it.

-So you would take the law into your own hands?

-Man, if the cops ain't doing it.

So I'm not the only one here with an exit strategy, only this poor guy can't sit back and play the odds, not in chair one.

-Would you say it's acceptable to kill someone who cheated on you?

-I'm not saying it's acceptable…

Don't back down, amigo. ¡*Ándele, ándele!*

…but if you let a dude walk over you, he won't be the last one.

That's what I'm talking about!

-I just want to be clear on this, Juror One. If you shoot someone who cheated you, should you be charged with a crime?

-No, he should.

Adiós, muchacho. Mr. Sloan consulted his papers.

-Juror Number Six, do you agree with Juror Number One?

-No.

Pale skin, long black curls, dark eyes. I wouldn't mind being sequestered with her.

-No?

-Not really. The police should handle it.

Mr. Sloan seemed surprised. What did he expect—all Hispanics would think alike?

-What if the police are too busy?

-I don't know.

-Shouldn't you do something about it yourself?

-Not if it means breaking the law.

I leaned to my left and whispered.

-He's gonna keep her.

My neighbor shrugged

-Maybe.

-She's not white.

-White enough.

-She's…she looks Mexican.

-If he keeps her, she's white.

I once had a sociology professor like that. You couldn't argue against her sophistry. Any outcome proved her proposition, it just required the proper analysis, which she generously supplied. We called her The Spinster. But if the guy on my left was a sophist, the woman on my right was a hypocrite. That disapproving glance when I pulled out my phone, reminding me the judge had insisted we give the proceedings our full attention, even us back-benchers, and now here she is with a paperback open on her knees. And she was smooth. She looked up, eyes on the jury box while turning a page, then dropped her head and returned to reading. Head lifting and dropping, like a swimmer coming up for air between strokes. Is it possible to read that fast? Oh, I know. It had to be. I caught a glimpse of the book's spine. Yep. Grisham.

According to the original twelve, at 10-1 with one abstaining, taking the law into your own hands is not acceptable. The abstainer was Juror Seven, who couldn't give a confident answer, he said, because he'd never been faced with such a decision. Is that honesty or stubbornness? He's the guy on the roof in the hurricane, so I'm going with stubbornness. Mr. Sloan will dismiss him—that was my prediction—and El Numero Uno of course, and I bet Number Four goes too, the allergic woman with the dog, for being dangerously stupid. That will be three of the prosecution's six allotted peremptory challenges. The defense I was less sure about. Mr. Lawson might toss Number Twelve, an elderly man thrice divorced who admitted to no regrets, and Number Nine, a mother of three including a military policeman. That would leave seven jurors in, five sent packing, and the court clerk calling five replacements into the box. Five out of the forty of us still sitting behind the bar, with only seven peremptory challenges remaining. I liked my chances.

-Juror Number One may be excused.

Judge Silverson had asked if there were any challenges for cause, both attorneys had declined, and now Mr. Sloan was jumping right in with the peremptory challenges. El Numero Uno picked up his jacket—a jacket in July? crazy *vato!*—and exited the box. You did it, bro. *Vaya con Díos.*

Mr. Lawson spoke next.

-Juror Number Two may be excused.

Huh? That's the woman who regrets her first marriage. She thinks cops are fallible—why would the defense toss her?

-Juror Number Eight may be excused.

Sloan dismissed an Asian woman who barely spoke English. I should have known.

-Juror Number Nine may be excused.

That's more like it—Lawson ousted the MP's mom.

-Juror Number Seven may be excused.

And next time listen to your wife and stay off the wet roof.

-Juror Number Twelve may be excused.

That seemed to be the end of it. Sloan and Lawson were at the bench, whispering with Judge Silverson. Three used challenges apiece, and I had picked four out of six. Not bad for an amateur. The remaining six included a black man and the lovely light-skinned Latina. No all-white jury today. I gave The Sophist on my left a smug grin. This ain't Alabama, brother, this ain't 1960.

-Juror Number Five may be excused.

The black MBA stood up. Mr. Sloan thanked him. The Sophist tilted his head toward me and raised an eyebrow.

-What'd I tell you.

It was like the NBA draft, only in reverse. You identify the most talented individual, the guy with the leadership skills and the presence, and if the opposition doesn't beat you to it, you use one of your picks to have him removed from the league. Ladies and gentlemen, with their first pick, the Chicago Bulls cut Michael Jordan. A reverse draft and then a reverse lottery. No number 51, please, anything but 51. The clerk called out seven numbers, none of them 51. Yes! Seven new candidates heading for the jury box, thirty-three prospective jurors still safe behind the bar, five total peremptory challenges remaining.

When we broke for lunch, I wandered the courthouse hallways, eating a sandwich and doing the math. At worst, if I was figuring this right, a fifteen percent chance of spending the week with Sloan and Lawson, attorneys at law, an eighty-five percent chance I'm eyeing bikinis while finishing my Grisham on the beach tomorrow, with my jury obligation satisfied.

After lunch, Mr. Lawson started again with the same question about a big mistake. One guy said he'd purchased a used car and the transmission blew. The next guy had even less imagination.

-Yeah, same thing, bought me an old Isuzu, never shoulda did that.

The website said trial lawyers try to identify leaders and followers in the jury pool. What they want is a jury filled with followers and a leader or two sympathetic to their side. Mostly I was seeing followers. A short Hispanic woman who regretted dropping out of high school with her friends. Follower. But now she was working on her GED to set a better example for her two kids. Leader? Maybe at home, not on a jury, no way. A young white woman who teaches yoga. Leader? Says she makes mistakes all the time, doesn't believe in regret, tries to live in the moment. Not real inspiring, lady. So who was going to lead this bunch? Anyone with even a hint of initiative—roof man, black MBA—was already on the freeway going home.

Mr. Sloan wanted to know more about the yoga instructor, who sat in chair ten.

-Do you have an open mind about this case?

-I believe so.

Duh.

-Would you be able to find someone guilty, even if it meant sending him to prison for the rest of his life?

-I think so. I mean, if he's guilty and everything.

-Did you grow up in Orange County?

-No, I'm from back east. Baltimore.

-Oh. What brought you to California?

-I needed, you know, a change. The yoga scene is better here.

-Have you ever been the victim of a crime?

-No, not that I…yeah, our house got robbed once, when I was little, but it was just some kids, nothing serious.

-Do you believe a person has the right to take the law into her own hands?

-You know, I was thinking about that when you asked it before, and I think maybe there are things we could solve ourselves. I don't mean like hurting someone, but you know maybe talking to them, telling them what they…what you think they did wrong.

-Okay. But what if they won't listen to you?

-I still think you should try.

Mr. Sloan smiled and thanked her. Would he want her on his jury? The Sophist to my left didn't think so.

-She's outta here.

-A white woman?

-A crazy white woman.

-He needs to save his challenges.

-He gets ten.

-Isn't it six?

-Criminal trials it's ten.

-You sure?

He was sure. And if he's right, I'm up to—I did the math: oh, shit—a forty percent of getting picked. Calm down. Even if I get called into the box, there's still Plan B, there's still stubbornness, there's still man, if the cops ain't doing it. That's it: I'm not staying without a fight.

-It's twenty.

What? The Hypocrite on my right had joined the conversation, but kept her eyes on her book, even when I whispered in reply.

-Ten each, right?

-No, twenty.

-Each?

-If it's for a life sentence.

She still hadn't looked up. Her nonchalance was troubling.

-Is there a problem, sir?

Judge Silverson! Her welcome-to-my office voice had become something sterner. Her stare honed in on me. The Sophist was suddenly busy checking his watch. The Hypocrite stayed deep in her paperback, not even a ripple on the pond. The Sophist and The Hypocrite—I was surrounded by Greeks, but I was in this alone, just me and the judge. Our eyes met, and she asked again.

-Sir, is there a problem?

I shook my head no. She held my glance a beat longer, a schoolmarm's reprimand, then instructed Mr. Sloan to resume his examinations. The bailiff, though, a rather extreme looking man—very serious, very short, very bald—continued sizing me up.

Is there a problem, sir? How many times have I used that tired line? What it means is I'm pretending to give you the benefit of the doubt, pretending that there might actually be a legitimate reason for you to be talking when you should be factoring equations or filling in bubbles on a standardized test, when we both know that if there was a legitimate reason for your conversation then you wouldn't be whispering while pretending not to be, only this way you can save face, and I can appear respectful, and we can both avoid escalation. What it means is shut up.

Actually, Your Honor, there is a problem. If The Hypocrite is correct, if each side gets to disqualify twenty, then I'm still in play, we all are. It's no longer about simple odds. If the attorneys don't like what they see, together they have enough challenges to march each one of us prospective jurors into the box and pop the question. A big mistake, immediately regretted? Actually, I'm regretting that I just missed my second escape opportunity of the morning, so please, Your Honor, could we try it again? Is there a problem, sir? Yes, Your Honor, I've developed such a crush on Juror Number Four that I can hardly think straight, I need to be dismissed. Is there a problem, sir? Yes, Your Honor, I neglected to tell you that I'm army reserve and I've just been called up, a text message from Uncle Sam, they've located bin Laden and need all boots on the ground, boo-yah! Is there a problem, sir? Yes, Your Honor, I'm having a stroke.

My pocket vibrated again: another text message. Wouldn't it be weird if it really was from the government, like the Pentagon is wiretapping brains now? You have a random thought—joining the army might be cool—and two minutes later a text message says Be all u can be and a recruiter is knocking on your door. That would make a great Grisham: a small town lawyer takes on the government, only the government can read his mind, so he has to think fake thoughts to misdirect them, then he sneaks out of town and plots his strategy in a cave in the mountains where the brain-tappers can't reach him. Can a person think fake thoughts? Could the small town lawyer drive down main street thinking he was going to his old aunt's house for Sunday afternoon pie when really he was heading for the cave? Wouldn't the brain-tappers know he was thinking about thinking fake thoughts? Probably too science fictiony for a Grisham.

The bailiff seemed to have lost interest in me, so I risked a quick peek at my cell phone: Get on the jury!

Huh?

Marissa works as a masseuse—forgive me, massage therapist—at a fancy hotel in Laguna, and when she has a time slot with no customers—sorry, guests—there isn't much to do except refold towels and send text messages to her few friends and her boyfriend—oops, guy she is seeing—so maybe she is just goofing around, but I don't get the joke. Or is the exclamation point supposed to be a question mark? I doubt it. But why would she want me on a jury? Maybe because when she has an afternoon off, she'd rather hang out with that artist guy, not the math teacher. Artist might be too generous a term. She says he paints landscapes, and in Laguna that usually means sun-drenched cliffs dappled with flowers overlooking a stretch of sand and a pale blue sea, sold to tourists wanting a splash of ocean in their suburban living rooms. Interior decorator is more like it. I'm sure he has a beard.

I typed Huh?, hit SEND, and waited for Marissa to reply.

Meanwhile, on the other side of the bar, Mr. Sloan was still working his way through the new talent. The guy with the bad transmission was the second Juror Number Five, having moved into the dismissed MBA's seat, and the difference was, well, night and day. Mr. Amiable replaced by Mr. Terse.

-Juror Number Five, have you ever met the defendant?

-No, sir.

-Do you have any independent knowledge of this case?

-No, sir.

-Any opinion on his guilt or innocence?

-No, sir.

His no-sir's had that aggressive matter-of-factness you hear from ex-military who, faced with the chaos of civilian life, take refuge in their certitude, their lack of ambiguity. The other guy with a bad car tried the same pose, but couldn't pull it off.

-Juror Number One, have you ever met the defendant?

-No, sir.

-Any independent knowledge of this case?

-No, sir. Uh, what do you mean by independent knowledge?

-Had you heard anything about this case before you came into the courtroom this morning?

-Oh. No.

-Maybe you read about it in the newspaper?

-Not really.

-So you don't have any opinion on his guilt or innocence?

-I don't know what he did, if that's what you mean.

In high profile cases, they sometimes have trouble filling a jury because most prospective jurors have already formed opinions about the accused, but that wasn't our situation. I read the newspaper, and I'm pretty sure this case went unreported. A drug deal goes bad in a rough neighborhood, some poor fool gets shot in the head—that doesn't even make the tv news any more, never mind the front page or even the local section. Rough neighborhoods don't matter. A guy named Jack is arrested, accused of first degree murder—murder!—and, yawn, nobody cares, nobody even knows.

I was beginning to think even the defense attorney didn't care. In comparison to Mr. Sloan's hurried efficiency, Mr. Lawson's friendly questioning now seemed lackadaisical. When it came time for challenges, he didn't even stand. He looked tired. Maybe the limp was real after all. Mr. Sloan employed four more peremptories, including one to dismiss the Hispanic GED mother. He was shaping a jury, he knew what he was looking for. Mr. Lawson disqualified only the bad car guy in chair one, an obvious move, and without much enthusiasm. Is Lawson bored? Ambivalent? Maybe he's sure his adversary will knock out anyone unpredictable, so he lets him do it, lets Sloan use up challenges, saves his own for when he needs them most. Like rope-a-dope. The slow guy with the bad hip wins in the end. That would be brilliant. Or maybe Lawson knows he's drawn the short straw, the losing card, knows once the damning evidence is presented the jury composition won't matter much at all. That's probably it. He's thinking let's just get this finished and go home. Or was it the other way around? A defense attorney excusing jurors left and right would appear desperate, and Lawson was sitting pretty with an ace up his sleeve. Hell, Sloan, you pick 'em this time, my witnesses are unimpeachable, my defense is jury-proof. Or maybe Lawson was just the typical public defender you read about—overworked, underpaid, uninspired, incompetent. Brilliant or incompetent, it's a fine line, right? If he was brilliant, he would have graduated top in his class and taken a big money job with a big money firm, like that character in my third Grisham. So, incompetent then. Maybe incompetently brilliant, like that genius mathematician who quit MIT and sought political asylum in France because he thought men in red ties were stalking him. Maybe crazy old Lawson has the perfect defense sketched out on his legal pads but won't reveal it, not even to the jury, fearing assassination if his legal genius becomes known? Or maybe his legal pads are completely blank, he's brilliantly incompetent, like Inspector Clouseau. Like he's actually the courthouse janitor pressed into service when he discovered the real public defender passed out in the bathroom. Don't worry, Jack, he'll bumble his way to an acquittal.

Or maybe I think too much. Marissa says so. Maybe that's why she likes the plein air artiste, whatever his name is, sitting dumbly at his easel, daubing distant seagulls onto his tedious seascapes.

Sloan and Lawson accepted Lady Yoga and Sir No-Sir, giving them seven total jurors. Judge Silverson asked the clerk to call five more numbers. Please, not 51. The clerk called 52. Whew, close call. The Sophist stood up. I hope they retain him—keep the black guy who predicted an all-white jury—how would he spin that? The clerk called 26, 18, 22. Sounded like a locker combination.

Suddenly, I could feel it. It's hard to describe, and I'm not psychic or anything, but sometimes when I'm concentrating intently, my mind will open up, my thinking will kind of relax, almost cease, and a physical sensation will emerge, at first just a hint, then growing stronger to where my thoughts and feelings reach perfect alignment, a unity, and then I just know. Only it's stronger than knowing. It's an awareness. Physiological certainty. I was now aware of what was happening, what was about to unfold. My number would be drawn.

And…bingo! When the clerk called 51, I was already standing. Five minutes earlier I had been dreading this moment. Now it was here, and I felt relief—the battle finally joined, nothing left to do but fight. And I was ready, I had my strategy: the stubborn, biased, obnoxious jury candidate was on his feet and heading for chair number one. Ready or not, Loan and Slawson, bumblers at law, here I come.

When Mr. Lawson, the brilliant or incompetent attorney or janitor limped or faux-limped toward me and repeated his perfunctory or crafty question, I finally got it. It wasn't a question at all, it was a mantra. Each time he said mistake immediately regretted, he was telling us that his man hadn't intended to kill, the gun just went off, an accident, regrettable, but not murder. It was a subliminal message aimed for a juror's unsuspecting subconscious, planting seeds of doubt in fertile ground. I should have been a lawyer. I mean, was anyone else catching all this? Does Juror Number Eleven, for example, a gray-haired woman with bifocals, realize she's being carefully cultivated? I doubt it, otherwise she would knock off the incessant smiling. She smiled at the attorneys when they questioned her, and positively beamed at me when I entered the jury box. What did the old bumper sticker say?—if you're not worried, you don't understand the situation. Something like that.

-What about you, Juror One, ever make a big mistake?

Mr. Lawson's face wasn't quite fat, more like round and fleshy, and, like most white people stuck indoors all day, his skin was closest to pink. He, too, was smiling—real or fake? or delusional?—as he waited for my big confession. But I wasn't ceding a thing.

-Sure, I suppose.

-Can you give us an example—a big mistake you made?

-I don't know. I try to forget them.

-I see. You're a teacher, right?

That was from the juror questionnaire: single, thirty-five, Dana Hills High School, no criminal record.

-That's right.

He paused, encouraging me to provide details. Not a chance, Mr. Public Defender, you're on your own.

-What do you teach?

-Math.

-Oh, math. How are the students these days?

-Fine. On vacation mostly.

-Right, yes, summertime. Do your students have trouble with drug use?

-No. They're experts at it.

Down in chair twelve, The Sophist laughed. Thank you, brother, I got a million of them. Judge Silverson wasn't amused. I could feel her eyes on me, waiting for me to go too far. Mr. Lawson managed a patient smile, but didn't relent.

-Ever make mistakes with students? I don't know, maybe yell at a kid and then wish'd you hadn't?

-Yeah, sure. It happens.

-Ever yell at the wrong kid? Like you thought he cheated and turns out he didn't.

-Actually, I try not to yell.

-Ever accuse the wrong kid of cheating?

-Probably.

-You don't remember?

Am I the one on trial here? Shouldn't we be asking Jack over there about his big mistake? Lawson hadn't shown this much interest in the other jurors. It was like my resistance had inspired him, and he was determined to break me. I didn't give an inch.

-Like I said, I try to forget.

-Right. Now tell me, can you look at my client seated at that table and say right now that you think he's innocent?

-Yes. No. I mean, I don't know.

-You don't know?

Don't blow it. Here's your chance. *Ándele.*

-I mean, when I see him sitting over there, I....

My phone vibrated in my pocket.

-Yes?

Mr. Lawson hovered over me, suddenly enthusiastic about his job. Blood rushed to my face. Focus, focus.

-It's like on tv, him sitting there, like the bad guy, and so I think something in my head assumes he's guilty. I can't help it.

Attaboy! That ought to do the trick.

-Thank you for your honesty. That's actually a pretty normal thought. Do you think you could set that thought aside and carefully, objectively, weigh the evidence?

-I'm not sure. I've never done this before.

Mission accomplished. Enough reticence to suggest stubbornness. Hints of sarcasm without bringing down a scolding from the bench. Clear admission of bias. And Mr. Lawson moving on to Juror Number Two.

Marissa's new message was burning a hole in my pocket, but it was too risky to check my phone while Lawson was talking to my immediate neighbor, while the spotlight was still so close. I waited until Lawson made it down to The Sophist.

-Juror Number Twelve, ever make a big mistake?

-I went up the Eiffel Tower, I thought I had enough time, but I ended up missing my flight back to the States.

-What were you doing in Paris?

-I had a layover, flying back from Morocco.

I leaned forward as if trying to get a better look at the globetrotting African American, propped my elbows on my knees, and read the new text message: Dude Angels game my place beers. That was Pete, not Marissa. If that was Marissa, I'd get down on my knees and beg her to marry me. I'd teach summer school for extra income. I'd give her the latest Grisham for Christmas. Her mother could move in with us. And bring her cats. But Marissa doesn't like beer. She doesn't even like sports. Sometimes I'm not sure she likes me.

From the box, I could now see the defendant's face. Jack looked to be in his thirties, six feet tall, lean—not all that different from me, actually, if I were wearing a coat and tie, not jeans and a polo shirt, and if I were a black man accused of shooting someone, not a white guy being accused of indifference. He was sitting at Lawson's table and staring, I swear, right at me. Stone cold. Like my future is in your hands, asshole, and you're playing with your cell phone? I'm usually suspicious of cops, but the two burly uniforms by the door were suddenly a comfort. I could easily imagine Jack with a handgun, no, a shotgun, and the same cold eyes watching his victim fly backward across the hood of a car. I looked away. I'd love to stick around and hear your side of the story, Jack, hear all the lurid details, hear your big regret, but it's seventy-five and sunny at the beach and summer vacation goes by in a flash.

Mr. Sloan wanted to hear more lurid details from my illustrious career.

-How long have you been teaching?

-Ten years.

-Would you agree that student behavior has gotten worse over time?

-I don't know. People say that.

-Do you consider yourself a disciplinarian?

-What do you mean?

-Well, do you tolerate student tardiness?

Okay, Sloan liked my bias against the defendant, thought I was a keeper, he just wanted to make sure I wasn't too forgiving. Time to shift gears.

-Students are going to be late. There's no point making a big deal out of it.

-Do you assign detentions?

-Rarely.

-What if a student is disrupting class?

The truth is, students don't disrupt my class because they know I'll send them out, call their parents, have them suspended, see them kicked off sports teams. And for tardies, same thing, zero tolerance. It's the only way to survive. But never mind.

-I usually ask a disruptive student to solve a few equations on the board. That calms them down.

If only.

-So let me ask you this. Would you be able to find someone guilty, even if it meant sending him to prison for life?

Competing mantras. Lawson says his client made a mistake he regrets. Sloan tells us to send the accused to prison for life. Judge Silverson must have understood what they were doing, trying the case in advance, yet she didn't halt their foreplay, their premature enunciations.

-I guess if I were truly honest, I'd say that life imprisonment is a waste of taxpayer money. Why keep a senior citizen locked up?

Sloan frowned and gave up. Fish Number One isn't a keeper after all. The only question that remained was who would excuse me first, Sloan or Lawson?

Well, there was one other question: had I committed a crime? Before jury selection began, we had all sworn to answer accurately and truthfully, failure may subject you to criminal prosecution. My responses to the attorneys now were definitely not in the spirit of the whole truth and nothing but. But did I actually lie? It would be tough to prove. They had mostly asked about my opinion, and opinions change. Did I really assume the defendant was guilty? Probably.

Probably I probably did, I can't be sure. Was I really skeptical about life imprisonment? In the context of public expense, probably. With regard to justice and deterrence, probably not, but again, I'm not certain. If they had framed more succinct questions they could have pinned me down. Sloan hadn't asked for my opinion on the value of life sentences. He had asked if I could find someone guilty, my answer was a non sequitur actually, and he let it slide. It's not my fault, Your Honor, if these bumbling lawyers didn't help me clarify my thoughts on issues I don't normally contemplate. That's it: I wasn't being dishonest, I was confused.

As it turned out, no one was concerned about my possible perjury. As it turned out, my ambiguousness wasn't interpreted as evasive or hostile. At least so far as I could tell. At the other end of the box, my friend The Sophist was far better behaved. He was cooperative and forthcoming, kept his cynicism under wraps. He presumed innocence but was willing to convict. He rejected vigilantism. He didn't know any policemen, agreed they could make mistakes, but had called them when his car was stolen and sure was grateful when they recovered it without a scratch two hours later. He managed a family restaurant and coached Little League baseball. Mr. Sloan sent him home.

-Juror Twelve may be excused.

Judge Silverson nodded. The Sophist shrugged and departed.

But neither the particular Mr. Sloan nor the brilliant or incompetent Mr. Lawson saw fit to dismiss the math teacher with the attitude. They were both sitting down, Sloan shuffling papers, Lawson whispering to Jack. It took a moment to sink in. I gave up on Lawson, but kept expecting Sloan to rise up and end my misery. Come on, buddy, you don't want a wild card like me, I'll hang your jury, I swear I will. Nothing. The clerk called two new numbers to replace The Sophist and one other lucky escapee. I stopped paying attention. It was over. I wouldn't be at the beach tomorrow, or the next day, or the day after that. I would be sitting in a stale courtroom, bored to tears, while Sloan, Lawson, and Silverson debated some arcane point of order.

My phone vibrated. A text from Marissa: **Bud Jack? Get on the jury!**

Well, there's a murder mystery for you, sports fans. Marissa rarely leaves bucolic Laguna Beach, avoids newspapers because they're too depressing, works in the hushed spa of a resort hotel tending to the aches of the rich, tan, and pampered, and somehow knows the name of a black man accused of murder sitting in the bustling county courthouse in Santa Ana, twenty freeway miles and a world away.

-Juror Number One, is that a cell phone? Sir?

Busted!

-I'm sorry, Your Honor. I—

-Perhaps you'd like to spend a night in lockup?

Busted, like my students say, big-time!

-No, I—

-I won't tolerate this.

-My dog is sick.

Where did that come from?

-I don't care. Is that clear to everyone? No cell phones in my courtroom. How sick? Mr. Fletcher?

-What?

How did she know my name?

-How sick is your dog?

-I took her to the vet last night. She was vomiting. And bleeding from the other end. It was pretty bad.

If you're going to lie, lie big, right? My heart was going a mile a minute. My face was on fire.

-Why didn't you say something earlier?

-I don't know. I thought it would be okay. But I just got a message from the vet. They needed my permission to run more tests. They said it was urgent, so I....

Judge Silverson looked out at the remaining jurors beyond the bar, then back at me. Her frown was gone. Maybe she's a dog person and knows what it's like when your little darling is hanging by a hair. Maybe I'm a better liar than I thought.

-Would you like to be dismissed?

That, then, is how you avoid sitting on a jury: lie through your teeth, perjure like a politician. Plan A was right from the get-go. Not that I'm proud of it. Not that I knew what I was doing. The dog story wasn't premeditated. I've never even owned a dog. Inspector Clouseau flashed to mind: Eet's naht mah dahg. The irony, too, was unintended. After all the calculating, all that agonizing, I'd finally found the way out, only there was one problem.

-No, Your Honor, I wish to serve.

Grisham's Juror

available in paperback and Kindle

published by The Disproportionate Press

GrishamsJuror@lunycrab.com • www.lunycrab.com

www.ingramcontent.com/pod-product-compliance
Lightning Source LLC
Chambersburg PA
CBHW021236130626
46554CB00004B/1510